DARK HOLE IN MY SOUL

Only love can redeem the pain

ELLEN FRAZER-JAMESON

FOURTH DIMENSION
of South Beach

Published by
Fourth Dimension of South Beach

© 2015 Ellen Frazer-Jameson

The right of Ellen Frazer-Jameson to be identified as author of this Work
has been asserted by her in accordance with sections 77 and 78
of the Copyright, Designs and Patents Act 1988

ISBN: 978-0-692-56381-6

Cover design and typesetting: Gary A. Rosenberg
www.thebookcouple.com

Contents

Acknowledgments

This book is dedicated to an angel—the beautiful and inspirational Dr. Juliet Ray, a trauma surgeon at Jackson Memorial Hospital in Miami, Florida. Juliet is without doubt one of the most gracious, caring and accomplished young women I have ever met. Truly beautiful inside and out.

She dismisses notions that she behaves differently than any other decent human being because it never occurs to her not to travel the extra mile to be of service. We did not meet in a hospital setting but I have her to thank for my recovery from a serious and life changing injury that I sustained during the writing of this book.

Without her compassion I would not be the healthy, happy and whole person I am today. Her husband of just one year, Eric Ray, a high-flying corporate lawyer, adores his Juliet, and the couple exude love and goodness.

Every woman deserves a champion and knight in shining armor. Their love story offers hope to all believers and romantics of that elusive Happy Ever After.

My thanks go to Clare Christian of Red Door Publishing and her creative team for their wide-ranging expertise and guidance. They never fail to come up with a solution. And The Book Couple for their calm professionalism during the production of this novel. Special thanks to Michelle Ruger who acted as editorial assistant and chief cheer leader.

Writing books is a pleasure but there can also be pressure and I offer my appreciation to friends and family members who consistently show up with support and encouragement. How lucky am I that there are too many to mention? I am well blessed. Life is grand.

With special thanks,
Ellen Frazer-Jameson
Miami Beach, 2015

CHAPTER ONE

Another Day in Paradise

A faceless member of the senator's staff who had been on duty at the mansion all day adjusted his mirrored sunglasses and hissed into a concealed radio.

"They're here. The Lady has arrived."

A high-speed cavalcade appeared. Leading the pack, leather-clad motorcycle outriders on Kawasaki motorbikes, followed by the black and white cars of the Miami Beach police department; blue lights flashed, sirens shrieked. Their demanding presence cleared the fast moving traffic and allowed free passage to the American flag-bearing black limousine that transported the Presidential candidate.

With the end of their fifteen-minute drive from Miami international airport in sight, the convoy made a sharp left off the MacArthur Causeway. The limo driver drew the attention of his passenger to the bay-crossing highway immortalized in countless action movies, scene of spectacular car chases and explosive multi-vehicle pileups.

He enjoyed passing on the information that the MacArthur Causeway bounds the Port of Miami, home to one of the largest cruise terminals in the world, and opens up an exclusive entryway to the private gated community of Flame Island.

Jagged shards of lightning illuminated the Miami Beach waterfront and threw into stark relief the menacing cloud-filled sky as the sound of thunder rumbled ominously out over the ocean.

Rain began to fall and the tropical storm that had been threatening gave full vent to its avowed intention to obliterate all traces of the endlessly cheerful Florida sun.

* * *

Serena Perez cursed under her breath. Then out loud. Damn, damn, damn. For added emphasis, she raised her tone ever louder, but even her professionally trained voice could not compete with the raging torrent. She struggled to be heard above the howling wind that forced the palm trees to sweep and swirl and bow to the inevitable force.

Surveying the picture-perfect grounds of her estate on a private island in sight of the Magic City of Miami, she resisted the temptation to scream out loud. Her meticulous plans were falling apart. Framed in the doorway of the hurricane-resistant glass patio doors, one elegant hand resting on the silver door handle, Serena looked as if she was about to deliver a scripted piece to camera.

"Welcome. Today, we are at the home of the super-rich and famous Miami television star, Serena Perez, awaiting the arrival of the Democratic Presidential candidate at an exclusive fund-raising lunch party. And the skies have just opened."

Serena knew how to handle drama, breaking news, and

developing stories on the Entertainment Channel, the national network where she was one of the highest paid and most popular presenters, but this was different. This was personal. This was her life.

She had spent months planning every detail and now the weather had betrayed her.

She considered whether to add her tears to the rain-soaked scenario or give in to her feelings of frustration and indulge in a diva tantrum.

She dismissed the crying option. Her personal makeup team from the Glam Squad would never forgive her if she messed up the flawless work of art it had taken over two hours to create on her beautiful face.

Instead, she screwed her features into a decidedly unladylike version of her best screen face, bared her teeth, and clenched her fists in frustration.

Wait till she got her hands on her colleague, the chief meteorologist back at the TV station, who had assured her, "No rain forecast." Today being the day of her ultimate social triumph. She vowed that every ounce of power she possessed would be utilized to ensure that nobody and nothing was allowed to rain on her parade.

Had she time, Serena would have gone up to the widows' lookout at the top of the house to get a grandstand view of the storm out over the Atlantic. She tried to imagine how it would feel to be a wife watching for a fisherman or sailor husband returning from a voyage. If a boat was lost this was the spot at which the wife first knew she was a widow. Serena was not a widow but she might as well be, she reflected. Perhaps the finality of knowing your partner was dead would be less painful than the uncertainty of betrayal.

Today of all days she would not allow herself to be distracted. She would not climb the stairs and risk being subject to the elements. Serena was determined to ensure that not even one drop of rain would be attracted to her couture Valentino pink, purple, and silver-threaded suit.

Ignoring the popular fashion dictate of not wearing diamonds at lunchtime, Serena was decked out in sparkling white diamonds at her throat and ears and on her engagement finger she wore a five-carat yellow diamond ring.

Detaching from the frantic activity going on in the Great Room that took up the entire ground floor of her mansion, Serena fixed her gaze on the private causeway, the only entry point to the exclusive island home.

"Casa d'Amore," the Mediterranean modern prime piece of real estate, was an architectural palace regularly featured in glossy magazines and television productions under the heading *"Multimillion Dollar Mansions of the Rich and Famous."* The subtropical home was visible behind sixty-foot high date palms and wrought-iron gold and black lacquer gates guarded by gold lion statues. Beyond the gates, tiled courtyards and manicured lawns, a magical Moorish wonderland of overflowing fountains and waterfalls, bougainvillea-draped loggias, classical marble statues, and decorated urns.

Welcome to Paradise.

Serena was anticipating the pleasure of inviting the Presidential candidate to a private guided tour. Woman to woman.

Out on the causeway, the official party was within sight of the Flagler monument, a white plaster obelisk on an island in the middle of Biscayne Bay. The railroad magnate Henry Flagler had been persuaded to bring his railroad south after pioneer Julia Tuttle sent him an orange blossom from Miami in the middle of the Northern states winter.

This early twentieth-century vision enabled the founding of the City by the Sea that would become a global show-place for art, fashion, culture, and architecture.

Serena kept her eyes firmly on the causeway.

A handsome senior member of the catering team appeared and in a carefully rehearsed game plan asked, "Plan B, ma'am?"

"You got it," said Serena, forcing a smile and hiding dis-appointment that the VIP guests would not be entering her palatial home via the circular driveway that bordered the paved terrace.

That route would have taken them past the dancing mosaic tiled fountains, the marble statue of Venus, and the yacht moored on the waterfront.

Instead, they were to be chauffeured to the front of the columned residence and escorted up a hastily laid red carpet under a waterproof canopy. From there through cathedral doors into the Italian-tiled inner vestibule with hand-painted murals—the centerpiece, a glittering Venetian glass chandelier that showcased portrait-lined walls and the gilt handrails of a sweeping stairway.

Uniformed waiters dressed in democratic colors of blue and white were already in place, standing to attention along the steps to the front entrance. Balanced on one hand they held silver salvers offering crystal flutes of two-thousand-dollar-a-bottle Dom Perignon champagne and passion fruit mimosas.

Arrangements for the fund-raising event had been carried out with military precision, and as benefactor of a million dollar campaign donation, chairwoman of the organizing committee, and chief fundraiser, television celebrity Serena Perez had been granted a private fifteen-minute audience with the Presidential candidate before other guests were scheduled to arrive.

Akin to being granted an audience with the Pope, after the private time, other members of the organizing committee would be released from their pre-lunch reception where they had been served canapés in the Great Room and be allowed exclusive access to the presidential party for a further fifteen minutes. Only then would the remaining supporters, who had paid ten thousand dollars a head for the lunch prepared by celebrity chef Simon Hall from one of Miami's finest restaurants, be welcomed into the reception. In an informal receiving line, guests stepped forward for a handshake and keepsake photograph with the candidate, one of the most recognizable and popular women in America.

Serena prayed that all arrangements would go smoothly. Time was of the essence and everyone had to do as instructed and keep on schedule. The candidate would be whisked away to her next appointment precisely forty minutes after lunch was served.

Out of the corner of her eye, Serena caught an unexpected movement as her personal assistant stepped out of the home office on the side corridor, made her way up the wooden floored corridor, and gestured to Serena that she needed to talk.

Striding to her employer's side, she said, "We have an emergency. The senior nurse at the hospice telephoned. Again. Your mother is very close to the end and she begs you to go to her. What shall I tell them?"

Struggling to maintain control of her emotions, Serena affected a tone of determination she didn't feel and said, "Tell them 'no.' I am not coming. I need to be here. I'm not leaving till the party is well and truly over."

Her shaking hands betrayed her inner turmoil but Serena walked with purpose and poise to the wide-open front door to welcome her special guest. She pasted on her biggest, brightest television star smile.

Serena was conscious she had reached the pinnacle of her social standing. The Presidential candidate was a guest in her home and she was not about to relinquish the bragging rights she had worked so hard to attain—not even to satisfy the demands of a dying mother. If she dies alone, then it is all she deserves, Serena told herself with a hardness of heart she did not feel.

"Showtime," she said under her breath as she stepped onto the red carpet and into the spotlight, presenting her best side for the official photograph and embracing her honored guest.

It's not every day that the future President of the United States comes to call, she reminded herself.

CHAPTER TWO

A Mother's Prayer

Hail Mary full of Grace, the Lord is with thee, blessed art thou among women and blessed is the fruit of thy womb, Jesus.

Perched on uncomfortable fold-up chairs, two nuns in floor-length black robes with white wimples framing their hairlines sat by the dying woman's bedside. They fingered their holy beads and prayed the rosary.

In the cancer charity's state-of-the-art hospice in New York City run by Roman Catholic nuns, it was a ritual performed day and night as terminally ill patients reached the end of their journey and prepared to succumb to death.

Difficult though it was to quantify the level of true conviction that a better world indeed awaited, most patients were of a religious persuasion and seemed to draw strength and comfort from the practice of a spiritual discipline that advocated prayer, priests, and preparation.

Inevitably, there came a time when the best medical treatment, tender loving care, and pain management could no longer hold back the ravages of terminal diseases. Even the best respite care and interludes of recovery offered only temporary relief, faint hope, and time to again await the finale.

Kathleen O'Shaunessey's frail, diseased body left barely an indentation in the pristine hospital bedding, but her voice was still desperate to make itself heard. Struggling to sit up she stared directly at the nun on her right side, daring her to stop reciting her constant prayer.

"Is she coming?" she demanded for the hundredth time that day. "Is she coming?" The nun looked at her companion, an older and hopefully wiser Sister in Christ who might have a suitable answer.

A downright lie would not pass their lips, but given the circumstances a softening of the truth was designed to offer comfort to the patient and relieve her agitated state.

The decision to contact Kathleen's daughter and tell her that the end was near had been taken earlier in the day. The priest had been alerted to administer Last Rites.

A point-blank refusal by her only known living relative to make a mercy dash to the hospital and see her mother one last time before she passed away had not been anticipated.

Genuine sadness for the dying mother whose request was being denied was tinged also with a disappointment that they might not get to meet her daughter, golden girl Serena Perez, a national television celebrity.

It seemed that everyone knew that Serena Perez's mother was in the care of the hospice.

Though there had been no visits from anyone, the jungle drum had started to beat when a call from the television star's office came to the administration offering to take care of the bills and giving a forwarding address in Miami Beach, Florida. Despite popular misconceptions about the

American healthcare system, terminally ill patients even without insurance are not turned away—but if a willing relative offered to foot the bill, so much the better. Serena Perez was willing to do that much for her own mother. Still, many at the hospice hoped that the glamorous news anchor-woman would appear in person.

In a world of suffering, and with the ever-present specter of death hanging over the inhabitants, a touch of stardust would have been welcome.

Serena Perez's high profile, nightly television appearances, her good looks, and ability to talk with intelligence and humor to anyone from presidents to victims of disaster and all manner of people famous and infamous, ensured her a huge fan club.

Unlike nuns in closed orders who live their lives in glorious seclusion, many of the nuns in the hospice movement had been in civilian jobs before entering religious orders. Their work with terminally ill patients in the community outreach programs gave them accessibility to the media and popular culture. They knew very well the name and image of the lovely Serena.

Despite their surprise at her refusal to visit her dying mother, none would have put their own disappointment at not getting to meet a celebrity at the top of a long list of reasons to be sad about the refusal.

The younger nun smoothed the bed sheets and gently cupped Kathleen's hands inside her own as she endeavored to still the inner turmoil forcing itself out through the thin, purple-veined hands, which constantly twisted first one way then the other.

"Is she coming?" she asked again.

"Shush, don't upset yourself," the older nun said in a voice that was barely above a whisper, her tone as loving and soft as if she were addressing a fractious baby.

Expecting Kathleen to settle, soothed by their expert ministrations, both nuns were taken by surprise when she gathered hidden reserves of strength, threw her arms out wide, and almost knocked out both of them with one gesture.

The older nun moved a little more slowly than her companion, and Kathleen's scrawny left hand swiped across the bridge of her nose and dislodged her large black-framed glasses.

"Now there's no need for that," she said. "You'll do yourself, as well as me, a mischief."

Turning to her nursing partner, she said, "Call the doctor, maybe he will give her something to calm her down."

Summoned by his beeper, Dr. Jonathan Traynor appeared and as he entered the room he smoothed down his tousled red hair, knowing that with all the rushing around he did from ward to ward, up and down hot hospital corridors, it would be looking far from tidy. He didn't consider himself vain but he did like to present a professional appearance, although this particular patient was past caring about how he or she looked. On his morning rounds, he had identified Kathleen as being in the late stages of her disease and in his opinion thought her unlikely to last the day.

Now here she was still raging against death, enough to be in need of sedation to take her back to the drug-induced coma from which she had so infrequently awoken in the week since she had been admitted.

But nothing surprised the handsome young American Irish doctor. He had seen it all in his few short years as a registrar on the cancer wards of the Sacred Heart hospice.

"Good on you, Kathleen," he said. "I can see you will not be going quietly into the night."

Kathleen clutched his hand and her once bright emerald eyes, now faded to a pale, watery green, pleaded, "Is she coming?"

Dr. Jonathan looked from one to the other nun and silently asked the question. They averted their eyes, avoiding answering.

"Now, Kathleen, we are going to give you a little injection to help you calm down and when you wake up, well, we'll see."

He nodded his goodbye to the nursing sisters and they prepared Kathleen's intravenous drip to take the sedative. The insistent bleep of his pager could be heard demanding attention as his retreating footsteps echoed down the polished wood corridor.

In minutes, the effects of the injection subdued Kathleen's nervous system and lulled her into a near unconscious state.

Only her interminable hand washing continued even in the deeper recesses of sleep and her voice demanded answers.

Her eyes flickered and a kaleidoscope of dreams and memories weaved a tapestry and played scenes from her life. Revisiting the days when she was the child, long before she had her own child. Dancing on the streets of New York while her father Padraic played the fiddle. Forgiveness.

Kathleen had to seek forgiveness from her daughter. Before it was too late.

Hardly audible or intelligible, but by now so familiar to her caregivers that they had no doubt of the words she labored to express, Kathleen repeated her refrain.

"Coming? Is she coming?"

CHAPTER THREE

Dancing in the Streets

Pressing her nose to the grimy, cracked windowpane, Kathleen watched from the family's dilapidated third-floor apartment at her handcuffed father being manhandled down the steep flight of concrete steps outside their home. They lived in a rundown, graffiti-covered brownstone building in Bay Ridge, Brooklyn, and Padraic was being escorted by two of the "finest" from the New York police department.

"Get your fecking hands off me," he yelled as he struggled to keep his balance, which in his intoxicated state would have been difficult even without his hands tied behind his back.

Fighting drunk and cursing everyone in sight, Padraic O'Shaunessey was well known to the uniformed cops. He spent many nights in the small, overcrowded drunk tank at the 68th precinct station. A court appearance and recurring fine completed the process and the judge's admonishment to "Lay off the liquor" always fell on deaf ears.

"Come on now, Padraic," Kathleen could just make out the good-natured cop, a fellow Irishman, attempting to reassure him, "We're taking you downtown to sleep it off. You'll be right as rain in the morning. Apart from a sore head."

Under her breath, through gritted teeth, she mumbled an old Irish admonishment, *"Hell slap it into him."*

Beyond caring at that stage, she was aware that the good cop act would probably not last much beyond their arrival at the station but at least her dad would be among his own kind. Half the cops in the NYPD were from his home county and some even the same town in Southern Ireland. He and they had left the Emerald Isle full of hope and in search of the better life in America and many of them had found it.

The O'Shaunessey family had not. A taste for booze and distaste for hard work meant that Padraic never even attempted to amount to anything.

"Come away from that window," his long-suffering wife, Caitlin called out as she raised herself up on her elbow. She leaned forward to better make herself heard from the depths of the unmade, bug-ridden bed where she lay nursing her bruises. Her injuries, as usual, inflicted by her drunken husband.

"Is it not bad enough that I have to bear the shame of the drunken eejit being arrested time and again?" she pleaded in her soft lilting Irish accent. Her distinctive County Clare accent had never diminished despite nearly a decade and a half living in the States, "Without you gawping like the rest of the neighbors?"

As he was thrown in the back of the police paddy wagon, Padraic looked up to the grime-covered sash window that Kathleen had struggled to open a few inches. She pushed and pulled against the warped jambs and was careful to avoid getting splinters in her hands from the crumbling woodwork and flaking brown paint. Even with three floors separating them, she could see the fury in his blazing, red-rimmed green eyes.

"Give the whore a message from me," he spat out, spraying the spittle that had built up in the corners of his mouth. "Next time, she'll be a dead woman."

Before he could repeat his threat the younger cop, who had no intention of pretending to be Mr. Nice Guy, grabbed his prisoner by the scruff of the neck and shoved him roughly into the caged back of the black prisoner transportation vehicle.

By the time he was released from custody, Padraic too would likely be nursing bruises. Funny how many times he was told by a totally credible police officer that in his drunken state he had fallen down the steps of the police station.

On returning home he would claim that he had no knowledge of what had taken place either there or indeed what incident had led to his arrest. "What happened to you?" he would belligerently ask his wife, deliberately turning his head from her bruised and swollen face and avoiding eye contact.

Kathleen vowed that no man would ever hit her. She could not understand why her mother allowed it to happen time and again. Why didn't she leave? It was obvious there was little or no love lost between them. In the tiny cramped and scruffy apartment the three of them shared, the only communication was conducted in high-volume screaming matches and constant bickering.

Yet her husband of fifteen years claimed that when he had brought Caitlin over from Ireland to join him in America, he had chosen her because she was the prettiest and sweetest natured girl in the village.

Kathleen swelled with pride when people told her that she looked like her still beautiful mother. Not that she believed it. As a gangly fourteen-year-old feeling like the ugly duckling, Kathleen doubted she would ever grow into a beautiful swan. Her mother assured her that it was only a matter of time. Give time, time.

"*Que sera, sera,*" Caitlin sang the popular Doris Day song to her only daughter. "*Whatever will be, will be, the future's not ours to see, Que sera, sera.*"

Her father's song was an obvious choice. "I'll take you home again, *Kathleen,*" Padraic sang at the top of his voice on many occasions as the two of them left the local watering hole. The irony that Kathleen was taking him home did not appear to concern him. Reality and fantasy were inextricably linked in his booze-addled brain.

A faded Polaroid snap taken on the steps of the New York City Hall showed his bride Caitlin as a fresh-faced Irish colleen with laughing eyes and shoulder-length wavy, jet black hair cut in a pageboy style.

Her cream-colored tailored suit topped off with a small veiled pillbox hat outlined a trim figure and the bride carried a dainty, hand-tied floral bouquet.

Smiling happily at the groom, Caitlin Courtney looked for all the world as if she were in love with the handsome, dark, curly-haired youth who hugged her to his side.

Times change.

"He brought me here under false pretenses," Caitlin complained with depressing regularity while speaking in a whiny, self-pitying voice that drove Kathleen to distraction, though she attempted to show understanding by holding her mother's hand and stroking her long wavy hair.

"How was I to know he was a fantasist and liar? He wrote me how well he was doing, working on the construction sites, earning a small fortune, and living the life of Riley."

Adding a disappointed sigh to emphasis her tale of woe, she would admit, "If he didn't actually say it, he certainly implied that the streets were paved with gold and he was just picking it up and spending it. Who can blame me for falling for it?"

Padraic had sent for Caitlin, writing her elderly father that he would be honored to meet her, take care of her, and legally marry her when she arrived in New York.

There was much excitement when Caitlin's family bought her a ticket on the inaugural Aer Lingus flight from Dublin to JFK just days after her eighteenth birthday in April 1971. She had traveled in style with two other girls from her small town of Ballyvaughan on the West coast of Ireland, on the southern end of Galway Bay.

Her two friends were also destined to join local lads who had taken themselves off to the new country.

Padraic had courted Caitlin for a short time when he took a break from his life of traveling and spent the winter months in Ballyvaughan, helping out on her parents' smallholding in a rural area of County Clare.

Caitlin was considered quite a catch. Dark Celtic good

looks, a well-brought-up young lady, beloved only child, indulged and cosseted by two loving older parents, not yet twenty years old, and with a promise of inheriting land in the old country.

An Irishman's dream. Now if her parents had owned a brewery as well, the dream would be complete.

Caitlin had received prior warning that marriage was in the cards when at a church lunch she had broken open a piece of barmbrack, an unleavened bread made with black raisins, golden raisins, and currants, and claimed the prize.

A small plastic ring was always placed inside the bread and superstition had it that whoever received the token would be married within the year.

Caitlin had been well educated by the nuns and she claimed to have not been aware when her suitor Padraic had asked her father for her hand in marriage that he hadn't written the letter himself—though if she had really thought about it she should have known he had to have had it written for him. He couldn't read or write.

There was nothing so unusual in that; even though the Catholic nuns ran the primary school and taught at the new High School, many children never attended classes and others were there only as and when it suited or until they were taken out to go to work and earn money for the family.

Padraic came from a large Roman Catholic family of a dozen brothers and sisters and, as he was a middle child, no one had any ambitions for him or expected anything of him. He was pretty much left to his own devices; he ran wild and free and rarely went to school. He had no use for book learning.

His family were gypsies, part of Ireland's itinerant population, traveling from town to town in modern motorized caravans; they bought and sold horses, ran betting rings, and did casual farm work as well as more questionable activities such as poaching, always staying one jump ahead of the gamekeeper and generally ducking and diving just this side of the law.

Padraic had turned his hand to most things since he had been obliged to join the family working party at the age of just six. However, he had a unique talent and this served as his own income-producing specialty—music making.

"He might not be the sharpest pencil in the box," Caitlin would joke. "But he could charm the birds out of the trees and make them dance to his tune when he played the fiddle."

Playing fiddle on the streets of New York City was how Padraic made his money.

"Go around with the hat—don't let the crowd just walk away," he would demand of his young daughter Kathleen from the time she was old enough to walk, "And be sure to smile at everyone, especially the men."

By the time of her sixth birthday, already an experienced street entertainer, she had added Irish dancing to musical skills on the flute and the tambourine.

"Don't she look cute," the ladies would comment on seeing Kathleen dressed in her little green kilt with a white silk blouse and shiny black shoes. She perfected the fast moving taplike dance movements with arms held rigidly at her side, and the brightly colored ribbons bounced in her long curly hair keeping time with the rhythm of her dad's vigorous fiddle playing.

"We play, you pay," was her way to encourage the crowd as she skipped around shaking the hat and making the money inside jingle. Knowing that she and her dad always put on a grand show made them feel entitled to the favor of the watching crowds. Dad in his element—proud, head held high, fiddle in hand. He was King of New York.

A master musician, he expertly managed to get the crowd going and the large black velvet hat in the center of the performance circle filled rapidly with quarters and dimes. Exhausted and exhilarated, after long days entertaining the crowds outside the theaters and cinemas and shopping malls of the big city, the tired duo would travel home on the A Train, Padraic carrying the bag of money inside his fiddle case and the fiddle in a small canvas bag.

"If anyone tries to mug me," he would tell her, "I'll hit them over the head with the case and you be off with the fiddle. I can always make money long as I've got the fiddle." Sitting close together on the train, smiling at their good fortune, and eager to be home and count the takings, they would amuse themselves telling jokes and laughing happily.

The rhythm of the music flowed from them and as Padraic drummed his hands on his legs, his young protégé tapped her foot in time to the unheard beat. They were partners, equals, confidants.

The pair shared enjoyable and exciting times and wanted to include Caitlin, but she refused to come out on the streets, not even to hear father and daughter play. She claimed to be too shy and embarrassed. The very thought of being with a large gathering of people on the streets of the city made her almost have a panic attack.

Padraic blamed her sad moods on homesickness and said she missed her parents and family. She was better on her own at home and though her nerves often got the better of her, on good days she tried to cheer up the family's squalid surroundings by collecting handfuls of flowers from the nearby Sunset Park and displaying them in a vase in the middle of the table.

A special though infrequent treat, if she had the money and the will to visit the local stores, was for her to welcome them on their return home with the aroma of a bubbling pot of Irish stew and large doorsteps of soda bread to dip in the rich gravy.

On those occasions the happy trio managed to make believe that they were a regular, loving family, and Padraic would eat heartily and call her "my own lovely wife."

If only he could have kept sober long enough, he might have been the husband she wanted him to be. Pleasing her was still something he tried to do though he wasn't always sure that his efforts would be appreciated. He'd have liked to be more generous with providing housekeeping, which may have made her happy, but he needed his money for liquor and tobacco.

"Don't forget to tell your mom about the nun," Dad reminded Kathleen as they made the homeward bound subway journey at the end of a particularly profitable day, "That'll cheer her up."

The crowd were entranced as they clapped and cheered the elderly bespectacled nun who hitched her skirts up and began doing her own Irish jig while Padraic played songs from the old country. Her favorites were "Wild Rover" and

"Molly Malone"—on the "a-live, a-live ooo" chorus she had kicked up her knees, displacing her long habit high above her knees and showing her bloomers.

On another occasion an Irish priest, a little the worse for wear, insisted on going around with the collecting hat, telling the enthusiastic crowd, "Support the artists and the children, you'll get your reward in heaven."

Fellow musicians, old friends, or kindred spirits often showed up with their instruments and joined in an impromptu session—until the call went out to warn the street entertainers that they were about to be moved along—or threatened with arrest.

"The polis is coming," would send them scarpering as they dispersed down alleyways, weaving and backtracking their way to safety.

"Padraic, tell us again how you gave the polis the swerve," his mates would encourage him. The tall tales of how he nearly landed in jail would be told and retold, getting more outrageous and further away from the truth with each telling. Like the fisherman's "one that got away," he had always escaped the biggest, most dramatic bust of all.

After a hectic day busking and performing on the street, more often than not his destination was one of the dozens of Irish shabeens in the predominantly immigrant neighborhood.

In the pub, surrounded by booze and loud company, Padraic was a star as he played and talked and laughed some more, sharing "the craic," a specifically Gaelic brand of fellowship. But inevitably the banter of fellowship and companionship would turn to fallouts and fighting as the booze went down.

If Kathleen could get out of the bar in time, she would run like the wind home before the mood turned nasty and before her father was ejected from the pub. The challenge was always to spare herself the humiliation of having to walk with her drunken father through the local streets.

His mood changes happened in a second without obvious external provocation. Singing, shouting, swearing, and incoherent ranting: he would switch rapidly from one to the other, all with equal intensity while they lasted and all inevitably lead to criminal charges of his being drunk and disorderly.

Caitlin would wring her hands in despair and twist and pull at her prematurely thinning hair as she heard of his latest exploits. Kathleen shrank in shame.

Nervous neighbors perfected their excuses as they stood up from the front door stoop outside the crumbling brownstone where the O'Shaunessey family lived on a half-derelict street, and more socially aware citizens gathered to meet and greet their neighbors. Innocent bystanders, they had no intention of being caught in the line of fire.

Although you could not hope to meet a quieter, more polite man when sober, drunk, Padraic's behavior was totally unpredictable.

Neighbors reserved looks of pity for his embarrassed daughter as they heard, usually before they saw, the noisy, staggering figure make his unsteady way home from the local pub.

Kathleen's cheeks burned as red-hot shame poured itself

over her and washed away all vestiges of self-esteem. Fervently she prayed that he would die or somehow be miraculously removed from their lives.

Love for her father fought deep inside with hatred for the drunkenness that blighted their lives.

CHAPTER FOUR

Counting the Cost

Drunken behavior was the order of the day. There was little to distinguish the night it all came to a head from every other night. However, it was to have life-changing consequences for the whole family.

On that fateful occasion, although he had had more than a few, Padraic avoided arrest on his journey home. It had been a few months since his last arrest but there was little expectation that he would avoid the consequences of his drinking for long. Among his mates, he claimed boasting rights with his long list of arrests for street fighting and being drunk and disorderly.

Perhaps because a light rain had begun to fall, even Padraic, his threadbare collar turned up and shoulders hunched down in his thin jacket, was subdued as he concentrated in his haste to reach home.

However, his progress was slowed somewhat by the fact that his lace-up Irish brogues, once so stout and sturdy, now had thin layers of cardboard covering the holes in the sole.

Putting new cardboard in his shoes was a job Kathleen studiously avoided, but even she could be prevailed upon when he told her in a small, sad little boy voice, "My socks have holes too, Kathie, be a good girl and sew them up for me and put fresh cardboard in the soles. It'll be like having a new pair of shoes. And God knows I need a new pair of shoes."

It was on the tip of her tongue to scream out that he could have afforded several pairs of new shoes had he not wasted all the money he earned on the street buying liquor. He knew, they all knew, but he didn't seem able to help himself. He had even stopped giving the lame promises that he would stop drinking.

God knows with the amount of money he spent in that pub, he could have bought the place several times over.

The overpowering beer and stale tobacco smell, combined with the escalating raucous noise, made Kathleen's eyes itch and her skin crawl. She craved fresh air and preferred hunkering down in her usual safe place on the steps outside the pub, away from the center of the action.

From her safe spot, she called out to one of her dad's cronies as he left the pub.

"Sandy, is my dad ready for leaving?"

"Don't think so, lass," he said. "He's setting up to play with some new boyos. You'll be here a while."

"Will you tell him I've gone home?" Kathleen asked, knowing that if she went through the doors she would be made to dance and accompany the impromptu band on either the tambourine or the ribbon-trimmed hand bells.

"You'll get me in trouble," he said. "My missus won't believe I'd already left the pub and went back to pass a message for you."

Still, he didn't seem too bothered and back in he went.

Knowing better than to wait for a response or permission, Kathleen ran home as fast as her skinny dancer's legs would carry her. She had good news for her mother. Before he got too drunk, Kathleen had persuaded her dad to give up some money.

She knew that her mother had been complaining she was again behind with the rent. Caitlin dreaded the fate of other neighbors who had been evicted without warning.

The landlord appeared to take positive pleasure in threatening to throw his nonpaying tenants out. And then doing so unceremoniously, their pitiful belongings left lying in the street.

Caitlin promised she would get him his money.

It was already twilight and the streetlights, such as they were, had come on. Kathleen ran fast and took the steep steps two at a time, then bounded up the three flights to the apartment.

"It's me," she shouted, puffing heavily and almost out of breath as she reached the top of the stairs, "And I've got a present from Dad for you. He's still in the bar"

Voices were coming from inside and Kathleen recognized the male one as that of the landlord. She pushed the door open; no one ever bothered to lock it and, had they done so, the battered, rusty lock would not have done its duty in keeping intruders out. Besides, there was nothing to steal.

The door creaked open and, in the light reflected from the one small low wattage bulb on a broken-down side table, Kathleen did a double take and felt herself go into shock.

She saw her mother in the arms of the landlord. Her light green cotton dress was disheveled. The pair were locked in a passionate embrace.

Kathleen stopped dead in her tracks. Frozen, wishing the ground would open up and swallow her or that she could run back down the stairs and pretend to not have seen what she had just witnessed. The couple caught in the act, turned startled faces to her, already forming words of denial.

"Kathleen, listen to me," Caitlin stammered, shaking her head. "Please listen to me. It's not what you think."

Her mom's stricken face was flushed a brilliant shade of red and she was visibly sweating as she untangled herself from the embrace and looked directly into her daughter's eyes. Silently she pleaded for understanding.

Turning from the two of them in disgust, in her efforts to distance herself and move her body too quickly, Kathleen's foot caught in the threadbare carpet on the cramped landing. She stumbled, put her hands out to break her fall, staggered, and ran headlong into Padraic.

Roughly he pushed her aside and let out a guttural roar.

As bad luck would have it, when Kathleen pushed open the door he had been coming up the stairs. Through the banister railings he had witnessed the same scene as she had been confronted with a few moments earlier.

Exploding like a raging bull he charged into the room. Bounding across the tiny room, he grabbed his wife by the throat and screamed "Whore." He slapped her, pulled her head back, and twisted his strong bow-wielding left hand in her loose flowing hair. Her eyes had widened, bulged and the veins in her neck stood out. Her body began to go limp.

"Please, please, let me explain," she pleaded, as she put both arms up to protect herself from her attacker and force the words out through her constricted windpipe.

Padraic looked about to squeeze the life out of her. He might just have done it had he not been distracted by the landlord attempting to slink furtively from the room. He had maneuvered himself almost to the main door when Padraic leapt onto his back, spun him around, and began beating him about the head and face with his fists.

"No, please, don't hurt me," he screamed. His cowardly response only made Padraic madder and he hit him even harder. Violence, which she'd already seen too much of, made Kathleen physically sick and, to hide her fear, she raised her hand in front of her eyes to block out the sight as she heard a bone-breaking sound and saw blood spurt from the landlord's nose.

"Gerry, are you alright?" Mom asked. For one split second Padraic caught Kathleen's eye as he realized they had never before heard the landlord addressed by his Christian name. All the tenants, behind his back, called him Sleazeball, though they knew his real name was Stephael.

Padraic was taller by at least six inches than Sleazeball and his drinking diet, which rarely included food, meant he carried no excess weight, unlike the fat cat landlord that he now knew was called Gerry. At least by those people who knew him intimately. Gerry lived the good life on the proceeds of his ownership of several rooming houses that were placed like Monopoly hotels in a row on one inner city street.

Pumped up like a wild beast, chest expanded, and breath

coming in gasps and heaves, Padraic counted himself out for a moment, before he regained his wide-legged stance, fists clenching and unclenching. His brow furrowed as he appeared to make a decision whether to continue to attack his male challenger or to turn his attention back to his terrified wife.

"Thinks he's man enough to steal my wife but squeals like a pig when he's getting beaten in a fair fight with a man," said Padraic, who in his time had competed in the brutal and unregulated fairground sport of bare knuckle fighting.

Calling upon all his acquired street-fighting skills, Padraic dismissed Stephael with one powerful punch that sent him crashing onto the landing and finished him off with a ferocious kick to his nether regions that caused him to gather momentum and be propelled down the entire three indoor flights of stairs, bouncing from step to step.

Watching the altercation from a safe distance, tenants and spectators had filled the stairwell. There was a party atmosphere as they cheered and roared their approval of the beating that was being administered to the money-grasping landlord.

Apparently Padraic was not the only husband to have discovered how their wives kept the rent man sweet when money was not available.

There was little sympathy for Sleazeball as more than one bystander called out "Give him one for me," and as he rolled down the steep flights of stairs he was helped on his way with boots to the rear and fists to the face.

The free-for-all ended as the warning sound of sirens

signaled the arrival of a police car on the street and two heavy-built Irish policemen made their way, puffing and panting, up the rickety stairway with the wobbly banisters and gloomy lighting.

Dad's knuckles were bloody and bruised as the defenders of the law grabbed an arm each, twisted it behind his back, and fastened on the steel handcuffs.

"You're in real trouble this time, Padraic," one policeman warned him. "You've got away with it enough times because your wife didn't press charges, but this time you're going down. It's jail time for you. You nearly killed the man."

"Yes and I will if he ever comes near me or my wife again," replied an unrepentant Padraic.

There was to be no repeat match. Padraic and Kathleen were left to share their disbelief when Caitlin decided that she had finally had enough of the violence, the lack of money, and of her husband. His fight with the landlord and brutality toward her had been the straw that finally broke the camel's back.

"I'm sorry," she told her teenage daughter, avoiding looking at the sad tear-stained face and accusing gaze as she watched her mother pack her meager belongings into a cheap, blue vinyl zip-up suitcase. "I've no intention of hanging around only to be used as a punching bag. Enough is enough. I'm leaving. I'll let you know where I am, and when I've got a place, you can come and join me. You'll be okay, as long as you're his dancing star. He won't hurt you."

Before Padraic was released from custody, his deceptively timid wife had feathered her own nest. Deserted her husband and the loyal daughter who had always tried to protect and support her. Caitlin left them to fend for themselves and moved in with her former landlord. She persuaded him not to press charges against her husband for the assault.

Obviously Kathleen and Padraic could not continue to live in their former landlord's property. As a priority, they needed to find a new place to live. Reluctantly they set out to find what they laughingly called a "home from home" for a lonely, scared teenage girl and a broken-down drunk who expected to be looked after by the one woman left in his life.

Kathleen's childhood, short as it had been, was now truly over.

CHAPTER FIVE

Paying the Piper

Hell's Kitchen, the location of their new home, sounded like Kathleen's worst nightmare, though the fact that it was technically in Manhattan almost misled her that they were moving up in the world.

The area was a noisy, teeming refuge for immigrants, mostly Irish and Italian, and its gritty reputation ensured that a degree of street credible skills were required to live there.

Padraic's avowed aim was to move as far as possible from his wife and her new live-in boyfriend, the former landlord, so with Kathleen in tow he moved from Brooklyn across the bridge to an apartment on Clinton at 11th Avenue in the city.

"Never mention that woman's name again," he warned her. "I have no wife and you have no mother."

Refusing to acknowledge the part he played in driving her away, his whole demeanor screamed righteous indignation that he should have been the one who was abandoned, but his eyes betrayed hurt and bewilderment.

Though she was not to be mentioned by name, "she," "her," and "the whore" were a frequent subject of maudlin, drunken conversation.

It usually started with the patently untrue, "I wasn't a bad husband, Kathie. I did my best."

His opening remarks gave warning that he would yet again be lamenting how badly he had been treated. Kathleen tried to suffer in silence but inevitably she would roll her eyes skeptically and that look alone was enough to set him off on a tirade against the downright unfairness of the situation and the disloyalty of his own daughter.

Caitlin moved into a renovated brownstone just one street from where her husband and daughter had lived. Her landlord boyfriend owned that block as well. Returning to the old neighbor and watching from across the street, Kathleen would spy on her mother and hope that one day she might turn and notice her. She never did.

There was no denying that she looked better than when the family were together. Her clothes were smarter and her hair looked shiny and clean. She walked with her head held high. No longer the shame-filled battered wife, now she was the mistress of a man of means. Kathleen did not begrudge her the change of fortunes but wished she had been included. Her thoughts had been consumed with the worry that now she and her dad had moved, would her mother know how to get in touch. Too scared to approach her directly, Kathleen prayed she wasn't to be forgotten. Her mother had promised she'd send for her. Surely she wouldn't go back on her promise?

The apartment Padraic found for them was in another turn-of-the-century multifamily block, with peeling brown paint and rotting black wrought iron banisters. Trashcans decorated the street level entryway and a damp, rancid smell permeated the building from the basement to the attic. The cooking smells, in an eclectic international mixture of ethnic cuisines, were enough to make anyone lose their appetite.

Kathleen's heart sank as he showed her the living quarters. One large room with bare floorboards, high filthy windows covered by a grubby floral drape, and on the ceiling a clanking rusty, metal fan.

"I've seen worse," her father tried to convince her; though even he would have been hard pressed to say where or when.

On either side of the room, there were two single metal-framed cots, each with a thin drape on a piece of string screening them off to offer a semblance of privacy. In the middle of the room were a rickety table and two plastic chairs.

Set into the wall was a fireplace that had once been a fancy carved centerpiece and now was soot blackened from a smelly gas fire. Above the kitchen table and a heavy-duty sink in the eating area, there were green painted wooden cupboards and a large meter, which needed to be fed with quarters to heat the water and fire. The toilet was down a flight of stairs and shared with other families. The tub was in the kitchen area and was used for bathing as well as all other domestic duties of washing clothes, laundry, and cleaning.

"We'll soon get it looking nice," said Padraic without conviction. "You can decorate and get some cushions and things."

And pigs might fly. He must have known as well as her that the chances of him ever giving any money to decorate the house were absolutely zero. Every cent he made went on alcohol.

Only by depending on charity at school and the church

did Kathleen even get a decent meal or any secondhand clothes.

"Please, God, get me out of here," she repeated to herself like a mantra over and over again. Refusing to express her feelings openly, she bit hard into the inside of her cheek and hugged her bony body as she shivered in the hostile environment. The room had not one redeeming feature.

Withdrawing further and further into herself, on the verge of bitter tears of self-pity, she vowed that one day her life would be better. She would be warm, well fed and, if she was *very* lucky, loved.

Despair threatened to overwhelm her and then she remembered the words of a song she had heard in an old-style musical some of the classes at school had staged called *"My Fair Lady."* There was a young London flower seller and she sang,

"All I want is a room somewhere, far away from the cold night air with one enormous chair, oh, wouldn't it be loverly."

"Oh, yes, wouldn't it be loverly."

"Come on, let's check out the neighborhood," her father cajoled her, but they both knew "the neighborhood" meant the nearest Irish pub. They had left Brooklyn several hours before and he couldn't last long without regular intakes of liquor. It was no longer just a desire to drink; now he was likely to have alcoholic fits if he was too long away from the bottle.

"Kathleen, I won't tell you again," Padraic said, "it'll be alright. Trust me. Come on, you can fix the place up when we get back. First we need to go and make some money on the street. Grab the hat and the bag and look lively."

*   *   *

Hell's Kitchen, a central area in New York home to a diverse and colorful ethnic community, had much to commend it. It buzzed with excitement, creativity, and the activity of diners, delis, restaurants, specialty stores, parks, schools, and churches all added up to a great neighborhood.

As the real estate boom of the eighties got into full swing, the area became gentrified and brick by brick floor by floor, father and daughter were able to drag themselves up to a better standard of living.

Kathleen and her father had come to an arrangement. He paid the living expenses from the money he made playing music, not always now on the streets as more often he was employed in bars or clubs. She acted as a housekeeper, providing food and clean clothes.

This suited both of them and allowed Kathleen to maintain an outward appearance of respectability. The pair lived separate lives, together.

Thanks to a scholarship applied for on her behalf by one of the nuns at her Catholic school, Kathleen was able to study performance arts at a local college.

"She's left me way behind," Padraic took pride in telling anyone who would listen. "I never had a music lesson in my life. This one, my daughter Kathleen, will be playing at Carnegie Hall next."

Occasionally he persuaded her to go to a bar or club where he was the resident act, and introducing his *"beautiful and talented daughter, the light of my life"* to the raucous crowd, together they would play up a storm. Padraic still knew how to please a crowd.

Drinking, of course, remained his favorite occupation.

Staggering home, reeking of the booze, his beery voice bounced off the walls and stairways as he made his unsteady way to their apartment. Home conditions had been transformed over the years and the small, neat apartment was Kathleen's pride and joy. She had her own bedroom and Dad had a private alcove screened off in the lounge. The furniture was best quality secondhand with pretty furnishings and drapes and a pleasing cheerfulness in the bright yellows and greens of the crockery and furnishings. Now they did have fancy cushions.

Everything had a place and was in its place—except when Padraic was too far gone to care and managed to create havoc, bumping into furniture, knocking over ornaments, and crashing into the kitchen pots and pans.

"Please, Dad, be careful," Kathleen chided him in her sternest voice. "I don't want you breaking up the house. You'll have to pay for it."

Thankfully their neighbors saw much more of the amenable Padraic than the drunken layabout from earlier days and, if he was a bit loud or liked a singsong now and then, no one made too much of a fuss.

He certainly wasn't the only one in the block who liked his drink. On Friday and Saturday nights the joint was always jumping.

Mostly Kathleen tolerated his addiction to the alcohol, having long since given up trying to persuade him to give up the booze.

Treating him like a naughty child, she reprimanded and scolded him. They were a team and worked together and there were tried and tested rituals for getting him into bed when he'd had too much to drink.

"Jacket off—let me help you pull your arms out of the sleeves one by one. I'll hang it up. Now, sit on the bed while I take your shoes and socks off. Unbuckle your pants, step out of them, and I'll hold your hand so you don't fall. Quick, into bed under the covers. Keep your shirt on."

Avoiding the flaying arms and blank look upon his flushed features, she assured him, "There now, you're alright. I'll look after you. You'll be right as rain in the morning. Apart from a sore head."

After a drunken evening, he would pass unconscious into a deep sleep. So deep that if the window rattling, nostril flaring snoring stopped, Kathleen couldn't rest until she checked that he was still breathing. In the morning he stayed in bed till she mixed his personal hangover cure of raw eggs whisked into milk.

To punish him, Kathleen refused to talk to him for a few days. Tiptoeing around the apartment, doe eyed and mumbling constant apologies, he waited to see when he was back in the good books.

Had she not been the one to let him down, this companionable arrangement could have gone on forever. It was par for the course back in the old country for unmarried daughters to spend their whole lives in the family home looking after parents.

"Will you come down to the club?" he invited her on the night of her seventeenth birthday. "We could have a bit of a party."

It was the last place she was planning to go. "You be off, I'll expect to see you later."

Almost jumping out of her skin with excitement, she had other plans to celebrate her special day.

Looking in the mirror, Kathleen congratulated herself that the gawky, frightened girl who had dreamed of being as beautiful as her mom, had indeed turned into a swan.

The attention she received from lads at school and at the local youth club where she hung out with friends had convinced her that she was on the verge of womanhood.

Seeming to have inherited the best of her parents, she was ready for her first romance. Kathleen was tall like her dad and had his dark curly hair and flashing green eyes. From her mom she had inherited a shapely figure and fine, even features with dimpled cheeks and full rosy lips.

Checking out her appearance in the mirror on the inner door of the dark mahogany closet, she offered a compliment, "Not bad, if I say so myself."

Marco Sanchez was on her course at the performing arts college. From a large Hispanic family, he was a Latin charmer with flashing dark eyes and slicked-back hair. His eyebrows were bushy and he refused to shave, preferring to show off his designer stubble. Marco was a natural performer and he carried his confident swagger from the stage into real life. Girls queued up to be noticed by him and Kathleen did not dare to stop and question why he had chosen to pay her so much attention. Tonight was their first official date, though they had spent some time together previously when they performed together in a musical production at college. On stage they had exuded a natural chemistry and the show had been a resounding success. The tutors said both had the talent to be professional one day.

Marco had arranged to meet Kathleen at the youth center and promised he had something special for her birthday present.

The outfit she chose to wear for their date was modest but stylish. Covered up but with a hint of intrigue, she wore a black dance leotard with a laced-up back and a short, wraparound skirt with a large buckled belt and knee-high boots.

She brushed her hair till it shone and left it long and loose, though the curls refused to be tamed, framing her face and tumbling down past her shoulders.

Marco approved, and when she met him at the front door of the youth center he made her blush as he whispered in her ear, "You look good enough to eat."

With his arm protectively around her shoulder, they walked into the club, obvious for all to see that they were a couple—for tonight, at least.

Loud music drowned out most of their conversation but Marco held her tight and whispered endearments. Working himself up to a state of excitement, his face flushed and his nostrils flared, Marco held her ever more tightly. Kathleen did not resist.

"Let's go somewhere private," he said and winked.

Kathleen had already told him that there was no one at home and the thought of enjoying more of his attentions appealed.

Hand in hand they walked the few short blocks to her building. As she climbed the stairs in front of him, key in hand, he patted her backside. Warning bells were sounding but Kathleen chose to ignore them.

"Which is your room?" he asked as they entered the apartment.

Without waiting for a reply he pushed open the door of the one bedroom and tenderly took her hand as he walked her across the room to sit on the bed.

In an effort to lighten the atmosphere, she joked, "Where's my present?"

"Don't worry, I've got something very special for you," he laughed.

"Lie down, you'll be more comfortable," and so saying he put his left hand under her knees and lifted her onto the bed. He pushed with his right hand on her shoulder until she lay flat out on the pink frilly covers on the neatly made bed.

He lay down alongside and stroked her hair, whispering words of encouragement as he kissed and probed her mouth with his tongue. First tenderly, then aggressively.

"Are you a virgin?" he asked.

Embarrassed by the question, Kathleen pursed her lips and nodded.

"Well, you won't be after tonight," he said. "That's my present to you."

Being the last virgin left in her circle of friends, she struggled with mixed emotions about whether it was a good or bad distinction. She nodded her head even while allowing him to slip the sexy black leotard from her shoulders.

Directing her to lift her buttocks, Marco helped her out of her tights.

He had unfastened the wraparound skirt and as she attempted to cover her nakedness and began to cry, he maneuvered himself on top of her reluctant body.

"Tell me if you want to stop," he said in an effort to gain compliance. Kathleen faced the wall to block out the inevitable.

Unzipping his pants, he proceeded to do what she now realized he had set out to accomplish—to take her virginity.

When it was over Marco asked, "Did you like it? Most girls don't the first time, but you'll get used to it."

All she wanted was for him to leave but before that could happen, all hell broke loose.

The sound of a key turning in the outer door turned her insides to ice. Being aware of an eerie calm she envisaged this might be what it was like before a tornado hits. The storm exploded. The bedroom door was slammed open threatening to come right off its hinges.

All at once a sickening feeling of déjà vu hit her as she heard rather than saw her father rampage into the bedroom. He grabbed Marco by the scruff of the neck and pulled him off her.

"Get out of here before I kill you," he said in a voice so quiet it was almost difficult to hear, though the message was unmistakable.

Marco did not need to be told a second time. He grabbed the jacket that he had such a short time before hung on the bedroom door handle.

To cover her nudity, Kathleen grabbed the cover off the bed. She stared at her father, petrified.

The pain in his eyes broke her heart.

"I came back to tell you we'd got a birthday cake for you at the club," he said in a voice filled with contempt. He looked right through her.

Kathleen shrank in fear as he pointed a finger. "Get out," he said in a voice filled with anger and menace. "Don't worry. I'm not going to waste my time hitting you. Just get out of my sight. I never want to see you again. Take your things and go join your mother, the whore."

His parting expression was that of disgust and humiliation as he turned and walked out of the bedroom.

Throwing a random assortment of personal belongings into a school bag, Kathleen was determined to make her escape before he could change his mind. She knew only too well that if Padraic started drinking he could all too quickly lose his resolve not to hit her. He had lashed out on other occasions, albeit that he was filled with remorse the next day. At least, she concluded, she should make herself scarce for the immediate future.

In two minds whether to at least risk his wrath and say goodbye, she hesitated, bag in hand in the doorway of the lounge.

Padraic was sitting in an armchair, his back to her, crying like his heart would break. Kathleen had no words to say. She left in silence.

CHAPTER SIX

Any Port in a Storm

"Don't move, little lady or you are going to get hurt." The rasping menace-filled male voice assaulted her ears and she sensed the presence that overshadowed her from behind. Kathleen smelled the all too familiar fumes of liquor on the pungent breath as it forced its way into her left ear. Her heart beat faster as a grimy, bony hand grabbed her throat.

Kathleen sat shock still as her mind frantically sought a solution. Fight or flight? Surprising herself almost as much as her assailant, she utilized fury born of fear to gain advantage.

"Get your filthy hands off me," she hissed matching menace with menace. Years of living with an alcoholic father, who constantly threatened but barely dared to carry out his threats, Kathleen had honed her survival instincts and perfected strategies to face down cowardly drink-fueled aggression.

Not judging it a sensible idea to turn around and face her would-be assailant, Kathleen reached up her own shaking hand and roughly ripped the grasping hand of the aggressor from her throat.

She was a kid raised on the streets and had learned at an early age to talk tough and act tougher.

The night air was cold but Kathleen was sweating; she wiped her palms on the arms of her thin denim jacket. She knew she had to conceal the smell of fear or, like a dog sensing weakness, her opponent would gain a psychological dominance over her.

All of her senses were powered up to full alert and in the stillness of the midnight shadows that concealed the immediate environment, Kathleen sensed another presence. There were sounds of a skirmish just out of her line of vision and she heard running footsteps. Out of the corner of her eye she caught sight of a small figure that scurried as defiantly and secretively as the rodents that inhabited the damp and putrid darkened passageways of the light-starved station concourse.

Relieved to see the back of the rapidly disappearing figure, she realized he was a kid probably not much older than herself.

In front of her an older man stepped from the shadows and like a conquering knight asked with impeccable politeness, "Are you all right, Miss?"

Not ready to put her trust in this new stranger, Kathleen refused to acknowledge his smile and instead stared straight ahead and answered his question with just the slightest inclination of her head.

To reassure her of his good intentions, the would-be Good Samaritan sought to engage her in conversation. "Damn punk kids, homeless, and looking for trouble on the streets."

Kathleen shivered involuntarily and anxiously wrapped her arms around her shoulders, endeavoring to offer her frightened little girl self some comfort and a sense of safety. As of tonight and for how long she knew not, she too was homeless.

Not knowing where to go after being thrown out of her home, she had headed to Penn station where she had tried to pretend that she was actually going to board a bus. The metal chair on which she sat was hard, uncomfortable, and her feet rested in litter that previous occupants had discarded: chip bags, a chocolate Hershey bar wrapper, and empty soda cans.

With few options and less money, it felt like she was glued to the chair. Head bowed, she held tight to the bag on her lap and struggled to hide her tears and ignore the rising fears.

"Do you need help?" asked the man in a voice that engendered trust. His soft voice was kind and Kathleen thought she detected an accent, definitely not a New Yorker she decided, probably not even American.

She would hazard a guess that the dark-skinned, short, stocky man wearing a thick wool overcoat, a small brimmed hat, and carrying a briefcase, was from Europe—but she couldn't pinpoint a country—probably because her geography was not good enough to allow her to explore possibilities.

Not that she had any intention of engaging in conversation. She just wanted to get rid of the enquiring stranger without giving away any information or showing her discomfort.

"Fine. Thank you for rescuing me," she said, "But I'll be okay now. I'm waiting for a friend. She'll be here soon."

Resisting the temptation to add, "Now please leave me alone," Kathleen stood up and, sweeping her eyes around the now practically deserted station concourse, pretended she was looking for the make-believe friend.

Walking quickly away from the man, she tried to compose herself and quiet her breathing, which was labored and threatened to shut down in the new atmosphere of close-up perceived danger.

The man followed her and when she increased her walking pace, he increased his. Catching up and walking along side her, he said, "Please, wait. I mean you no harm. I've been watching you. That's how I knew that other wino kid was bothering you. You've been sitting there for hours; I sense that you need help. I am perfectly respectable, I missed my bus and there is not another to my destination tonight."

His voice was reassuring, persuasive, and Kathleen desperately wanted some relief from her lonely vigil. Perhaps she could allow him to wait with her a while.

As the hour had moved toward and past midnight, into the wee small hours, there were fewer buses, fewer passengers, and fewer fellow travelers with whom Kathleen would even, as a last resort, chose to share a long, dark night.

"At least will you let me buy you a coffee?" asked the persistent erstwhile rescuer, who seemed determined to be her protector. In need of a friend and deciding to trust her instincts, Kathleen surprised herself by agreeing.

By the time the morning buses started running, Kathleen

and her new friend, Sami, had talked all night and forged an unlikely alliance. She told him about her early days dancing on the streets and her dreams of becoming a professional performer. Sami expressed his delight and told her that he had contacts in the entertainment business in New York.

Sami suddenly had a grand idea. Like in an old Hollywood movie he proposed, "Let's do a show here!"

Persuading Kathleen that he needed to audition her, he took her by the hand, steadying her as she climbed up on the bench in the twilight zone of the predawn station and sang for him one of her father's favorite numbers, "Danny Boy." Sami was entranced. This girl has real talent, he decided.

It seemed that fate had brought them together. Sami proposed to postpone his previous intention to leave the city.

He had a better plan—and Kathleen was an integral part of that plan. She was young, beautiful, and talented and he dreamed that she would be his passport to fame and fortune.

CHAPTER SEVEN

Pass the Hat

"Slow down. Please, don't leave me. Wait for me. I can't keep up with you," Kathleen pleaded, as Sami rushed out of the station with such speed he threatened to disappear entirely from her line of vision.

Cursing her high-heeled shoes, she debated whether to take them off and run barefoot. Despair swept over her. Sprinkles of tears spilled from her night-tired eyes and, feeling vulnerable, Kathleen wanted to cry out loud for her mother to rescue her from this frightening situation.

The station filled up with early morning commuters and the army of cleaners, food peddlers, and shopkeepers who would service them. All around were signs of dawn activity as employees noisily wheeled trolleys, wrenched open shutters, unlocked metallic doors, and turned closed signs to open.

Welcoming smells and sights from the food court pumped up the volume with the lifesaving aroma of fresh coffee and newly baked bread, bagels, rolls, and cinnamon buns designed to entice hungry clients in for a wakeup call and an energy-giving carb-filled start to the day.

51

Kathleen was not traveler or worker or a sleeper-on-the-streets stray. Fear and pain jarred her tired body as she was forced to face the fact that albeit temporarily, she was indeed a misfit, a person of no fixed abode. Tears of frustration that had previously formed a two-track line down her face increased to a veritable downpour of self-pity and self-recrimination. Sami was the only person offering her any solutions.

It would be a calamity if she lost him now.

Sami had no intention of letting Kathleen lose him, but once he got a fixed idea in his head there was no stopping him. He prided himself on being a fast thinker and a fast mover. His mind raced with all the infinite possibilities of how he would turn his new protégé into a star. And he knew exactly where he was going to start. Ducking and diving his way around New York's awakening streets, Sami checked that Kathleen was behind him.

Like a guide marshaling tourists, he took off his hat and waved it in the air to provide a visual sign of his whereabouts.

"Not much further," he called to her, though the human ocean of commuters between them meant that his voice was swallowed up and Kathleen had to keep running on faith.

Without warning, a gaping hole opened up at her feet and she skidded to a halt. Cellar doors yawned ajar and gave the appearance of the devouring jaws of a prehistoric wooden, scaled monster greedily swallowing barrels of beer from a truck parked on the sidewalk.

Having arrived ahead of her, Sami was already inside the

establishment. She struggled to make out his disembodied voice as he urged her to take care and step over the threshold, being careful to avoid the cellar doors.

Kathleen blinked as she stepped into the gloom of the darkened bar and wrinkled her nose in distaste at the stale smell of beer and tobacco. The wooden paneled bar was ancient and smelled damp, probably running live with termites. It was a real spit and sawdust kind of place. From a floor way above her head Kathleen became aware of a loud thundering noise, as simultaneously she saw and heard a huge bear of a man come charging down the winding wooden stairs.

Sami had second thoughts about trying to hide under the stairwell and walked forward to confront boldly the force of nature that was bearing down physically and verbally upon him.

As the new arrival came into view at the foot of the stairs, Kathleen pressed herself into a far-off corner of the bar and watched in fascination as the man twanged bright red suspenders over his broad shoulders and finished tucking his shirt into the back of his pants.

A red mist surrounded him and with his color coordinated suspenders, bright carrot red hair, and red balloon face he looked like he was about to audition for a movie part as Mr. Angry.

"Get out, get out," he bellowed at Sami who was standing bravely in the way of the tomato tornado.

"I told you never to come here again—and I meant it," he said.

Without pausing even to catch his wheezing breath, he

squeezed himself through the small opening in the bar counter, after raising the flap and securing it. His expanded body did not look as if it would go through, but after what must have been years of practice he first deflated the bulk around his waist and re-inflated it once behind the bar.

Knowing he was unlikely to be about to offer them a drink, Kathleen wanted to be well out of the way before the next act played out. She decided to make use of the deflation trick and like Alice in Wonderland make herself appear smaller and smaller.

"Just hear me out, Big Mac," Sami said in his most pleasant and reasonable voice, as he launched into his version of a highly plausible explanation for ignoring previous instructions to stay away.

He plowed on gamely, even though he was required to address the man's back and watch him help himself to multiple measures while filling a glass with whiskey from the optics lined up behind the bar.

Big Mac was silent, but anyone familiar with tornadoes would have realized that while all was calm in the eye of the storm, the outer rim of the whirling weather system was about to hit—with exaggerated force.

Gathering all his reserves, Big Mac spun around at great speed, surprisingly agile for such a large man. In his ham-fisted right hand he held a large kitchen knife snatched up from the cutting board, where the outer ends of last night's garnish of lemons and limes rested in a small puddle of citrus juice.

"I'll count to ten," he threatened, "If you're still in my bar when I reach ten—the knife will do the talking."

Sami's eyes betrayed his fear; the whites were plainly visible and his Adam's apple worked frantically up and down as he swallowed and twice removed his hat and put it back on again immediately, seemingly unsure whether to stay or go. He did not look at Kathleen, for that she was grateful, but all her senses were alert as she stood by awaiting a silent instruction from him.

"The police raid was not my fault," Sami started out, talking fast and furious. Then he slowed right down and spelled out the information he needed to impart. One word at a time. "Your wife set you up."

Now he had Big Mac's attention. Thinking fast and talking faster, Sami enlightened the landlord of one of the roughest pubs in the Hell's Kitchen area of New York: "Your wife called the cops and told them you were hiring illegals. She wanted you arrested and she tried to get me in on the scam."

All the fight went out of Big Mac as he absorbed the information, but he wasn't about to give up yet. He insisted on retaining some semblance of dignity.

"I'm still counting," he warned Sami. "You're at five. Keep talking."

"Don't make me be the one to tell you." Sami chose his words carefully, allowing him to be the bearer of bad tidings but hopefully avoid being the messenger who got shot. "All the bar knows, she's at it again," he said in a small voice.

Mac stopped counting and stabbed the knife into the counter top.

"This time I swear I will kill her," he said in a low, menacing voice, while lifting the knife and stabbing it again into the counter top, to ensure his point had been made.

Pressing home his advantage, Sami gestured to Kathleen to come out of the shadows. She shook her head in a small but adamant gesture and tried to signal with her eyes that she had no intention of drawing even the tiniest amount of attention to herself.

Sami was in no mood to take "no" for an answer; like a chess player he had already planned his moves several steps ahead.

"Allow me to introduce, the answer to at least one of your problems." Sami helpfully presented the solution, seamlessly implementing his well-honed salesman strategies. Identify what the customer needs and provide it. Make sure the customer knows you are doing them a favor.

"The first people taken to the slammer were the sexy, singing sisters from Brazil," Sami reiterated, knowing that Mac was so drunk by the end of most nights in the bar, he often had no idea what had actually transpired on his own premises.

"You are going to need a new act to draw the crowds back in—police raids are not good for business—and she can also work as a barmaid. That is if you really are going to kick your wife out once and for all." Mac scowled and, knowing that he had overstepped the boundaries, Sami backed down.

"None of my business, of course," he said, "but at least give the girl a chance, you won't regret it."

Kathleen had not said a word and had barely moved a muscle, but she had a horrible premonition of what was coming. The embarrassment of singing to vagrants in a deserted late-night station was bad enough; this humiliation had all the potential to be even worse. Her face was flushed as red as Mac's had been earlier.

Now with the first medicinal measure of whiskey inside him, Mac was already mellowing. Just to be sure that he was treating the cause, he jammed the glass up to help himself to another mega measure.

Sami walked slowly toward Kathleen as if approaching a frisky young colt and took her arm as he led her to the front of the empty bar. "Time to sing for your supper, my pretty."

Kathleen took a deep breath and put on the mask of her performance face, perfected over the years with her father on the streets. She was a trooper and, even when singing and dancing was the last thing she wanted to do, she could always step up to the plate. Padraic had never shied away from calling upon a good cliché to prove his point.

"The show must go on," he said regularly and with such certainty that it sounded like an Eleventh Commandment.

Always the true professional, Kathleen positioned herself in the best light, even in the smoky darkness of the bar, and invited her audience of two to sit back and enjoy the show.

Her young voice rang out crystal clear, as she sang the haunting melody of a traditional Irish folk song; the second piece she chose for her impromptu audition was a popular hit parade ballad, and she finished off with a grand old sing-a-long "When Irish Eyes are Smiling." Treating the audience to a rousing final chorus, Kathleen added the extra touch of theatricality that always made her performance at once unexpected and extra special. She launched into her ritualized traditional Irish dancing, arms and hands straight by her sides, feet moving at the speed of light and rapid-fire taps on the ground sounding out an ancient drum beat.

Rat a tat tat—heel toe, heel toe, kick, flick, constantly increasing the speed and powering up the energy. Spinning and twisting and weaving a magic spell, faster and faster, her beautiful long black hair joined the dance and fairy tale curls framed her bewitching nymph face; it was as if a divine, mythical creature was dancing to enchant a royal court. Sami and Big Mac looked on in awe at the sheer power the self-assured teenage performer generated.

Then the storm passed. Kathleen gradually decreased her spinning and visibly made a physical change as she reentered her body—human once more. The spell was complete. Standing still and silent, a whirling dervish came to rest. Kathleen was startled when a whole battery of applause greeted the finale of her inspired performance.

Only then did she discover that she had not only been entertaining Sami and Mac, whom she was deliberately setting out to impress, but her singing and dancing had drawn a crowd.

Draymen who had been delivering the beer direct to the cellar came to collect their money and stayed to see the beguiling creature who had turned the dreary early morning bar into a palace of entertainment. Even a couple of passersby had been enticed by her siren song. They hovered in the doorway, clapping enthusiastically.

Mac did not hesitate. To Sami's delight, he hired Kathleen on the spot. "She can start tonight," he said and with more than a touch of sarcasm, added, "I'm presuming you are her agent."

"Of course," said Sami. "She's the best thing you've had in this establishment for years. Better than the Sao Paulo sisters."

Before Mac could react and start the wheels of his mind working on just who had benefited from the sudden incarceration of his previous star performers, Sami was quick to take his leave.

"You've got a star attraction on your hands, Mac. She'll make us both a fortune."

Kathleen was not consulted on what she thought. Just as well. She was too street smart to trust an opportunistic conman and a drunk with murder in his heart.

For the time being, at least while she had no other options, she proposed to hand herself over to The Fates and "seize the day."

CHAPTER EIGHT

If I Can Make It There

A noisy chorus of *"Why are we waiting?"* signaled to Kathleen that her audience was restless. For the twentieth time she checked her appearance in the cracked, peeling backstage mirror and reapplied high-gloss scarlet lipstick.

The excruciating cramps in her stomach reminded her of the early nerves she had suffered when she had first performed at the raucous Irish bar The Magic Harp, known throughout the city for a well-pulled Guinness, a lively music scene, and nightly fist fights. The nerves she experienced then had soon subsided as Kathleen had quickly established a loyal following and become a star attraction: the beautiful and very young Irish colleen who had been trained on the streets of New York and danced and sang with all the vigor and emotion of the homeland, the beloved Emerald Isle.

As seductive to the homesick audience as a map of Ireland, Kathleen's coal black hair reminded them of the peat rich soil; her alabaster white skin seemed nourished by the creamy milk of the well-fed plump Irish cattle, her lips held promise of chaste romantic summertime kisses, and her smiling emerald eyes exerted a magical power over the bewitched audience.

Kathleen had stolen every man's heart and every woman secretly yearned to be her.

"Come on, Kathie," Big Mac's unmistakable bellow spurred her into action. "Get out here and shut this lot up. What do you think I pay you for? For the Lord's sake, get yourself a wiggle on, Missy."

For over three months Sami had been grooming Kathleen for her Big Break and he had convinced her that she needed an attention-grabbing stage name. Now only those closest to her still called her Kathleen—though Mac and a few friends chose to call her Kathie, a nickname her father had often used for her.

Kathleen had been transformed into *Angel Kennedy, Heaven's Gift.*

The grubby single curtain of old tapestry material that separated the backstage area from the bar was held open by one of the male waiters and Big Mac thankfully made his nightly announcement.

However many times he had rehearsed his MC moment, he still got it wrong more often than he got it right. Mac was a man of few words and even in the few words it took to give a fitting introduction to his star turn, he still fluffed his lines.

"Here she is now. The lovely young lady you've all been waiting for—Kathie, no, wait a minute, bear with me, I'll start again. Here she is now, Miss Angel Kennedy, a Gift from Heaven."

Mac's stumbling introduction was not heard. As soon as

the curtain opened, the audience erupted with enthusiastic applause, cheering, whistles, and catcalls.

Angel Kennedy stepped into the spotlight that was trained on a small raised platform at the end of the public house, almost directly in front of the restroom doors. Dressed in a light-reflecting, dazzling green velvet off-the-shoulder dress, her ample breasts and small waist were shown off to a breath-catching "ooh, la la" by the wide corset belt accentuating her curvy, feminine form. Shiny black tights encased her long lithe legs and silver buckles glinted on her black patent dancing shoes. Ribbons of green, white, and gold streamed like sunrays from her luxuriant ebony spiraling hair.

In her new incarnation, Angel truly did look divine—an angel, a goddess. The effect was magnified as she opened her mouth to sing. A reverential hush settled over the previously untamed crowd and the audience breathed as one, quiet as church mice.

Angel stood at the microphone, composed, in charge; she had the audience in the palm of her hand. It was standing room only in the jam-packed bar and even the jostling for position stilled while Angel waited for perfect silence and rapt attention from her adoring fans. Acknowledging the waves of love that were directed toward her, Angel blew a kiss to the audience and every man there believed it was directed at him.

"Thank you," she said. "Let's get this show on the road."

The deliberately sentimental opening number was designed to evoke memories of the old country and she began her repertoire with the ever popular, Irish classic, "Mountains of Mourne." As Angel conjured up images of the mountains rolling down to the sea, tears smoothly rolled down the cheeks of Irishmen who dreamed of one day going home and, not to be left out, those who had never even been home, but who too dreamed of a joyful return.

Kindred spirits all. Singer and audience became one as they traveled on a carefully choreographed musical journey through the highways and byways of a bygone and largely mythical Ireland. A land of green fields, blue waters, and abundant good-luck four-leaf clovers. An imagined idyllic pastoral scene that many had fled and few would ever behold again—except in their dreams. But who cared for reality and news of The Troubles when there was nostalgia on tap and ale to fuel the imagination.

Angel played her audience like a well-tuned musical instrument. She could make them laugh, she could make them cry, and without too much effort, she could cajole them into accompanying her in sing-a-longs.

Her empathy with the audience was genuine. Her soul yearned for the same union of family, home, and hearth they craved. The emotional roller coaster invoked by her choice of songs and dances stirred memories of her mother and father, drove her on, and ensured that her performances transcended the ordinary.

The incorrigible dreamer, her father always exhorted her, "Ordinary is for those without the imagination to soar beyond the stars. You need extraordinary to power the life force. Never settle for mundane—only the best is good enough."

Angel dared to soar. Her music carried her up to the

celestial spheres and she sang her way joyfully through traditional folk songs, popular ballads, hymns, and anthems—finishing as always with multiple choruses of "When Irish Eyes are Smiling."

The experienced musicians who had accompanied her all through the show used well-tried techniques to bring the concert to a close. A fiddle player, an accordionist, and the man with the drum all slowed their rhythm to allow Angel to acknowledge the applause, which showed no signs of ending, and exit the stage. No virtuoso entertaining the glitterati at a Carnegie Hall concert could have attracted a more appreciative audience.

Angel exited the stage—gulped down a large glass of water—and made a run for the poky staff bathroom. Into the grubby, chipped porcelain bowl, she threw up. Now that Dr. Theater no longer carried her on a wave of euphoria and adrenaline, her stomach cramps returned, worse than ever.

Concepta, one of the older barmaids who had befriended the younger girl since the two came to work at the bar a few days apart, put her head around the bathroom door. Kathleen splashed her face with water from the faucet. Concepta had temporarily deserted her serving position behind the bar and would soon be missed. Leading Kathleen gently by the arm to an old armchair the staff used to prop Big Mac in, when he could no longer safely stand, she sat her down. "You look terrible," she said. "What's wrong?'

The beautiful young would-be star, who a few short moments before had held an audience spellbound, now looked washed-out and drained of all energy.

"Perhaps it's something I ate," Kathie replied, as she tried to find an explanation. Anxiously screwing up a piece of toilet tissue in her clammy hands, she loosened the corset belt that was now feeling like a vice.

"Wait and I'll get one of the men to walk you home," Concepta told her. "I'll come around to see you when I've finished here."

Kathie lived just a few doors from the bar in a rooming house owned by Big Mac. "You're very kind but I'll be alright, I've got to meet someone," she insisted.

Seeing her fellow worker's puzzled look, Kathie enlightened her. "It's a friend of my father's. One of the musicians. They used to be in a band together. I promised to have a drink with him and catch up on old times."

Concepta, a well-padded, dark-haired down-to-earth motherly type, a good ten years older—maybe more—than her new best friend Kathie, considered whether to try to play the heavy-handed parent and order her young friend to go home, but decided she would be wasting her breath. Kathie might be young but she was strong willed and, to give credit where it was due, she was also sensible.

Apart from Sami, who was still spinning her his dreams, she lived a quiet life without the benefit of family or friends, and Concepta had never heard her mention a boyfriend or show any interest in the many men who tried to offer her a better life—with them as her protector. Sami might have been ineffectual, but he also appeared harmless and was genuine in his admiration of Kathie's considerable talent and his efforts to move her career along.

Unfortunately, so anxious had he been to get back into Big Mac's good books and accept his spontaneous offer on day one of bringing Kathie to his bar, Sami had made a potentially costly mistake. On the basis that a bird in the hand was worth two in the bush, Sami had fallen into the kind of trap desperate men are often prone to often fall into.

He had signed Kathie to Big Mac exclusively. She was not able to sing at any other establishment for the duration of their six-month contract and that was only just over halfway completed. If she were offered a recording contract, that would be a different matter. Mac would have no objection whatsoever to having a famous singing star entertaining his drinking crowd. Perhaps one day Sami would pull it off and negotiate that break for his protégé. In the meantime, he rather grandly described the interim period as "artist development."

Kathie took singing and dancing lessons and even studied drama with a crazy Russian acting coach who was teaching her to create a public persona—*Angel Kennedy, Heaven's Gift*—and inhabit her new flamboyant stage presence.

Sami treated Kathie respectfully, almost like a daughter—he was actually old enough to be her grandfather—and he got a kick out of introducing her to his contacts and friends in the music business. Stealing a clichéd Hollywood movie line, Sami had assured his teenage discovery, "Stick with me, kid, I'm gonna make you a star."

Kathie couldn't be sure but she thought she had heard that very speech on one of the old black and white movies her mother used to watch on television. *Banish the thought.* She missed her mother and desperately wished she had the courage to go and visit her. However, the thought of having to face her new boyfriend, and a sense of loyalty to her father, stopped her.

In the meantime, Kathie took the Magic Harp by storm six days a week and Big Mac's profits soared.

Concepta had Kathie to thank for her job. Kathie's popularity was the deciding factor that made the Magic Harp stand out from the other drinking establishments in their less than salubrious area of town. In common with most drunks, Big Mac was unpredictable and Concepta knew that he was likely to start shouting and roaring when he discovered she was still missing from behind the bar.

Without will or inclination to argue with the younger girl, Concepta settled for a friendly admonishment, "Well, make it a quick drink or you'll be in no condition for tomorrow night's show. I'm amazed you got through tonight without passing out on stage, judging by the state of you now."

Making her way back to the bar, Concepta identified one of the musicians, his accordion already stowed in its case and placed securely by his feet under the wooden trestle table.

"Are you waiting for Kathie?" she asked him.

"That's right," he agreed, lifting his glass of Guinness to his lips and leaving a small white mustache of cream that he wiped away with the back of his hand. Pride of Ireland's brewing, the black and white ambrosia of the Gods had as its universal advertisement, *Guinness is Good for You.* Concepta issued the musician an instruction. "I'll send over a small glass of that for Kathie, she looks like she needs the iron. Now don't be keeping her, she's very tired. She needs to be away home."

"I hear you," said the affable red-faced Irishman. He raised his glass to his lips again and stared into the black sea of goodness as Kathie appeared by the table and prepared to sit down.

She had changed out of her stage costume and now resembled more the fashion-conscious young lady she had become since joining the ultracompetitive female world of a college of the performing arts. She was dressed in denim jeans and a trendy faux fur coat. Her lovely long tresses were tied into a ponytail and she had removed most of her stage makeup.

"It's good to see you again Seamus," she told the visiting musician, as she made herself comfortable on the opposite side of the table to him and avoided kicking the large reinforced cardboard carrying case that held his precious accordion.

"Thanks for the great playing tonight. You and your guys are the best. Dad always said so." Seamus smiled and thanked her. He had chosen a quiet place at the back of the still crowded bar.

"The barmaid said she'd send over a glass of Guinness for you," Seamus passed on the message.

"That's fine," replied Kathie. "And no doubt there will be another one for yourself. I'm not a beer drinker, or any kind of drinker come to that, but I'll not turn down her kindness; she means well though I'm already feeling better. That'll be thanks to seeing you here, you and Dad always were good friends. I miss seeing all the old gang. You'll have to tell me all the news." Seamus smiled again and revealed gaps where teeth used to be.

Kathleen was embarrassed about the estrangement between her and her father. Although their bars were only a few blocks apart, in a big city it might as well have been the other side of the world. Each small area is a village and drinkers tend to stay in their comfort zones. If anyone had information about Padraic, they weren't saying—and Kathleen did not ask too loudly. Dirty linen was not for washing in public.

However, in her three months of working at the bar, Kathie had tried on a number of occasions to go and see her father and put matters right between the two of them. He was never at home when she called and her house key did not work—the locks had been changed and the apartment appeared to have been boarded up. Just one neighbor, an Arabic-speaking lady, had volunteered any information as to his whereabouts—all she had to say was that he had "gone away."

Concepta urged Kathie to "drink it up" as she placed a small tumbler of Guinness on the table in front of Kathie. Filled expertly to the rim without a drop being spilled, the black of the body was the texture of crushed velvet and the white head was smooth as silk—with a smiley face drawn in the center.

Seamus raised his glass to toast Kathie and as he placed the drink back on the table with care, he took the volume down on his voice, lowered his chin, and tried to make himself look smaller. Still, he would not avoid saying what he needed to say and, being careful not to avoid Kathie's eyes, much as he wanted to, he said respectfully, "I'm sorry about what happened to your father. He was a good man."

Glass halfway to her lips, a proposed toast still reverberating in the jaunty angle of the airborne glass, Kathie froze mid-gesture, as if in a child's game of statues. For a silent moment her world stood still. All sights, all sounds, all action ceased.

Fearful she would drop the full glass, Kathie returned it to its resting place in the center of the thin cardboard beer mat on the wooden table from where she had lifted it a moment and a lifetime ago. Looking directly into Seamus's eyes, Kathie asked the question to which she already dreaded the answer. Exhaling and gathering courage from the familiar sensation of her own breath in her body Kathie spoke up. "What happened?"

Seamus could not reply and stay connected to the pain in her eyes. "Oh, God, Kathie, I'm sorry," he pleaded, using again the childhood name by which he had known her so long ago, not her stage name. "Please forgive me. Until this minute, I didn't know, you didn't know."

Reaching out a hand to cover hers, he gave her the devastating news: "Paddy, Padraic, your father, he was murdered."

Kathie swayed forward and her head connected with the tabletop. She fell toward the sea of blackness in her glass and as she fainted it seemed that all the lights had been switched off. Kathie was out for the count.

CHAPTER NINE

No Time to Say Goodbye

Coming to in her own bed, Kathie was befuddled and could not remember how she got there. As she tried to raise her head from the pillow, Concepta gently held her down and continued applying an ice pack to the bruised area where Kathie's forehead had hit the tabletop, narrowly missing smashing into glasses.

Two strong-arm men from the public house had volunteered to carry her home and Concepta, released by Mac from her bar-tending duties, had hurried along in attendance.

She held Kathie's hand and assured her, "You're okay. Don't worry. We'll soon have you home and in your own bed." At the door of the rooming house, Concepta had stood aside to let the men transport Kathie up the narrow flight of stairs.

The rooming house, under the direction of Mac's erstwhile wife Gloria, who was given to delusions of grandeur, had seen its lowly status elevated to hotel, but a lick of paint and a change of name from Mac's Guest House to the Dubliner Hotel fooled no one.

Kathie's room was on the first floor at the back of the

hotel. Staff accommodation was generally up further flights of the rickety staircase, but Sami had negotiated a discount rate for his favorite artiste. He had persuaded Mac to allow Kathie to have the small double room previously shared by the singing Brazilian twin sisters.

The room was cramped even for one person and the few pieces of furniture were basic, but Kathie had made her living space homely. She endeavored to keep the place spick 'n' span, as she had strived to do at home with her parents. Cheap secondhand fabric throws, cheerful bunches of flowers in colorful vases, and a poster of the Notre Dame in Paris made the room appear cozy and welcoming.

Also there was no denying the luxury of the double bed, which the sisters had shared, and fresh bedding courtesy of the departing girls—they had traveled light when they fled the country rather than face deportation—and there was a water filled washstand in one corner of the room. Kathie had known and lived in worse; she did not waste time complaining.

Even though she had not expected visitors in the shape of the two good Samaritans from the Magic Harp, Kathie's room passed inspection.

The men left before Kathie was fully compos mentis and Concepta promised she would make sure Kathie had an opportunity to buy them a drink and thank them next time they came to the bar.

"Now stop worrying about other people and think about yourself," said Concepta pretending to be annoyed.

"What happened?" asked Kathie, and immediately her

mind flashed back to the freeze-frame moment when she had asked the same question of Seamus.

"This is not the time to try to get answers," said Concepta, fearful of the reaction from Kathie if she began to unravel the reasons for having passed out. Preempting further questioning, she told Kathie, "I asked Seamus to come and see you tomorrow; he was already on his way to play at another bar tonight. You need to make sure that you're alright first and if you don't follow my advice to stay quietly resting here, I may be forced to take you to the hospital emergency department in case you have concussion after your knock on the head."

Both women knew it was a threat intended simply to allow Concepta to keep control and avoid Kathie having to face situations which for the time being had no resolution. Kathie struggled to sit up and Concepta decided to allow her patient to win one battle.

Setting down the ice pack, she helped Kathie get upright, plumped her pillows, and made a bargain. "If you can sit up without any pain in your head, I'll treat us both to a nice cup of tea."

In the corner of the room, beside a tiny sash window, a small gas ring on a narrow makeshift counter held tea-making equipment: a whistling kettle, an economy sized teapot, and a diverse assortment of china cups and saucers. Another gift from the previous occupants. Alongside the meager cooking facilities, there was a meter. Concepta crossed her fingers and checked the dial. She was pleasantly surprised to find there was enough gas available to boil the kettle. She hadn't wanted to go rousing neighbors to try and borrow tokens for the meter.

She busied herself with the ritual of the tea making, taking as much care as if it really were afternoon tea at the best hotel in town.

Her intention was to keep talking, keep bustling around, and avoid a conversation with Kathie about her father.

Seamus had confided to Concepta the tragic news that he had imparted to Kathie and that had led directly to her fainting fit.

"The poor girl didn't know that her father had been murdered," he told her in shocked tones.

"I could have bitten off my tongue when I realized that I was the one to tell her. I don't think she even knew he was dead, never mind the way he died."

"WHAT happened? I want to know," said Kathie adamantly. "I have a right to know."

Concentrating on her tea-making duties, Concepta pretended not to hear. She had no answers and knew no more than Kathie herself. Although he would happily have gone into details, Concepta judged that it was more appropriate that Seamus tell the whole story when Padraic's grieving daughter was able to hear and process the information.

Kathie and her best friend and confidant drank their tea in silence. The evening had taken a huge strain on both of them.

"Budge over," said Concepta after she had used a small amount of the water in the nightstand to rinse out the empty cups. "I'll stay with you tonight."

Extinguishing the gas mantle on the wall near to the

head of the bed, Concepta enquired again about Kathie's condition. "I'll be here if you need me," she said kindly. "I'm a light sleeper. So, no snoring."

Both women laughed, some light relief finally releasing their heightened emotions. "Night, night, don't let the bugs bite."

More laughter as Kathie let out a yell, "I wish you hadn't said that. One of the little buggers just got me. Now him and his family will be feeding on me all night."

"So, what's new?" said her visitor. "We Irish have sweet blood."

* * *

Exhausted and heartbroken, Kathie cried herself to sleep. On awakening, the throbbing pain in her left temple was eclipsed by the stabbing pain in her heart.

Kathie was at a loss to identify which ailment was causing the nausea and sickness she suffered. It happened almost every morning as soon as she woke up. A cup of hot tea and small piece of dry bread generally helped the feeling to pass and before leaving home she took both to fortify herself for the day ahead.

She had not been aware of Concepta waking, dressing, and leaving for her midmorning shift at the Magic Harp. Kathie's name didn't appear on the daily roster though she was still called upon to help out waiting tables at particularly busy times. So popular was she with the customers that even being on the premises socializing attracted more drinkers to the bar and put more money in Mac's till.

Seamus had promised to come by the bar during the

lunchtime drinking session and Kathie wasted no time in getting up, dressed, and out the door on her way to meet him.

Her mind was already working overtime; it tortured her with terrible thoughts of what fate had befallen her father that he should now be described as "a murder victim." The truth could not be worse than her wild imaginings. Seamus would have some answers.

Kathie made the short journey to the Magic Harp and had time to thank Concepta for her many kindnesses before Seamus arrived. He was not alone. With him he brought a young man who Kathie knew from the streets around her former home in Hell's Kitchen. The lad was a known troublemaker, a small-time crook who liked to fancy himself as a member of a larger, more powerful criminal crowd.

His sheepish look betrayed the fact that he had not come altogether voluntarily. Seamus gave him a small shove forward to indicate that he should offer his condolences to Kathie.

"Sorry about your Dad," he said without raising his eyes from the ground. Seamus sat at the table and nodded for the lad to do the same. Kathie sat down in the same place she had sat the night before, across the trestle from Seamus and the tall, skinny young lad whom she knew by the nickname, Spike, on account of his slicked skyward hairdo.

Concepta was already on her way over bearing a tray with a pint of Guinness for Seamus, a half pint for the underage kid, and a glass of soda for Kathie.

Taking her by surprise, Seamus pointed to the lad beside

him and sneered as he explained, "He knows the whole story. HE was there when your father died."

"But I didn't have anything to do with it," Spike interjected. "It wasn't me, the old man was dead when I got there."

Seamus shot him a dark look. "Mind your language. This is the man's daughter you're talking to, show some respect."

Kathie stared directly at the youth who she judged to be not much older than her. It was obvious he had been coerced into coming to talk to her and she was determined to hear his side of the story before he clammed up or took flight.

"Me lado here works for some of the less desirable elements in the neighborhood," Seamus offered by way of explanation. "They don't know he's here today and certainly wouldn't want to know that he's talking to you. Still, your dad's friends have their own ways of doing business too. No doubt that's why they went to such lengths to try to prevent us hearing about what had happened.

"It's as if they all joined a secret society and took the vow of silence. But there's always a little bird that sings—for glory or revenge."

Seamus's tone was serious. "This young hoodlum has been promised that we'll keep his name out of it if he can set your mind at rest and give you a little peace. Maybe his conscience was bothering him."

Anger flashed in his eyes as he barked, "Spike, Pike, or whatever your name is, tell her what you know."

Spike took a long fortifying swallow of his drink and, in a voice rich with bravado and a boastful tone, he talked to Kathie about the night her father died. He seemed torn between trying to minimize his part and wanting to show off the fact that he was a go-to man for some powerful street criminal types.

"Some friends of mine have been helping out the owners of properties in Hell's Kitchen. The building where your father lived being one of them. We've been 'persuading' tenants to move out because the developers are coming in and they won't pay the money for the old houses if there are people still living there. We 'suggest' that they might be happier living somewhere else."

Seamus scowled, not appreciating Spike's attempt at humor.

Switching to a sales pitch as if he were a realtor talking up the project to a buyer, Spike continued. "It might look like an old slum but the developers are buying all the old properties and sending in the demolition crews. They are going to make it a high-end development like Midtown or even Manhattan. This will be prime real estate, rents will be sky-high, and anyone who gets in on the ground floor will make a fortune."

"Fascinating," said Kathie trying hard to keep the sarcasm out of her voice. "But what's it got to do with my dad?"

"He wouldn't move," said Spike. "We gave him warnings and even when the building was practically empty, he hung on. The landlord asked him nicely but your dad turned nasty and threatened to go to the Rent Commission. He was a stubborn old bugger. I talked to him myself a couple of times."

Kathie wasn't sure that she understood the situation.

"They had him killed because he wouldn't move?" she questioned.

Spike was no longer boastful; in fact he was sweating and looked decidedly uncomfortable. Running a bony finger inside the collar of his grubby work shirt, his spiky hairdo looking seriously in danger of collapsing, he declared, "It's very hot in here. Could you see your way to getting me another drink? A pint this time."

Kathie nodded to the young barmaid who had taken Concepta's usual place behind the bar and held up two fingers while also indicating that the running total should be put on her personal tab behind the bar. It was a small price to pay to get the inside track on what had happened to her father.

"Drink's on its way. Go on," she encouraged Spike.

"It was an accident," he said, "But I wasn't there. I went around to help after he was already dead."

"Tell me what happened. From the beginning," said Kathie beginning to despair that she was ever going to hear the full or true story.

"Some of the boys went around to 'talk' to him. Well to give him an ultimatum. Move or be thrown out on the street. He got lippy and wouldn't listen to reason. They said he was drunk. No one meant to hurt him bad, our orders, I mean *the* orders were, to rough him up a bit. He knew what they were there for. Somebody hit him and somebody pushed him. He collapsed. He was lying on the floor and I was told he just stopped breathing. Just like that. One minute he's alive and giving aggravation, the next he's dead on the floor.

"The boss called and said I should go around and give them a hand.

"Clear up things. A baseball bat had been left behind but our boys insist that no one used it on him; it was just to put the frighteners on him. He hit his head when he fell down."

Seamus had stayed silent up to that point, and now he looked at Spike and said one word, "Scum."

Spike had the grace to hang his head in shame.

Kathie had heard more than enough but she had to hear more.

"When was this?" she asked.

"A couple of months ago," Spike recalled, before continuing his story. "We set a small fire in the house and called the fire department. One of the lads kept watch till they arrived and took the body away. The landlord told us to remove all traces of his identity and he denied knowing who the guy was when the police questioned him. Said he'd probably used a false name anyway when he rented the apartment.

"Seems he was listed as a John Doe at the morgue. Dead on arrival."

Seamus took up the story and offered what information he had gleaned from asking around the neighborhood. "The construction crew went in and demolished the whole building a few days ago. The city condemned the block and put a compulsory purchase order on it.

"Most convenient for the landlord and developers who promptly bought it back. They plan to build high-end residential apartments on what is now a vacant lot."

"Two months ago," Kathie repeated. She was remembering the night of her birthday, three months previously. Her dad had never even told her that there was a problem with their accommodation; he had kept the worry and concern to himself.

If only he had shared the information about the harassment with her she might have been able to help. Even if they had had to move, it wouldn't have been the first time and they would have managed. Of course, he knew how much effort she had put into making a comfortable home for them, but it was nothing that made it worth losing his life over.

She wanted to rage and scream at Spike and kick out at all the despicable low lives that prey on those weaker than them. Instead, as the tears streamed down her lovely face, she thanked Spike.

Thanked him for having the courage to face her and for telling her the real situation so she did not have to go on making it up in her head. Even while acknowledging that in his behavior there was nothing to be proud of, she still hoped that just maybe he would experience remorse.

However, worse still was the contempt and shame she felt for herself. The feeling of guilt was already overpowering and making the bile and nausea rise again from her cramped stomach into her foul-tasting mouth. She sipped a tiny amount of her soda. Her thoughts crucified her.

You are as much to blame as that bunch of thugs, she told herself. You had a responsibility to your father, your own flesh and blood. He loved you. He took care of you. You should have protected him. If you had been there, it wouldn't have happened. You'll pay for your wickedness.

An overwhelming feeling of doom swept over her whole body as surely as if it were a raging wave. *You will never be happy in this life. Thanks to your selfishness and lust your father is dead. God will punish you.*

Spike was obviously anxious to be off after his confession; Kathie hoped that maybe he would feel the relief of confession. In his own heart of hearts he knew the part he had played that fateful night.

Seamus too, reaching under the table for his trusty companion the accordion, was more than ready to be on his way.

"You're a good friend," said Kathie as she took his arm and walked Seamus to the door of the bar. "Thank you, my dad would have been proud of you. You're a decent human being and I thank God for that. Please don't be a stranger. Keep in touch and I'll be sure to see that Big Mac invites you to play for me whenever you choose. Thank you again, Seamus."

To Spike she offered forgiveness knowing that allowing her anger and resentment against him to fester would serve no purpose. Her father had always told her, carrying resentment is like drinking poison and hoping the other person will die. Perhaps by being treated right he might even have his eyes opened to the dangerous and murderous path he was already treading.

"Your life will end violently as surely as was my father's," Kathie told him. "Thank you for coming today. It can't have been easy to face me. You can rest assured; I promise I won't pass on the information you've given me to the authorities.

"I don't know yet if there is any action I can take, but you won't be implicated. Not by me anyway. Goodbye, Spike."

Kathie leaned against the solid bar door and watched Seamus and Spike walk down the road. She felt sorry for Spike. He was a street kid with little chance of ever making a decent life for himself. He was not a big-time criminal, just a scared little boy, acting big.

At least her dad had instilled good values in her and the nuns had ensured that she knew right from wrong. *Oh, God, in heaven, how many Hail Marys will it take to set right the wrong I've done?*

Kathie was forced to brush Concepta out of the way as she ran to the restroom. The waves of nausea and chronic sickness were upon her again.

CHAPTER TEN

Matters of Life and Death

With no clear destination in mind, Kathie left the Magic Harp and stumbled along the familiar city street past her lodgings, blinded by tears and choked with sadness. She found herself standing alongside the small opening in the double wooden doors with rusty iron locks and bolts that led into the tiled entrance hall of the Church of the Sacred Heart.

She ducked her head, though it was not strictly necessary as there was plenty of room to pass, and stepped into the safety of the church. Automatically she dipped the tips of the first two fingers on her right hand into the holy water in the marble font that was strategically placed on a pedestal beside the inner glass-paneled doors. Before crossing the threshold into the ornate gilded and statue-filled church, she made the sign of the cross with the holy water on her forehead, at the center of her chest, and alongside her shoulders blades.

The afternoon sun, high in the sky, shone radiantly into the silent church. The aisle was bathed in fragmented reflections from the jewel-colored stained-glass window that depicted Jesus with his welcoming arms outstretched illuminating the blazing Sacred Heart.

Kathie walked straight to the front of the church, genuflected in front of the altar steps, and proceeded to the wrought-iron candle stand situated beside the chapel of Our Lady of Lourdes. She dropped coins in the offerings box and lit several votive candles. Kathie stood reverentially with her hands clasped and head bowed in prayer. She made her way to her favorite pew, beside the aisle, two rows back on the right-hand side opposite the pulpit. She checked her watch and confirmed that a priest was scheduled to hear confession. So far she was the only penitent. The thought brought shame and she began to cry softly.

Kneeling on the hard wooden foot stool, hands covering her eyes, and cradling her head as it rested against the hard ledge at the top of the seat in front, Kathie slumped forward and allowed herself to fall apart.

Emotions threatened to completely overwhelm her. Her tears were fueled by a toxic combination of rage, powerlessness, and a deep sense of loss. Her breathing became uncomfortably shallow and the airways felt as if they were blocked; she gasped for air. The constriction in her chest coupled with the tears running into her mouth made her feel as if she was drowning. She fought an insane urge to hit her head against the bench in front; maybe physical pain would stop the hurt inside that drove her to force her fingernails into her hands and long for them to bleed.

In the moment of her greatest pain, Kathie opened her eyes and looked up at the figure of Jesus on the cross hanging above the altar in front of her. *Father, why have you for-*

saken me? she pleaded. In His eyes she imagined she saw an echo of her own hurt and despair.

She was startled to hear a concerned male voice respond. Kathie had not been aware of anyone entering the church but as if in answer to her prayers, the priest appeared at her side.

"Can I help you?" he asked.

Regaining her composure, as if social niceties mattered in her time of despair, Kathie took a deep breath and answered. "I'm fine, thank you, Father."

He put a hand on her head gently, muttered a blessing, and walked on purposefully about his business. As he reached the confessional at the back of the church, he took time to slide the door indicator to In Attendance, then disappeared inside the freestanding box, and closed the red velvet drape that covered the opening.

Kathie was grateful for the solace of his touch and it was only when she followed the priest's path and was about to take her place inside the confessional that she noticed the name of the priest In Attendance.

The name board stated Father O'Malley—but the priest who had spoken to her was not Father O'Malley. He had been a young fresh-faced novice whom she had never seen before. That's a mystery alright, she told herself. Pity the young priest wasn't taking confession, she thought.

"Father, forgive me, for I have sinned."

Kathie knelt on the tapestry-covered wooden hassock in the small confessional cubicle. She addressed the priest through the metal grill that separated them as she had hundreds of times before at weekly sacraments of reconciliation.

She was not as regular an attendee at mass as she had been in her convent school days but still she recognized the stern countenance of Father O'Malley as she prepared to admit her sins before God. *If she couldn't have the novice, why could she not have got the older, more kindly Father Hart?* On second thoughts she was not about to ask leniency from the clergy or from God. She had come primarily not to seek forgiveness but to have her penance handed down.

Inside the holy space of the confessional, Kathie spilled out her anguish. "I broke the commandments," she confessed. "I did not Honor my father and now he's dead. Because of me. I'll never forgive myself."

The priest admonished. "It's God's job to forgive," he told her. And it's in God's time that people are called from this life. You are not powerful enough to make these things happen."

Offering more understanding and compassion than Kathie felt she deserved, the priest allowed her to tell her story and, after gently guiding her to understand the part she may have played, he made ready to offer absolution.

"There is one other thing, Father," Kathie told him. "I feel I need to take revenge for my father's death. How can I reconcile that with God's will?"

Seamus had indicated that, although he was not advocating it, he would be an ally for Kathie if she chose to take action against those responsible for the brutal killing of her father and the heartless way they had disposed of his body, lying now in an unmarked grave in the city graveyard.

"The Lord giveth and the Lord taketh away," Father

O'Malley told her gently. "Let God cast judgment on those responsible. Now go in peace. Your penance is to say the rosary every day for the next month and to come to mass every day. The blessed Mary will bring you comfort and the Lord blesses you with His forgiveness. Go in peace, child, to love and serve the Lord."

Kathie signed the cross, thanked him, and walked out filled with a sense of relief, happy to undertake the penance of saying the rosary. Confidently she accepted that her sins had been forgiven, but she knew that despite the ritual of the Catholic sacrament and her faith, the aching pain for the loss of her father would remain.

However, years of indoctrination in the Catholic Church did offer Kathie a profound sense that a burden had been lifted from her heart.

She was grateful she had been absolved of the responsibility of pursuing her father's killers. Deep in her heart she knew she would not have tried anything had she thought there was the possibility of achieving a satisfactory conclusion.

A young girl on her own, even with loyal support from friend's of her father, she accepted she had no power to fight the evil forces and the tragic circumstances that had conspired to take her father's life. The priest had assured her she was not expected to take matters into her own hands.

The wrongdoers would get their just rewards in the fullness of time.

Kathie had offered forgiveness to Spike just as she had been shown mercy and forgiveness by God, but she would not forget. One day she prayed that there would be justice for the death of an innocent man. She vowed to keep the promise alive in her heart.

Before exiting the church, Kathie said the first rosary of her penance—and lit one more candle. To justice.

CHAPTER ELEVEN

Facing the Music

"Where have you been?"

Concepta stepped directly in front of Kathie as she arrived back at The Dubliner Hotel and demanded an explanation. "I've been worried sick about you. Last I saw you were rushing out of the bar without even stopping to tell me what Seamus told you.

"Where were you? Are you alright?"

Kathie took her friend by the arm and steered her into the hotel and up the stairs leading to her room.

"I'm sorry, Concepta," she said. "I didn't even know myself where I was going. But I went to the church. It seemed the best place and I made my confession."

Concepta, a Catholic, nodded knowingly, though she wasn't sure what Kathie had to confess.

"You sit down while I put on the tea and I'll tell you the whole story," Kathie urged her friend. "Seamus brought the boy, Spike, and he knew what had gone on."

Concepta held Kathie's hand as she reiterated what she had learned about her father's death. "Spike insists it was an accident, not murder," said Kathie, "and I can't deny him when he says that my dad was drunk and got aggressive."

"Still no excuse to kill him." Concepta exploded.

"No," said Kathie. "And if there was any way I could change what happened I'd give everything I have to do it. But it all happened months ago now and even the building has been demolished. I don't have anywhere to start to make any further enquiries.

"Saddest thing of all," she continued, "even if I was able to find my dad and get a positive identification on him, I don't have the money to give him a decent funeral. Even though it breaks my heart, what's done is done and nothing is going to bring him back."

Concepta crossed herself and said a prayer. "May his soul rest in peace."

"What did the priest say?" she asked, acknowledging that being good Catholic girls, they were accustomed to bowing to the authority of the church, and a pronouncement from a member of the clergy would be enough to confer a settlement on the matter.

Kathie explained what had occurred in the confessional and shared with her friend the penance that had been imposed.

Sipping thoughtfully at her hot tea, Concepta told her friend, "I'm still not sure why you were the one confessing. What did you do wrong? It was your father who threw you out and you did go back and try to put matters right."

Kathie blushed. "Mostly it was because of the fourth Commandment," she admitted. "About honoring your mother and your father. I did not honor my father and I never went to find my mother and tell her I was living away from my dad. She might have let me live with her but I didn't give her the chance."

She hesitated and took a deep breath before continuing. "But there was something else. Something I meant to confess and just couldn't bring myself to say it. The priest was so understanding about my father's death. I refused to shame myself by telling him the other thing."

Concepta put down her cup, moved to sit next to her friend on the bed, and clasped both hands in her own.

"Do you want to tell me?" she asked kindly. "Remember you are as sick as your secrets."

"It's the real reason I was put out of the house," said Kathie. "I've almost convinced myself and everybody else that it was just because my Dad was drunk. He wasn't on that occasion. Unusual as that may be. He was playing at a social club with his band and he came back to invite me to a party for my birthday."

Kathie uncoupled her hands from Concepta's and proceeded to twist them into knots. It seemed that she might not be able to say the final words even to her best friend.

Eyes misty, she looked away and in a barely audible voice admitted, "When he came to the house, I was in bed with a boy. We had made love. Had sex. It was my first time. My father threw the boy out, called me a lot of horrible names, and told me to go. He told me, 'Go join the other whore, your mother.'"

Kathie's shame inflamed her face and she added to the hundreds of tears that she had already shed that day.

"Concepta," she said as she put her head in her hands and sobbed, "I think I might be having a baby."

If she had a cent for every time she had heard a single unmarried friend utters those words, Concepta would have been a rich woman. Fortunately, it often turned out to be a false alarm. Unfortunately, Kathie's mysterious sickness and symptoms over the last few days took on a new dimension and suggested that her self-diagnosis might be right.

"You're not alone," said Concepta, "I'll help you through this. First we need to get you to the doctor and get a test done."

To break the unbearable tension and take the forlorn look from Kathie's stricken face, she smiled. "It's not the worst thing that can happen in the world. Thousands of women have babies every day."

Kathleen hoped Concepta wouldn't ask, but it was an obvious question. "Who's the father?"

"Do I have to tell them?" asked Kathleen.

"Do you have to tell who?" asked Concepta.

"The doctor."

"No, of course not. It's your business. I was just curious. I never even knew you had a boyfriend."

Reluctant as she was to admit the circumstances of her pregnancy, Kathleen was relieved to unburden herself and tell her friend the truth.

"It happened the first time I had sex. That night I told you about when my dad caught us and threw me out. I was a virgin and he wasn't even really my boyfriend. Just another student at the college. His name was Marco and although I went back to the college to see the Principal and explain why I left so abruptly, I never saw Marco. Nor would I want to. I certainly wouldn't want him to know I'm pregnant."

"He should take some responsibility," said Concepta. "We could confront him and at least make him aware of what he did to you."

Kathleen looked panic-stricken.

"No, no please don't. I'd die rather than face him again."

Concepta stopped short of trying to force the issue.

"Don't worry. I'm not going to do anything you don't want. I promise. But if you want me to go around and bash his brains out, I will."

The two women laughed. "It'll be alright," said Concepta. "Trust me. You're not on your own. I'll look after you."

Under her breath she mumbled, "Bloody men."

Kathie was still far from being able to see any positive side of the situation but she smiled at her friend. She could not have been more grateful for the love and support she received from this caring woman.

"But you do have one big problem right now," said Concepta in a mock serious tone. "Big Mac will have your guts for garters if you're late for tonight's show. We better get back to the bar sharpish."

"Are you kidding me? I don't think I can get up on that stage," said Kathie.

"Of course you can," Concepta encouraged her. "Dedicate tonight's performance to your dad. Didn't he drum into you? 'The show must go on.'"

*   *   *

True to her word, Concepta took loving care of Kathie and after her pregnancy was confirmed she ensured that for as long as was possible she was able to go on performing at the Magic Harp.

"The fewer people who know about the baby, the better," Concepta counseled her. With Kathie's agreement, the two made arrangements for her to go to a Catholic home for babies and mothers in upstate New York. The official story was that Kathie was suffering from TB, a lung sickness picked up during her performing days on the streets of the city.

Sami feigned disappointment but truth was that having failed to turn Kathie into an overnight sensation—at least in the wider world outside the Magic Harp, through no fault of his own, he was quick to point out—he had moved on to promote the career of another "favorite artist." Stars were dime a dozen in his world. Mr. Big Producer was more a figment of his imagination than anything else and he had long since settled for more modest successes. He talked a good game but credible results had so far eluded him.

"Give me a call when you are back in town," he told Kathie.

Kathie had already had her heart broken by her father's death and the disappointment of the consequences of that fateful night when she had so badly let herself and him down.

She wished the circumstances could have been different but she was glad to be leaving the city. Sami was the least of her worries. Big Mac promised he would welcome her back to her old job any time she wanted and Concepta promised to visit regularly.

Life was not turning out as she had anticipated but

Kathie was determined to focus all her love and care on the baby she was expecting.

Even if her life depended on it, she would not let down her child. Giving herself a personal challenge she vowed, *I will work every day of my life to be a better mother than I was a daughter.*

CHAPTER TWELVE

Mother Knows Best

Alighting from the daily Amtrak train in a small town beyond upstate New York, Kathie O'Shaunessey bid goodbye to the kindly conductor who had befriended her on the six-hour journey. Fall had just turned to winter and although the prettily painted station with well-tended tubs of bushes and foliage that lined the platform was bathed in a buttery late afternoon sunshine, there was a definite chill in the air.

"You take good care of yourself, Miss," her new friend Raymond called out as he leaned out of the carriage door and checked to make sure that the sweet young lady he had taken such a shine to was indeed being met as she anticipated.

He hoped to catch a glimpse of her husband. Now that was one lucky young man.

Kathie was not proud of the fact that she lied to decent people who took an interest and went out of their way to help a woman in her condition, especially when she traveled by public transport. Nor was she willing to admit the truth. She was an unmarried mother-to-be.

"My husband will meet the train," she had told the guard when he expressed concern about her ability to carry the two small suitcases that, did he but know it, contained all her worldly possessions.

One suitcase was needed just for her stage costumes. She had been so proud of her lovely outfits—courtesy of a seamstress of Sami's acquaintance—and she was determined not to leave them behind in New York. Besides, she told herself, she didn't know when she might need them to enable her to make a living. Strange as it seemed, she was practical enough to realize that she might actually find herself in a position where she would be glad to take up Big Mac's offer of returning to her old job to support her and her child.

Concepta, who thought of everything, had provided a cheap wedding ring bought from the five and dime store and Kathie now called herself Mrs. O'Connor. Her imaginary husband they had named Eamonn.

Times and attitudes to single motherhood had changed dramatically in the twenty years since the contraceptive pill had become more widely available, but there were many communities where such modern behavior was considered unacceptable. The Irish community was one of them.

Kathie had been brought up in the traditional ways and, out of respect for her dead father and her long lost mother, she felt the need to keep up appearances and mask the true circumstances of her pregnancy.

Kathie looked about her anxiously and, with a final wave to the conductor as the train pulled out of the station, she attempted to identify the driver she had been told would come to collect her for the onward journey.

She observed one other young lady standing on the platform, and though she wore a loose-fitting oatmeal colored wool coat, it did not completely conceal the fact of her condition. Kathie was wearing a similar cover-up.

The two smiled shyly at each other and began to walk toward the exit sign. Parked directly outside the station was a small black station wagon and sitting in the driver's seat, a young nun.

She beckoned the girls over with a barely there smile and pointed them toward the open trunk to deposit their luggage, indicating that they should sit in the back seat. Gestures rather than words were her preferred method of communication.

On the fifteen-minute journey to their destination she uttered not one syllable. So neither did Kathie nor the other young woman who shared their car space. Kathie actually wondered whether the nun was a member of one of the silent orders and hoped that would not be the case for all of the religious community that she would be living with for at least the next six months.

First sight of the *Sisters of St. Bernadette's Convent and Convalescence Home* was impressive. The sandstone turreted property lorded it over a lavishly landscaped estate, and a mile-long gray gravel drive up to the building was lined with huge redwood trees.

The young nun drove the car around the building to the back of the property and pulled up on the small pathway outside an open door. She waited for her passengers to exit the vehicle and collect their luggage. A final nod toward the open door and she drove off.

Kathie raised her eyebrows and the other passenger giggled as they allowed themselves to express their confusion.

Without putting her case down, Kathie smiled, indicated that she would normally have shook hands, and introduced herself.

In reply the other girl acknowledged, "I'm Margaret, pleased to meet you."

"We best be going in then," said Kathie, gesturing to the open door and affecting a cheerfulness she did not feel.

"Hello, girls," sang out a welcoming voice as they entered a cheerless room. The room appeared to be a classroom and alongside a blackboard propped up on an easel sat the owner of the voice.

A metal name badge pinned to her dark robes identified her as Sister Mary Magdalene. Having made herself perfectly at home behind a square white metal desk she reclined in an armchair with her feet propped up on the desk showing off a pair of white tennis shoes.

"Don't be scared. I won't eat you," she said jovially, observing the girls' obvious nervousness. "But the dog might. Here he comes now."

Kathie and Margaret felt their anxiety levels rise alarmingly as they turned to see a large St. Bernard dog with a deep-pile cookie colored fur coat come bounding into the room. The only thing missing was a brandy barrel around his neck.

"Here Bernie," said Sister Mary Magdalene, slapping her ample thigh and encouraging the dog to stand up on its hind legs and give her a sloppy kiss.

"Now, down to business, just a few formalities to complete and we'll get you girls something to eat and then you can have an early night after your long journey.

"You'll find us a friendly bunch here at St. Bernadette's, though some of the nuns take themselves a little more seriously than others. In the service of Christ Our Lord, which I may say I entered rather late in life, I absolutely insist on being happy, joyous, and free. Before taking Holy Orders I taught Latin at a Boys' School, so you could say I have inflicted quite enough misery for one lifetime."

Sister M and M, a nickname by which she was known throughout the community, let out another full-bodied laugh, took her feet from their desktop position, and planted them firmly on the floor. She opened an A4 brown leather register.

"Now, who have we here? Kathleen O'Shaunessey, seventeen years old, last known address in New York City, and Margaret Platt, eighteen from good old Philly.

"Correct?"

As both girls nodded and acknowledged their names, with an ostentatious flourish she ticked two columns in the register and closed the book before returning it to a desk drawer, which she locked with a key hanging from a clanging bunch on a thick black leather belt at her waist.

"Suppertime," she informed Kathie and Margaret as she led them from the classroom, along a corridor, and into a refectory with trestle tables and wooden benches.

"The other girls have finished eating but I made sure cook put some aside for you. I'll get one of the girls to take your luggage from the classroom to your dormitory and I'll take you up there myself after you've eaten."

Sister M and M left them to their supper, a delicious cold plate of tasty sliced meats and garden fresh vegetables. Dessert was a homemade sponge cake with creamy custard and they washed it down with a good strong cup of tea served in half-pint mugs.

Sharing their stories, Kathie and Margaret talked of their home lives, families, schooling, and hobbies, but neither mentioned the details of the events that had brought them to St. Bernadette's.

There would be plenty of time in the intervening months to get to know each other. However, they did confide the dates when their babies were due to be born and were more than delighted to find out that they were expecting in the same month, April, just days apart.

Right on cue, as they finished eating, Sister M and M came to show them to their sleeping accommodation. Two flights up in an outer wing of the one-time family mansion, former girls' boarding school and now convent, the ten-bed dormitory was clean, comfortable, and fit for purpose. Kathie would have been reluctant to admit it to anyone, but it was actually a lot more amenable than most of the places she had lived growing up.

Sleep came easily and she was enveloped in a pleasant reassuring feeling that she and her baby would be safe here.

An innocent abroad she could not in her worst nightmare have guessed that the whole reason for her status as a "non-paying guest and patient" was to separate her from her baby.

Under the guise of being loving, protective, and God-fearing, the nuns pursued their own agenda.

The Sisters of St. Bernadette's sold babies.

CHAPTER THIRTEEN

Baby Blues

Mother Michael, the Mother Superior and ultimate authority at St. Bernadette's Convent and Convalescence Home, was not one to mince her words or beat about the bush.

"I want an answer now," she said menacingly.

The heavy metal crucifix that clung to a black leather thong tied loosely around the collar of her white wimple was gyrating like a divination crystal as it swung dangerously between her ample bosoms. It was propelled by the rapid hand movements of its devout owner, who seemed to be trying to wrench it from its restraining cords.

With her free hand she pushed into place the small gold-rimmed round-framed glasses that had been dislodged with the frantic motion and now rested near the tip of her nose.

Her whole body appeared to be on the move. Demands for an answer to her question had brought upon a state of perpetual motion, relief from which would only come when Kathie signaled acquiescence.

Kathie was defiant. She crossed her arms on her chest, rested them on her huge stomach, and anchored her hands under her armpits. Without so much as a single blink of her eyelids she focused her vision straight ahead. Few dared but Kathie stared out the Mother Superior and repeated her answer.

"No. Never. I'll burn in hell before I let you take my baby."

Mother Michael, a middle-aged nun who had been Mother Superior at St. Bernadette's for almost two decades, feared she had met her match. Kathleen O'Shaunessey gave no outward indication of the steely strength that forged her personality and made her intractable. Mother Michael had tried all the methods she knew to coerce frightened young girls into giving up their babies for adoption. Even when they declared that it was the last thing they wanted.

Over the years Mother Michael and her team of nursing sisters had used reason, entreaties, threats, bullying, and peer pressure.

Young unmarried girls, more often than not completely estranged from their families, had quickly seen the wisdom of allowing their newborn babies to have the opportunities offered by well-off families who could give the child a better life.

With no real evidence to the contrary, it was difficult to dispute the fact that the nuns genuinely believed they were offering their charges and the newborn babes a practical alternative to a life of hardship with an inexperienced, homeless, or destitute teenage mother who had no support system and no resources, financial or otherwise.

Married couples, desperate for a baby, who for one reason or another could not produce their own children, were prime candidates to offer loving homes to healthy, white, Anglo-Saxon newborns. And they were more than happy to pay the price.

Often the potential parents were referred by local parish priests, who were able to vouch for their parishioners and identify those who were able to pay the "referral fee."

Challenged to explain their actions, the God-fearing nuns and clergy had ready explanations: the money was used to give the girls a new start in life and church funds benefited from the fees paid by adoptive parents.

A winning situation all round, if the perpetrators' good intentions were to be believed.

Kathie had heard all the arguments. She remained skeptical.

In her months at the convent she had stood by and watched as new mothers reluctantly handed over their babies weeks after birth, knowing they would never see them again.

At night she lay in her small bed in the dormitory, listening to those same mothers cry themselves to sleep night after night. By day their tortured eyes and forlorn expressions told of their despair as they haunted the corridors of the convent as if seeking the lost child.

The administrative offices of St. Bernadette's welfare charity did offer a "resettlement" allowance, but few of the girls had homes or lives to which they could return. Some stayed on at the convent to work with the fresh intake of new pregnant recruits, living vicariously through their precious time in the convent nursery, looking after the newborn babies and befriending their brainwashed mothers.

Mother Superior had all her arguments in place. She had tried every one of them with Kathie. The trump card Kathie knew she held was that her agreement was required to progress the adoption process. Although she would not put it past the convent authorities to forge a signature, unless they were to act in a totally criminal manner, procedures had to be followed.

Mother Michael had run out of patience. "If you do not agree to have your baby adopted, then I must ask you to leave. You are exerting an unfavorable influence on the other girls and I am no longer willing to shelter you under our roof."

Kathie had not expected the ultimatum but she did not flinch. "The answer is still no," she said.

"Then I must ask you to vacate the premises," said Mother Superior, curling her lip and offering a weak but thinly disguised smile. "Please pack your bags and leave first thing in the morning. I am sure you can find your own way to the station. After all, you will have to fend for yourself from now on."

Kathie stared at the Bride of Christ in disbelief. Where was compassion? Where was love? Where was her sense of humanity? Kathie shivered now she knew how it felt to be completely and utterly alone in the world. It appeared that even God—or at least his representatives here on earth—had forsaken her.

Kathie eased herself up using the arms of the chair in which she had been sitting to gain leverage and maneuver her large bulk upright.

With as much dignity as she could muster while navigating a bump the size of a baby elephant out of the office door, she turned to cast one last disdainful look at the woman who had just robbed her of hope and forced her to face a perilous future.

But the future was already upon her. At that moment, she experienced a searing pain in her lower stomach and let out a muffled scream, "I think the baby's coming," she gasped.

The well-trained nursing staff did not hesitate; the procedures were tried and trusted. Kathie was transported to the care and comfort of the delivery room.

On awakening she remembered little of the birth but was grateful for the painkilling injections that had eased her physical distress.

Barely conscious she was startled when a smiling young nun handed her a squalling baby.

"A beautiful girl," said the nursing sister.

Her first visitor was the last person she wanted to see. Mother Superior was wearing her best holy face and full of exaggerated goodwill.

"Congratulations, Kathie," she said exuding sincerity. "You have been safely delivered of a healthy baby girl. Her new parents will be delighted."

Struggling to comprehend what she was hearing, Kathie beseeched the smiling woman. "New parents? I don't understand. What do you mean? Tell me. Please tell me."

"Oh, you don't remember? During labor, while you waited for a painkilling injection, you kindly agreed to sign the consent form to have your baby adopted. I assure you, your baby will have the most loving parents and best life you could envisage for her. Thank you, Kathleen. I knew you would come around to my way of thinking."

Kathleen handed her crying baby girl to the nurse, turned her face to the wall, and cried bitter tears which left deep pain lines on her cheeks and heart.

As soon as she could find the strength to raise herself from the hospital bed, Kathie planned to leave the place she now thought of as a prison.

Fighting against all her natural instincts, she refused to go and see her baby in the nursery. She was adamant that she would not bond with the precious little bundle she had been tricked into giving away.

Gradually her resistance was broken down as she struggled to set aside her own feelings and focus only on what was best for her baby.

Visiting the nursery several times a day she would bath, change, and play with the baby that she knew was on loan. Her heart ached and she wondered how she would ever endure the constant bleeding wound that inflicted a dark hole in her soul. Moments of exquisite pleasure as she sat cocooned in a large armchair holding her sweet smelling, dainty, dark-haired baby were brutally replaced with the sorrow of the upcoming parting.

She stroked the infant's face and imagined that her baby watched her even though the child's vision was still misty. "Mama's here," she dared to croon soft as a whisper. "Don't forget me baby. I love you. Don't ever forget. Write it on your heart. Your mother loves you, precious child of God."

The angel touch of the baby's tiny fingers as she curled them so trustingly in those of her mother assured Kathleen that she was known. Her very being reverberated with the unique sight, sound, and smell of her child. *I will never forget you,* mother promised daughter. *One day I will bring you back to me. Where you belong.*

Kathleen went along with the charade that was meant to sever the bond between natural mother and transfer ownership to the new parents. If the rite of passage was designed to offer closure, Kathleen refused to even entertain the notion that it was anything other than a sales event. It would have hardly surprised her if she had been invited to a pink ribbon-cutting ceremony with cake and popping champagne corks. Mother Michael wins again.

She railed inwardly against the unholy justice of an immoral ritual whereby she had agreed to hand over her child in exchange for a chemical solution to take away her pain. She had traded mere moments of relief for a lifetime in purgatory. Betrayed her child for less than forty pieces of silver.

Kathleen struggled with the dilemma. On one hand she wanted nothing to do with the physical and emotional handing over of her baby. On the other hand, she wanted to exert a moral obligation by looking into the eyes of the new parents and making them aware that her daughter's real mother was holding them accountable for her daughter's lifelong well-being and happiness.

"Kathleen, meet Mr. and Mrs. Perez," said Mother Michael standing up to welcome the expensively dressed, handsome couple as they were shown into her private sitting room by one of the young mothers. Wearing her most false smile she introduced the three of them and launched into what sounded like a prepared speech, no doubt one she had delivered many times. Kathleen kept her eyes firmly downward, desperate to try and avoid looking in the direction of her baby.

"Kathleen, as I have explained to you, Mr. and Mrs. Perez, Maria and Humberto, are to be your daughter's new adoptive parents. I am delighted that they are willing to offer your baby a spirit-filled Catholic life. Your daughter will have every advantage and two loving parents." She smiled obsequiously. "They have also been most generous to the Convent and that will enable us to help and support other unmarried mothers who are in need."

The main rationale for the bizarre ceremony appeared to be the minimizing of any guilt felt by the adoptive parents, and their assurance that the birth mother was giving her consent willingly and with a sense of gratitude for the new life the child would enjoy.

Kathleen still burned with resentment that she had been outwitted by the Mother Superior. She held fast to her emotions as her feelings threatened to overflow and overwhelm her. In a wild moment she contemplated grabbing the newborn baby who lay peacefully sleeping, unaware of the drama all around her, racing from the room, and running as far away from the tragic scene as possible.

Instead she put what she now perceived to be the greater good of the child above her own deepest desires.

"Please look after her," said Kathleen as she tenderly lifted the baby from the bassinet that Maria had purchased from her favorite New York department store, Macys.

The look of genuine love and compassion in her eyes,

answered Kathleen's plea. "We will always hold you in our prayers," said Humberto. "You have given us the precious gift of life. We thank you and Mother Michael for the service you have done in God's name."

Kathleen could stand no more. "Thank you," she said quietly. "Goodbye."

Job done, Mother Michael had already turned her attention back to Maria and Humberto.

"Goodbye, Kathleen," she called, and almost as an afterthought, "God go with you."

Refusing to give Mother Superior the satisfaction that her spirit was completely crushed, before she left the convent, Kathleen asked her friend Margaret to help her make one last stand. For this final act of rebellion, she needed an ally.

Kathie and her friend from that first day when they arrived together at the convent were no longer as close as they had been in those early days. The rift had developed when Margaret succumbed to the nun's propaganda, signed the adoption papers, and started to say, if not altogether believe, that her baby would be better off with the parents the convent supplied through the adoption service.

Now Kathleen needed a favor and she was sure her former best friend would not refuse. She asked Margaret to help her break into the locked desk drawer where the register of all the girls was kept.

She knew what she was looking for. Now she had met them and knew the names, she was determined that Maria and Humberto would not disappear into the night like thieves with her baby. Kathleen wanted their address.

Sneaking into the downstairs office, the two accomplices had their story ready in case they were spotted.

"I'm checking for my wallet," Kathleen would explain. "I think I left it on the desk earlier when I came to sign paperwork for Sister M and M."

Kathleen had come prepared. Fishing a sharp kitchen knife from the pocket of her loose outdoor jacket, she urged Margaret to stand look-out at the doorway while she set to work on the lock.

"I didn't know you had a previous career as a burglar," Margaret joked, as Kathleen systematically wiggled and jiggled the knife in the lock.

"I should have brought some butter from the kitchen," said Kathleen, "to soften it up." The image of a buttered lock made them both laugh and Kathleen was taken by surprise as the lock suddenly retracted and sprung open. "Lock breaking, just one of my many talents," she winked at Margaret who still stood guard at the door.

"Good for you, now get a move on, and let's get out of here," she urged.

Kathleen pulled the drawer wide open, located the brown leather ledger, and in one movement turned to the date when she and Margaret had entered the convent. With beating heart she tried to speed up the process as she ran her finger down the columns and checked the neatly written records. Trust M and M, the former classics teacher, to use Roman numerals.

"Got it," said Kathleen out loud aiming to assure Margaret that she was almost finished. In the "adoption services transfer" column, Maria and Humberto Perez were identified as the parents of her child. Kathleen grabbed a pen and a green post-it note off the pad on Mother M and M's desk.

She copied down a Florida address. XV111 East San Maria Drive, Venetian Causeway, Miami Beach.

"Mission complete," she called to Kathleen across the empty echoing office space.

"Best not hang about," said Margaret, "in case there are any repercussions. Come on, you've got a train to catch."

As they walked, Margaret was quiet. "I should have asked you to check the address for my son," she said. Then as quickly as she had contemplated the possibility, she changed her mind.

"No, best to make a clean break," she concluded and breathed a deep mournful sigh. "I'll get over it. One day."

Margaret and Kathleen walked arm in arm to the end of the convent driveway and hugged goodbye. "Take care," they told each other.

Kathleen carried only the two cases with which she had arrived. She refused to take anything else and even stubbornly refused the "resettlement payment" that was offered.

Proud and defiant, despite the offer of a ride with the young nun in her open-top jeep, Kathleen insisted on making her own way to the station. She refused to accept charity.

Her heart was heavier than her suitcases as she left St. Bernadette's Convent and trudged the long lonely journey back to the railroad station.

Like Lot's wife, she could not resist one last lingering look. Seared forever in her memory, the turreted tower where her newborn baby lay, awaiting its new life, Kathleen knew her own life was over. She would never be happy again.

CHAPTER FOURTEEN

Breath of Fresh Air

Kathleen had only one place to go, back to the only friends she knew, at the Magic Harp in New York City.

But out of sight, out of mind. Big Mac was pleased to see his former songbird turn up, but he had a new girlfriend and she was running the show. Kathleen was relegated to occasional singing spots in between her waitressing duties.

Concepta, who had carried her through the early days of her pregnancy, had moved in with a new man and, although she was pleased to welcome her best friend, the two were no longer as close.

What am I going to do with my life? Kathleen asked herself over and over. *Am I to accept that at eighteen years of age, I'm already washed up, a failure?*

She made a few feeble attempts to find her former so-called agent and manager, Sami, but he had left town and, besides, her heart was not in her singing.

Standing at the microphone, Kathleen clasped her hands tightly to stop the nerves and at every sad song her tears would flow and threaten to choke her.

To sing was painful; to dance required an energy and

exuberance she did not feel. Kathleen was a shell of her former self.

"I feel like my heart has been ripped out," she admitted to Concepta during one of their snatched girl-to-girl chats in the darkness of the bar.

Concepta, wise and kind as always, told her, "You're suffering grief, for your baby, for your father, for your mother, and for your own lost innocence. You need to put the past behind you and look to the future.

"My advice to you is to leave the city for a while. Go somewhere you can rest and recover. You'll be able to find a job just as good as your bar work here."

Kathleen was doubtful. "Where would I go? I've never been anywhere in my whole life except here and Hell's Kitchen." Kathleen deliberately omitted to include mention of her prolonged stay at the convent.

Two days later Concepta introduced Kathleen to a businessman friend of hers. "Manny owns a restaurant out by Sandy City," said Concepta. "It's only half an hour from the city and it's on the ocean. A great place to work on getting your health and fitness back. You won't know yourself."

Kathleen liked Manny, though he wasn't much to look at. Balding, middle-aged, down to earth and overweight, he obviously carried a torch for Concepta. If he could put himself in her good books, it would be a win-win situation. She had assured him that Kathleen was a good worker, reliable, and a great draw for the customers.

"The restaurant is on the seaside," he told Kathleen. "Not fancy but a good family restaurant and that keeps us busy when the season is over and the tourists go home.

"There is accommodation available. A month's trial, either side. Usual wages and you keep your own tips. Want to give it a try? You can start right away."

Kathleen felt an excitement she had not experienced for a long time. "Yes, why not? What have I got to lose?"

Eyes shining and with a genuine smile on her face, she reached out to squeeze Concepta's hand. The two friends were sitting at the back area by the restroom in the Magic Harp, where they always took their breaks and had their heart-to-heart conversations.

"You are a real pal," she told her. "One day I'll be able to do something for you. I'll give Manny's restaurant a shot, who knows it might be just what I need. Thank you, Concepta."

Manny was staying overnight in the city on business and returning to Sandy City the next day.

"Meet me here at ten o'clock and I'll give you a ride," he said. "Don't be late."

Kathleen had no intention of being late. She was back at the lodgings Mac owned but this time she was staying in a poky single room, unable to afford anything better.

"I won't be hanging around here a minute longer than necessary," she told Concepta. "Promise you'll come to visit me?" she asked.

The two hugged and Kathleen was happy to report to her friend, "I feel hopeful and happy and it's all thanks to you."

With her spirits raised, Kathleen made a decision.

"I'm going to ask Mac if I can give a goodbye performance tonight. I want to sing 'When Irish Eyes are Smiling' just once more, without crying."

CHAPTER FIFTEEN

A New Start

Good to his word, Manny collected Kathleen from outside the Magic Harp right on time. She had been unable to sleep the night before, first excited at her new adventure, and then worried about whether she was making the right decision.

Although she was squashed like a sack of potatoes in the small backseat of the transit van, among all the boxes and bottles and packages that her new boss had picked up from his preferred wholesaler in the city, Kathleen felt as spoiled as if she were being driven in a limousine.

The congestion of the city was soon left behind as they exited through the tunnel and drove on out on the Garden State highway toward the New Jersey Shoreline.

In short sentences shouted above the noise of his over-loaded vehicle and the rattle of engine noise, Manny told Kathie they were headed for the small seaside town of Ocean Bay, a rural former farmland community that had been attracting vacationers from New York City for well over a hundred years.

In an ideal location that boasted pristine, sandy white beaches and a well-preserved boardwalk, from which could be seen breathtaking panoramic views over the Atlantic Ocean and a landmark historic lighthouse, two decades earlier, Manny had found his spiritual home—and the perfect site for his business.

"It's a small town with a lot of community events and activities," said Manny proudly. "A great place for families, and I say that even though my wife walked out on me and took the two kids. The life of an innkeeper is not very compatible with family life, but that's no reflection on the town. The kids still love it when they come to visit during the summer vacations.

"I've got two boys, an eight-year-old, Hank, and ten-year-old Manny junior. They get a kick out of seeing the town "Welcome" sign each time they arrive. The great big "smile" on a billboard reminds them that they're going to have lots of fun here. Swimming, fishing, surfing.

"Their mother says I spoil them," admitted Manny, "but why wouldn't I? They're only here for a few weeks and then they go back to real life with her."

Manny had made himself sad at the thought of his kids and to hide his embarrassment, he abruptly brought that particular line of conversation to an end.

"Want a soda," he asked, "Or a beer? Here take this penknife and open up one of the boxes on the back seat. Coke or beer?"

Kathleen did not hesitate, "A Coke will do fine," she said. "I don't drink. What'll you have?"

"Same as you," Manny told her. "I drink, too much, best not to start while I've got a long day ahead of me."

Kathleen flipped the ring to open the can, leaning over to put it directly into Manny's free hand—it had been resting on his thigh as he drove one handed. She flipped the ring on her can, took a satisfying swallow, and settled back to watch the passing scenery on the hour-long journey to the shore.

She decided that she liked Manny; she'd been too quick to judge him by appearances when they met in the Magic Harp the previous day. Mr. Tall, Dark, and Handsome he wasn't, but he was a nice guy. The two could be friends. And God knows, she could use a friend.

As they neared their destination driving along the picturesque beaches and bays, Manny resumed his tour guiding.

"Smile, you are entering Ocean Bay," he called to her. "Almost home."

On a quiet street within a breeze of the seafront, Manny pulled the van to a halt outside a well-kept, white clapboard two-story building with a painted metal sign declaring itself "The Best Little Bar House in Town."

"I'll get your case, the lads will unload the van," Manny told her as he swung himself down, with surprising agility, from the front seat of the transit.

"Come on in and you can meet everyone."

Inside, "The Best Little Bar House" looked like a traditional old-fashioned tavern. Wooden beams, brass beer pumps, black metallic old-style candlesticks, moody black and white prints crowding the walls, and tables covered with cheerful gingham-checked tablecloths.

Behind the highly polished red mahogany bar, optics containing jewel colored liquids glinted and glasses of every size were neatly arranged along the mirrored back shelving, sparkling invitingly.

The wide open barnlike space with booths on two sides was lovingly cared for and cozy as surely as if it had its welcome mat newly shaken and laid at the front door.

Kathleen felt an immediate affinity with the homey atmosphere and looked forward to her new job and life.

"Out the back," said Manny, with a nod of his head, walking swiftly across the bar, and exiting through an opening alongside the open alcove of the activity filled kitchen.

"It's all yours," he said, as Kathleen came alongside him outside a small wooden structure at the outer edge of the yard.

"Small but private. Come and see."

Kathleen did not need to be told twice. She was intrigued. Turned out to be a small former stable block constructed with the original inn over sixty years earlier. Kathleen toured the premises and observed that it really would be difficult to swing a cat, but for her it was perfect. Two tiny windows provided the light into one simply furnished open-plan downstairs, with a wobbly wooden staircase up to an attic room with two beds, a small built-in closet, and two cupboards.

On the ground level alongside the front door, Kathleen had her own surprisingly modern toilet and bathroom suite.

"Oh, Manny, it's perfect, thank you," she said, only just resisting the temptation to throw her arms around him.

"My sons sleep here when they come to visit," he explained. "I had it renovated for them. The summer vacations are over now, so you can use it, at least until they come back."

The sadness Kathleen had noticed earlier was upon him again. "But that's probably not going to be anytime soon."

He didn't elaborate. Kathleen didn't ask.

"Now," he said, getting back to business, "there are customers to be served. The lunchtime trade can be hectic. I'll get someone to show you the ropes, but it won't be that much different from what you're used to at your other establishment."

I shouldn't be so sure of that, Kathleen thought.

She was anxious to get to work and asked Manny, "Just give me ten minutes to change and I'll be right in."

The one case she had with her contained just a few outfits and she happily unpacked her brightest colored blouse and a smart skirt. In the bathroom she brushed her hair and tied back her long ringlets with a red ribbon.

I look quite respectable, she told herself, but first wage package I'm going to buy something really pretty.

*　*　*

Kathleen quickly settled into her job serving first-class food in the family friendly restaurant. Seafood, steaks, and grills were the specialties of the house with a few quirky signature dishes of beer-battered fish 'n' chips and lamb stew with dumplings.

She had never been to the Homeland but Kathleen believed those customers who told her that The Best Little Bar House in Town reminded them of old-fashioned pubs back in Ireland.

They lived on in her father's memory and she had heard him reminisce often enough about the attractions of the Celtic bars, their home-style cooking, live entertainment, and of course for him the main attraction, the beer.

Strangely, in a way that had never happened at the Magic Harp, Kathleen also felt at home in The Best Little Bar House in Town, and connected to her roots.

Kathleen loved her job and the customers loved her. A natural cheerfulness that for too long had been suppressed now bubbled to the surface and Kathleen was soon one of the most popular servers on the staff.

She worked her way up the pecking order and, in all but name, became manager and assistant to Manny.

The two worked harmoniously together through a couple of tourist summer seasons and party-filled holidays. Just once had Manny made a feeble attempt to cross the boundaries between work and personal life and that was when he had had too much to drink.

Waiting until he had sobered up the next day, Kathleen challenged him about his unacceptable behavior. "You made a pass at me and tried to kiss me," she told him, knowing that she would embarrass him. "If you ever try that again I'll walk out."

Contrite and determined not to lose his best waitress, Manny apologized profusely. "The drink makes me do stupid things," he admitted. "It won't happen again."

"You're a good girl and a real asset to the business." Then he added with a grin, "I'd rather have you behind the bar than in my bed."

"You cheeky beggar," laughed Kathleen, flicking out at him with the dish towel she had been using to dry glasses. "In your dreams."

Concepta may have told Manny about Kathleen's history and the baby, but it was a subject well off-limits as far as Kathleen was concerned. She had closed that door firmly and intended to keep it locked forever.

Since the fateful encounter with Marcos that had tragically led to the twin events of suffering one birth and one death, Kathleen had not had a boyfriend.

Not that she lacked for offers. Her beauty and lively personality attracted many male admirers but she always refused dates and claimed she had to work, adding, "And on my night off, I wash my hair."

Life in Ocean Bay rejuvenated Kathleen. Away from the oppression of the city, she discovered that she loved the open doors and fresh air. On days off she strolled the couple of blocks to the beach and walked miles along the shorefront, reveling in the feel of the soft, snowy sand and the Atlantic Ocean lapping at her feet.

Kathleen later claimed that she rediscovered her faith in God on those solitary invigorating walks.

Lost in thought and silent meditation, her soul was restored and a healing process took place. She learned to talk to God, instead of being angry at Him.

Absentmindedly throwing small pebbles into the sea,

Kathleen started to pray again and with nothing to lose, she opened her heart.

"Dear God, I've managed to forgive you for taking my baby away from me and now I want a favor from you.

"I know the pain will never go away completely and I'm not asking for that because it might mean I forgot her, but the huge burden of loss is being replaced with a deep longing.

"I want someone to love."

A perfect peace settled on her. A peace almost immediately shattered by a small white dog running up to the tartan blanket where she sat near the water's edge and kicking up the sand in a scramble to retrieve a ball that had been thrown.

"Come away, I said," called a male voice. "Leave the nice lady alone."

Kathleen looked up and saw him striding toward her. Leash in hand. Kitty's owner was tall with tousled black hair and piercing blue eyes.

"Come away," I said. He looked at Kathleen and laughingly admitted, "Just one word from me, and she does what she likes."

Kathleen gave a small shrug accompanied by a laugh and took a closer look at him as she shaded her eyes and pushed back her hair, which struggled to break free from her black velvet hair band in the mischievous breeze.

"No problem. It's not the first time I've had sand kicked in my face. But you do know she's a dog, not a cat. That might be why she ignores your instructions."

The dog owner laughed. The cleft in his chin was clearly visible. He showed a set of perfect white teeth and his dazzling blue eyes sparkled and reflected the sky blue of the ocean, as he looked appreciatively at Kathleen.

"Touched by angels," her mother called those who had the cleft in their chin.

Kathleen felt herself well up with emotion and gratitude.

A divine sign. At least a promise that maybe one day she would be sent someone to love. God was answering her prayer and encouraging her to believe.

Not that she expected it to happen out of the blue, but she was struck with a crazy thought, *"Maybe I should get a dog."*

What happens next? Should I say something else? Will he prolong the conversation?

The decision was made when the dog bounded off down the beach, chasing the ball, which she had retrieved, and was now intent on giving herself and it a bath in the ocean.

"Bye, then," said Kathleen.

As Kitty's keeper turned to follow her, he called back over his shoulder, "Are you local? What's your name? Can I buy you a coffee to say sorry for Kitty's bad behavior? Will you meet me at the beach café up by the lighthouse in say half an hour?"

"Won't promise but if I do, my name's Kathleen. What's yours?"

Kathleen already knew that she had no intention of not showing up, but she wanted to give herself an out, just in case. Besides she didn't want to look too eager.

Just because she had finally found Mr. Tall, Dark, and Handsome, he didn't need to know that he was shaping up to be the answer to a maiden's prayers.

*   *   *

Sitting at a weather-beaten table in the late afternoon sunlight, outside the beach café, Kathleen and her new friend, Kieran, talked and laughed and shared stories.

"Kitty is named after my mother," he explained. "A beautiful Irish colleen from Kerry called Catherine. She passed away a few years ago. She lived in Ireland. It was me who left. I decided to seek my fame and fortune on the gold paved streets of New York. Now I work as a computer programmer in the casino trade. For a while I lived in New York and commuted to the shoreline. Then I had a brainwave. I could live here and commute to New York when necessary, which is not often. I rented a little beach cottage for me and the woman in my life, Kitty."

Kathleen wanted to ask the question but was shy. He answered it for her. "And no, there is no Mrs. Kieran Fairley. There was, back in Ireland. That's history."

Kathleen was relieved. She told Kieran about her job at The Best Little Bar House in Town, the idyllic little cottage where she lived, and about her kind landlord, being careful to stress that the relationship was purely professional.

"I too have a history," she told him. "Maybe one day I'll tell you. But there's no man in my life. Even the bar cat is a female."

Kieran and Kitty walked Kathleen home when it was time for her to get ready for her evening shift.

"Meet me at the beach café tomorrow," said Kieran as they parted. "If you don't show up, just remember, I know where you live."

The huge smile on Kathleen's face was proof enough that she would keep the appointment. Kitty showed approval of her owner's new friend by licking her hand and jumping up to kiss her face.

"I'd like to do that," said Kieran with a cheeky grin.

"Don't you dare," said Kathleen. "Just because you're from the old country, doesn't mean you can push your luck. Let's take it nice and easy."

CHAPTER SIXTEEN

Love at Last

Walking hand in hand on the sandy white beach, Kathleen and Kieran talked and laughed and shared secrets. The lovebirds were in a world of their own.

"Who was the father? Did you know?" Kieran asked.

Kathleen felt as if she had been slapped. Eyes blazing she stared at Kieran. "Of course I did. I only ever slept with the one boy and it happened on the very first and only occasion."

With a defiant shake of her head that made her ringlets bounce up and down, she challenged him. "You obviously don't know me at all and now you won't get a chance to have that pleasure."

In less than a month, taking it easy, one step at a time, they had gone from breakfast, lunch, and early dinner together every day to talk of marriage.

The whirlwind romance had taken both them and their friends by surprise, but the powerful forces behind the commitment had suggested real potential for happily ever after.

The first kiss had cast a magical spell and the two felt they had known each other forever. Now reality had intruded.

Shaking with hurt and humiliation, Kathleen turned and ran as fast as her bare feet would allow. She retraced the two sets of footprints back across the sand in the direction from which they had come.

Hearing Kieran's footsteps behind her, she ran faster and then turned and called to him over her shoulder, "Leave me alone. There is nothing you can say. Go away."

Kitty, thinking that this was a new game, joined in the chase.

The overexcited dog weaved in and out of Kathleen's legs, causing her to lose her balance, stumble, and trip into the sand.

Putting on his most authoritative dog-training voice, Kieran tried to regain control. "Kitty. Here. Now."

Misunderstanding, as usual, Kitty took a flying leap into his arms and knocked him to the ground. He landed on the carpet of sand alongside Kathleen.

Kitty, her white fluffy fur still matted and wet from her last dip in the ocean, jumped on top of both of them, licking and poking her nose into their faces, seeming to say, "Now kiss and make up."

Kathleen was still furious and not yet ready to let go of the anger, but she struggled not to laugh at Kitty's antics.

Getting to his feet, Kieran held his hand out to Kathleen, "At least let me help you up. Did you hurt yourself?"

"Not as much as you hurt me," Kathleen replied sharply.

"I'm so sorry," he said and although she tried to look away, Kathleen could not deny the pained expression on his face. "Please forgive me. I was angry and I lashed out at you."

Kathleen remained sitting where she was on the sand, pulled her knees up to under her chin, and wrapped her arms around her body. She looked straight out across the horizon.

Sitting stiffly beside her, Kieran too stared out across the water.

"I told you I had history," he explained. "Back in Ireland, there was a girl. I was in love with her. When she told me she was pregnant and it was my baby, I told my wife about the affair and walked out of my marriage.

"I wanted to do the right thing by the girlfriend.

"More fool me." He gave a cynical laugh. "Turns out it wasn't my baby and she was only using me to make the ex-boyfriend jealous, and hopefully get him to marry her.

"I was made a laughing stock of and the worst part of it was that my mother was so disappointed in me. The wife wouldn't have me back. She insisted on a divorce. Not that I blamed her, but I decided the best thing was for me to leave Ireland and start again in America.

"I hope you can begin to understand why I reacted like I did. It's no excuse and I know I should never have said what I did to you. Please accept my apology. Forgive me."

He acted with such sincerity and was so contrite Kathleen decided she would trust her instincts and take a leap of faith. The connection the two of them had experienced in their short time together was too good to throw away for a matter of pride.

Yes, she had been hurt but she'd get over it.

The two sat close together on the beach as Kitty explored and the early winter sun completed its journey across the sky and sank into its western nighttime home.

At first they held fingertips, then hands. Finally, they cuddled together for comfort against the chilly evening breeze and thankfully accepted the extra warmth provided by Kitty, as she lay stretched out across two sets of legs like a rug.

"Let's go home," said Kieran, "And get warmed up by the fire. You can even wash your hair at my house on your night off. Although I can think of other ways to keep you occupied."

* * *

Waking with Kieran's arms locked around her as the sun arose the next morning, Kathleen smiled. He looked so beautiful and content lying there asleep, eyes closed, jet black hair tousled, and long dark eyelashes flickering shadows on his cheeks.

She reached out and softly stroked his handsome face.

"You were worth waiting for," she whispered.

"And so were you," he replied, rewarding her with a smile and a wink.

131

CHAPTER SEVENTEEN

Happily Ever After

A hushed silence descended on the wedding party as Kathleen stepped into the single spotlight shining on the small stage in the decorated restaurant setting.

The bride, a vision of beauty in a simple floor-skimming ivory lace gown with a garland of fresh flowers in her free flowing curly hair, became once again that singing sensation Angel Kennedy whose life held such promise and innocence.

"Amazing Grace" evoked the divine presence of the occasion and a powerful version of the Whitney Houston classic "I Will Always Love You" was rewarded with thunderous applause. Kathleen had been persuaded out of early retirement to sing at her own wedding party.

Kieran walked proudly across the stage to his new wife's side and embraced her. "Please show your appreciation for Mrs. Kieran Fairley," he said into the microphone.

"Perhaps we will be able to persuade her to sing again later. If I haven't already whisked her off. Now we'll take to the floor for a first dance but I am no Michael Flatley and I can't do the River Dance, so it will have to be a slow shuffle. Make sure you all join in."

The marriage ceremony earlier that day had been an intimate affair held at Ocean Bay Town Hall with just two witnesses, Concepta and Manny.

Back at The Best Little Bar House in Town, Manny had pushed the boat out and treated the invited guests to a feast of seafood, surf 'n' turf, and a traditional old recipe of laverbread cookies, one of which he claimed had a special coin in that would grant the wish of marriage to one young lady.

Together, Kathleen and Kieran had chosen the theme for the wedding day and, in honor of the happy couple's Irish backgrounds, the restaurant was decorated in green, white, and gold.

Manny ordered a special two-tier wedding cake, and instead of traditional bride and groom figures on top, there were Mr. and Mrs. Leprechauns sitting on a red and white toadstool playing Irish musical instruments, little shillelaghs.

The decision had been made to dispense with official speeches, as neither bride nor groom had family at the event. Kieran's best man, René, his casino manager boss, proposed a toast to absent friends, including Kathleen's mother whom Concepta had tried without success to track down at her last known address in Brooklyn, New York City.

Manny, proud of his honorary title of "Father of the Bride" replied to the toast and handed his special friend and favorite employee, Kathleen, into Kieran's safe keeping.

"You may, with my permission, kiss the bride," he said, shedding a whiskey tear and slurring just a little.

"Here's to a happily ever after," he proclaimed.

✳ ✳ ✳

Kieran's small beach cottage was a romantic first home for the newlyweds and Kathleen was in her element as she made it into a little palace.

Looking up from the interior design magazine she had been studying, a thought came into her mind.

"Why don't I sign up for a course at the community education college?" she suggested.

Her husband agreed it was a great idea.

"I know you like working at the restaurant," he said, "but you've never had time to develop a career. Now's your chance, especially since I have to work several nights a week at the casino.

"Talk to Manny about switching you to daytime shifts and sign up at the college."

Kathleen took to her new hobby with enthusiasm and was delighted to discover that she had a natural flair for color, design, and innovation.

Inspired by the natural resources and treasures that she observed in the local ocean and beach, Kathleen found the confidence, combined with a new level of expertise in the interior design classes, to create original crafted items and paintings.

"We never had any money for special accessories or furnishings when I was growing up," she told Kieran, "but my dad always said I was a born homemaker."

Kieran gave her a mysterious smile and said, "I'm pleased to hear it, for I have a project for you. Let's go for a walk on the beach and I'll tell you all about it."

Intrigued and excited, Kathleen called to Kitty, who never needed to be asked twice, and told her, "Walk time."

Speeding up, she made her way out of the door and declared, "Last one at the water's edge is a cissy."

It was a fresh spring day and the trio walked briskly, but as she made to take their familiar turn to the right on the boardwalk, Kieran stopped her. "Follow me."

With the ocean on the right and the dunes on the left, they walked toward a row of pastel-colored clapperboard houses, with front porches overlooking the beach.

"Close your eyes," said Kieran guiding her gently from behind. "Trust me. Don't open your eyes till I tell you."

He walked her forward and stopped in front of the last house in the row, he wrapped his arms around her from behind and, with his hands gently over her eyes he said, "Make a wish."

"That's not fair," said Kathleen, "you know I have only one wish. To live happily ever after with you."

"Okay," said her husband. "Do you think you can live happily ever after here? Open your eyes. Welcome to our new home."

Kathleen was speechless. In her dreams she had never dared imagine that one day she would live in such an idyllic home.

Overlooking the waterfront yet secluded by the dunes, the house was attached to its neighbor on just one side and open to the beach on the other. In need of a new coat of white paint, the wood was weatherbeaten and peeling. The window frames were rusty and the small garden area around the porch was overgrown.

"It's perfect. I love it," said Kathleen, throwing her arms around her husband.

Kieran laughed. "I hoped you wouldn't be annoyed at me for buying it without letting you in on the secret, but it was a last-minute thing and too good an opportunity to pass up."

The house, an estate sale, had been put up for auction and Kieran's boss René, the best man at his wedding, had urged him to make a bid. "It's never too early to get on the property ladder," he had told him, "and with a new young bride, you can't go wrong, Waterfront is prime real estate."

From his jeans' pocket, Kieran pulled out a set of keys that unlocked the front door of the rickety old house.

"René is finalizing arrangements through the company to get me fixed up with a mortgage," he explained, "but for now, there's no one living here and we can pay rent and make a start on the renovations."

Inside, the house was dusty, musty, and badly in need of modernization. The downstairs lounge had wooden floorboards and a huge carved wooden fireplace dominated the room.

A small kitchenette was basic but did have working electricity and fifties-style appliances. The bathroom was eighties chic, obviously a newer addition.

"Watch yourself on the stairs," Kieran called out in warning.

"Grab on to the banister and follow me. If it holds my weight, it'll hold yours."

Upstairs there were two bedrooms, the front with a wooden balcony giving spectacular views of the shoreline.

The interior decoration was in need of tender loving care

as was the outside. Crumbling walls revealed cracks and peeling wallpaper.

"It's a big job," Kieran pointed out, beginning to look uncertain for the first time since they had entered the house.

"Are you game for it?"

Kathleen was busy trying to open the French door that led out to the balcony. "This is man's work," she said. "It needs brute force."

After much pushing and pulling and the discovery that the doors needed not just brute force but to be unlocked, Kieran and Kathleen stood lost in wonder on their balcony gazing out to sea.

In the magic of the moment, Kathleen turned to face her husband, gazed into his eyes, and smiled.

"You're not the only one who can keep a secret," she said. "I have one too. We're going to have a baby."

Kieran almost backed into the wobbly balcony railing with excitement. The happy couple hugged and laughed and then cried.

"This is the most perfect day ever in my life," said Kathleen.

"You have made me the happiest man in the world," said Kieran.

"Now let's go and check out the nursery," said Kathleen, bubbling over with joy. "There's not a moment to lose getting this house knocked into shape."

* * *

In the frantic activity of the next six months, there were

times when Kathleen felt like Snow White, with the seven dwarves clambering from the roof to the foundations and all floors in between.

To the sound of hammering, banging, screwing, and sawing was added whistling, humming, singing plus occasional cursing and shouting from the team of painters, plasterers, electricians, plumbers, and carpenters.

Kathleen made endless pots of coffee and Kieran wrote endless checks. Kitty played the role of foreman, bouncing upstairs and down, eagerly checking out each craftsman's work.

Finally, the renovations on the house were complete and Kathleen organized and coordinated deliveries of new furnishings, furniture, and appliances. Beach chic was her preferred style and the colors of the ocean, azure and deep navy, and the violet blue of the sky and vibrant mellow yellow sunshine, complemented and contrasted in each room. The white of the playful sea-gazing clouds formed the tapestry on which everything else was painted.

Proudly observing from the shoreline the transformation of their beautiful seaside home, Kieran and Kathleen agreed that the eau de Nil, "water of the Nile", glossy paint they had so carefully chosen for the window frames, front door, and the new awning over the porch, accented the house to perfection. And to top it all off, there was a shiny red chimney spout complete with smoke rising from locally grown cedar logs.

"A home made in heaven," they congratulated each other.

"All that is needed to make it complete is our baby."

Neither spoke the last thought out loud. Silently they remembered the losses that had robbed each of them of a family life.

CHAPTER EIGHTEEN

Cruel Fates

Kathleen was home alone when her labor began. Timing the contractions as too close together for comfort, she called her husband who did not pick up his phone. It went to voicemail. Without hesitation she pressed the preprogrammed number in her cell phone for the private ambulance service Kieran had arranged. Even as they transported her to the hospital, they called her husband at work telling him to make his way to the maternity unit.

Receiving the message and furious he had missed the crucial call he had been expecting and waiting for, Kieran dropped everything. As he ran from his office, he struggled into his suit jacket. René was on duty behind the main reception desk. Kieran called out to him

"Baby on its way. I'll call you from the hospital."

Kieran slowed just once in his mad dash; he stopped and rubbed his hand on the paw of the life-size bronze lion that gamblers at the casino rubbed to bring good luck.

Pushing through the side door rather than waste a precious second waiting for the automatic doors, Kieran headed for the curbside where a valet had brought around his car from the staff parking lot.

Thinking for a split second that it was a car backfiring, Kieran heard but did not process the sound of the loud crack that filled the air. Without warning a gunshot rang out and a bullet flew through the air. Suddenly, as if in slow motion, Kieran fell forward. His eyes frantically scanned the faces of passersby to find an explanation.

"He's been hit," screamed a panicking middle-aged woman.

Kieran's blood splattered the sidewalk as his white shirt-front turned crimson and he slammed with a sickening thud face first into the concrete.

The frightened middle-aged woman who had seen the whole incident up close, as if in slow motion, ran from the scene desperately brushing Kieran's blood from her clothes.

Casino security staff jumped into action, dialed 911, and summoned police and ambulance. Kieran lay face down unmoving as a sea of blood spilled around his prostrate body.

"Clear the scene," they shouted, endeavoring not to generate anymore panic than had already ensued. "Everyone, clear the scene, there's a gunman on the loose."

* * *

Through the long hours of her labor, Kathleen asked constantly for her husband. "Why hasn't he arrived? What could be more important than to be here at my side for the birth of our baby?"

In a fog of sedatives and disorientation, Kathleen cried out, "Kieran, Kieran. Is he coming?"

Kieran was indeed at the hospital but in no condition to visit his wife as she gave birth.

"A tragic accident. He just happened to be in the wrong place at the wrong time," the paramedic relayed his report to the senior nurse at the admittance station.

"Her husband was the victim of a random act of violence outside the casino where he worked. Rushed out of the building and got caught in the crossfire as an angry customer fired at another employee."

The nurse stopped briefly in her duties of checking the patient's vital signs. She had been on duty in the maternity unit and attended the gunshot victim's wife, a lovely young girl earlier that day. With genuine concern, she asked. "Will he be alright?"

Shaking his head, the paramedic looked doubtful.

"Bullet pierced his heart. Lost a lot of blood but he's young and fit, he's been given a transfusion. I wouldn't bet on it but maybe he'll survive."

The nursing shifts changed and Kieran's condition was recorded as having deteriorated from "Serious" to "Critical."

Kieran lost his battle for life in the intensive care unit during the long nighttime hours.

In a parallel universe in a ward just one floor below, his wife Kathleen gave birth to a baby girl.

All through the pregnancy she had promised herself that she would refuse all chemical relief no matter how bad the pain. Now the absence of her husband was a source of greater anguish than the excruciating physical discomfort of childbirth.

Hospital staff gently persuaded her of the wisdom of

taking medication. "Your levels of distress aren't good for the baby," they told her. "It will make the delivery more difficult for both of you."

Distraught and scared, Kathleen became more and more frantic.

"Please will someone tell me what is going on? Where is my husband?" she shouted at nurses who were not in a position to enlighten her. "I need to know, is he coming?"

Enveloped in a dreamlike state, drifting in and out of consciousness, through twenty-four long hours of labor, Kathleen was exhausted and delirious when the reluctant baby finally arrived.

After the cord was cut and the baby washed and enfolded in a snowy white hospital gown, Kathleen clung tight to the strangely quiet newborn.

Kathleen could not shake the terrible overwhelming feeling of impending doom. She prayed that she was simply imagining it but deep down sensed that there was something wrong with the child. Her instincts were correct.

The medical delivery had already identified a heart defect. Without surgery the baby would not survive.

A hurried consultation took place in the doctor's office. "Someone must be with her when we tell her the devastating news. She's still drowsy and sedated, that's a blessing. Apart from her husband, who is her next of kin?"

Concepta had been summoned from New York City; Manny drove frantically to the city and collected her to be at the hospital when Kathleen was given the unbearable news of the double tragedy. Kieran, her beloved husband, was dead and her unnamed daughter needed lifesaving surgery.

Concepta and Manny held a vigil at Kathleen's side. In silence they sat as she gazed with rapt attention at her tiny child hooked up to the tubes and machines in an incubator.

Kathleen had asked Concepta to bring her a rosary. Now she reverentially fingered the sea blue glass beads. Praying as if her life depended on it to the Virgin Mary.

Holy Mary, Mother of God, have mercy on me. Hail Mary, full of grace, the Lord is with thee. Blessed art thou among women.

The thought that the tiny body would be mutilated with surgery broke Kathleen's heart. She prayed more fervently than she ever had before.

"Blessed Mother, don't let them hurt her. Give me her pain. She's an innocent child. Don't inflict this upon her."

Kathleen's newborn survived just another twenty-four hours. Her delicate heart and weakened body could not withstand the rigors of the best medical treatment.

She was a beautiful butterfly destined to live for just one day.

A priest baptized the baby and administered the last rites.

Her mother named her Angel.

Concepta knew there was no answer but she raged and asked Manny, "In the name of God, how can any woman be expected to survive this tragedy? Her beloved husband and newborn baby girl are both dead. How will she ever cope with the loss?"

Kathleen was prescribed heavy sedation and put into an induced medical coma. Her friends did not leave her bedside.

Their hearts ached for the tragic young widow and bereft mother.

Forced to return to reality and wake from the ignorance of oblivion, Kathleen had only one plea. *Let me sleep and never wake up. I don't want to live. I can't live without my husband and baby. Please let me die.*

CHAPTER NINETEEN

Beloved Child

Tiny ballerinas skipped daintily down the short flight of steps of Miami City Ballet's headquarters alongside the Bass Museum of Contemporary Art in the tourist Mecca of Miami Beach.

Proud of its origin as one of the few facilities in the world built from the ground up specifically for dance, huge loft floor-to-ceiling windows and mirrored studios with lightly sprung Marley floors and custom-made barres offered unobstructed front-row viewing into classrooms and practice workshops.

Interested passersby enjoyed unprecedented access to the enchanting world of warm-up sessions and dance rehearsals. Sidewalk audiences are treated to early performances of works in progress and presentations of up and coming choreographed segments of the Miami City Ballet's modern and traditional repertoire.

Like a well-drilled mini army on the march, the student classes of in-their-dreams prima ballerinas, and pre-professional dancers, wore color-coordinated leotards of yellow, red, and purple, designed to offer unrestricted movement and to show off lithe, slender bodies and coltlike legs encased in white, hint of pink, or flesh colored tights.

Every hair, systematically scraped back from tiny delicate features, succumbed to being brushed into submission, pulled into a tight bun, and secured with pins and a net. Ballet shoes or practice pumps were stored, as per regulations, into shoe bags with the leaping dancer motif and MCB logo. Conformity being the order of the day, each child was a vision of femininity, discipline, and grace.

Serena was a star pupil who had been attending Miami City Ballet since baby classes and through her years at Miami Beach High School. Every season she had a lead role in the holiday spectacular, *Nutcracker*, and she had progressed in her career through featured roles in the classic *Swan Lake*.

In a community where spoiling children was a national pastime, Serena Perez was the most beloved.

Just six weeks old the day her new parents collected her from St. Bernadette's Convent, she was seamlessly transported into a fairy tale world of money, prestige, and privilege.

Snuggled in a lace-lined bassinet in the back of a top-of-the-line Cadillac sedan, the chauffeur drove while Maria and Humberto Perez held court and gazed at the baby they had longed for. Happily married for almost ten years, their successful and contented life had been marred only by a heartbreaking inability to produce a child.

Not to be defeated and knowing that everything had its price, the couple were more than willing to pay to achieve their lifetime ambition. Humberto did not hesitate when asked to open his checkbook on being presented with an opportunity to buy a baby.

Maria thought she had died and gone to heaven the day the phone call came saying that their baby was available.

"Mrs. Perez, I have the most welcome news for you," said Mother Superior, trying to keep the gloating tone out of her voice. "God is good and I am pleased to tell you that your prayers for a baby have been answered.

"As I informed you previously, I was confident that the young lady in question would agree to my request when I explained that her baby was to be lovingly brought up by parents of the highest caliber. Our young mother is relieved that her baby will have the upbringing that she desires. I have assured her she will have no cause for concern when her baby is in your capable care. It is a blessed solution for all concerned."

Maria had thanked God for this blessing and her husband Humberto wore a permanent grin, suffused as he was with happiness.

"Tell me again about our baby," said Maria. The couple had compiled a wish list and now their designer shopping spree was about to manifest itself into a real life human being.

The wish was for a baby girl, healthy, light skinned with dark hair and dark eyes. To all intents and purposes, the adopted child should pass for their own.

Hispanic, good-looking, even featured with gently sun-kissed skin, Maria and Humberto, immigrants from Cuba, were proud of their Spanish ancestry.

Exiles from their homeland of Cuba, they had been

forced to flee the revolution that made freedom fighters of the population after the dictator Fidel Castro had turned their idyllic Caribbean island into a communist state.

Like their compatriots, the dream was that one day they would return, when Castro was overthrown. In the meantime they were determined to preserve the culture and traditions of the land that in the intervening decades, had assumed a mythic quality of fantasy, romance, and legend.

Over the course of several visits to St. Bernadette's, they had identified Kathleen O'Shaunessey as the poster child mother whose dark good looks, black hair, and delicate features would produce the beautiful baby they desired.

Even had one been available, it would have gone against their principles to have adopted a baby of genuine Cuban birth born to an unmarried. In an ideal world, they would rather not believe that those things happened to girls from their own country.

* * *

A high-end apartment on Park Avenue close to her new father's business address had been Serena's first home but she would always consider the family's waterfront property in Miami Beach, her childhood home. Before she could walk, the family had moved into a vine-covered red tile Spanish villa, with stucco walls, wrought iron balconies, and tiled walkways. Prime real estate, it was located on a palm tree-lined street on a manmade island on the Venetian causeway with views overlooking Biscayne Bay and the downtown Miami skyline.

In elementary school, being a pupil at an exclusive

private girls' Catholic school ensured that her friends and classmates were from Miami's premiere rich and influential families.

Her mother, Maria, the daughter of a wealthy Cuban landowner, had lived the elegant and sheltered life of a debutante, before leaving Cuba for America as a teenager. Castro's communist revolution had soon disdainfully swept away the aristocratic pampered mode of existence.

Humberto was a real life hero of the Bay of Pigs invasion, when President Kennedy had sent an army made up of members of the CIA to join Cuba's Brigade 2506 to overthrow Castro. The invasion had been a disaster. Eighty men were killed, thirty-seven drowned before they reached the beaches, and 1,180 members of the 1,400 man assault force quickly surrendered as Castro's forces drove them back into the sea. In a humiliating defeat, the US had paid a $62 million ransom in food and medicine to have the young Cuban males released from Castro's jails.

Humberto was one of the young freedom fighters and he had joined an early airlift from Havana that transported Cuban refugees to the processing center of "Freedom Tower" on Miami's Biscayne Boulevard from where they would be resettled in the States.

As a "brother in arms" he was accorded a special position of honor and held an esteemed place in the Cuban community, revered and respected.

A cultured, charming man and handsome silver fox, by the time he met Maria, ten years his junior, he had achieved affluence and power as a wealthy real estate developer and benefactor. An unofficial civic leader and man of influence, he was looked up to and admired. A one time revolutionary he had become a pillar of the community, living the American dream with his successful businesses, expensive homes, and flashy American cars.

Being part of an exiled community, there were plentiful opportunities and obligations to support other families and it was a matter of honor to integrate the new exiles who continued to arrive in Miami and other parts of the United States for the next twenty years. Fidel Castro had solved a homegrown problem by exporting those who opposed his regime, and on arrival in their new country, many idealistic Cubans still saw themselves as embattled heroes in an ongoing struggle where good must ultimately triumph over evil.

The US took them in and through the federal government refugee program and enthusiastic support from local Catholic charities, helped whole families resettle on the mainland.

Coming from rich families in Cuba, many of the members of the new community had left behind substantial lands and properties on the small island ninety miles from the tip of Florida, and even poor immigrants fantasized that they had been members of the elite, educated, privileged Havana families. Serena was constantly told that Cuba was the most beautiful land human eyes had ever seen.

Maria and Humberto Perez were the real deal, Golden Exiles who soon established substantial lifestyles in the USA.

Growing up, Serena never tired of hearing stories of her father's bravery and she was proud of her beautiful socialite mother who had readjusted to her new life with grace and style.

"Tell me again about the suitcases," she would urge them. "Why don't you unpack?" she would ask.

Three black leather suitcases were permanently on display in a corner of her mother's bedroom. Serena knew the answer but still she loved to hear her mother tell her yet again, "We never unpack because the day Castro is overthrown, we will go back to Cuba."

As a child the prospect both excited and scared Serena. Along with her parents she waited for the day of the homecoming. The years turned to decades and the teenager liked to tease asking, "Have they overthrown Castro yet? Are we going back to Cuba?"

Serena knew she was privileged but could not help but take for granted her gold-plated lifestyle.

The family enjoyed every luxury money could buy and entertained lavishly at their elegant mansion location, with its infinity pool seeming to overflow directly into the tidal Bay. At the tree-lined water's edge sat Humberto's ocean-going yacht.

A dedicated staff of maids, a pool man, and landscapers kept the property immaculate.

Visits to the beach and swimming in the ocean were high on the after-school schedule, either being chauffeured or hitching a ride in friends' convertibles.

Serena lived the American dream. A popular sporty girl and chief cheerleader, she was chosen for every school team and always had the lead role in plays, concerts, and dance performances.

A high achiever, it seemed that there was nothing she couldn't do. Fluent in Spanish and English, a straight-A student, she worked conscientiously to make her parents proud as she excelled both academically and socially.

For the first sixteen years of her life, Serena led an idyllic, indulged existence. International vacations, designer clothes, and her own charge card—with no limit—at the exclusive stores, Neiman Marcus, Nordstrom, and Saks Fifth Avenue.

Her "Sweet Sixteen" party, a Latin tradition, had been held at the Vizcaya mansion, a grand neoclassical building with ornate Italianate grounds and sweeping views out over the Bay.

The invitation list to her birthday party was a who's who of the rich and powerful of Miami, it was reported in the local paper, and photo spreads appeared in glossy magazines including *Ocean Drive* and *Aspire*.

A Bling and Diamonds party, the claim in the media, not denied by her high-spending father, was that the event, complete with Emmy award-winning musicians from the Miami Sound Machine and world famous singing star Enrique Iglesias, son of Julio, cost almost $100,000.

Serena was a princess, prom queen, and the girl most likely to succeed.

However, her parents were also civic activists and apart from their glittering beach social life, they stayed close to their Cuban roots with regular visits to family and friends who had settled in Miami's downtown SW8th Street area, Calle Ocho, known as Little Havana.

Together the family enjoyed regular trips to Festival Culturals in "Calle Ocho" and the annual street festival where hundreds of performers, dancers, puppeteers, and vendors of all forms of ethnic food, including Cuban black beans and rice and paella, celebrated their origins and colorful traditions.

Serena was a Golden Girl but few saw her other side. She was fiery and strong willed. "You should have been born with red hair," her mother joked.

Her ballet mistress was not amused the day she found her entertaining fellow pupils with a noisy and energetic performance of Irish dancing in the hallowed confines of the Miami City Ballet studio.

Serena's parents refused to be outraged but nor would they offer an explanation as to why their classically trained daughter might be so proficient at traditional Celtic dances. They privately expressed the view, "It's in the blood."

In a perfect life, Serena was a perfect daughter and her parents chose not to allow any shadow to darken the fairy tale life by telling her about her true origins.

However, her parents' best intentions did not stop reality from cruelly bursting into her life the day Serena's birth mother Kathleen showed up on the doorstep of their luxury Miami Beach home.

CHAPTER TWENTY

The Secret's Out

Loud hammering at the main doorway scared Serena who was home alone in her bedroom listening to music and reading celebrity and fashion magazines. She put down her copy of *In Style* and listened.

Who could be demanding entry? Police, ambulance, emergency services? Even in secure residential neighborhoods in wealthy Miami Beach, home invasions were not unknown. But surely they wouldn't knock on the door?

The real mystery was that anyone should have evaded the security system and bypassed the video camera at the gated entry point.

Maybe the maid had inadvertently locked herself out. Or the pool man was requesting payment? Serena tried to think of sensible explanations that would stop her heart from pounding.

She threw on a wrap over her underwear and reluctantly made her way down the grand winding staircase that led from her bedroom on the upper floor to the public rooms on the main mezzanine level.

To avoid having to open the door, she tried once more

to arouse the maid. "ChiChi where are you?" she called, "Can you answer the door?"

No response, though her cry for help reactivated the person on the other side of the door and the hammering continued even louder than before.

What a ridiculous situation, thought Serena. I'm sixteen years old and can count on the fingers of one hand the number of times I have answered my own front door—and never, that I can remember, when no one else was at home. Examining the locks and bolts she tried to work out the process that would produce an "open sesame."

Should I phone my mother? She wondered.

Little did she know that her mother was the one demanding entry.

Serena checked the image on the video camera—she didn't recognize the slightly disheveled dark-haired woman who was staring angrily into the lens.

Against her better judgment she decided to open the large double doors, but not too wide. The woman had her speech prepared.

"I'm a friend of your parents," she said. "I was in the neighborhood and wanted to say 'hi.'"

"How did you get through the security gate?" asked Serena.

"The maid was leaving, her lift was waiting," she explained. "She let me in to make a delivery."

In her hand the woman held a small grocery store bouquet of flowers. "These are for your mother," she said.

Serena held out her hand to take the gift.

"Thank you, I'll give them to her," she said, "She's not here right now. Who shall I say they're from?"

Not ready to relinquish the advantage of the flowers as a bargaining tool, the visitor snatched the flowers, which were already leaking from the bottom of their plastic reusable bag, out of reach.

"I'd rather give them to her myself," she said. "Can I wait for her?"

Taking Serena by surprise, she made her move and barged past her into the marble floored hallway of the house. Serena followed. She didn't know how to stop the situation that unfolded and was rapidly getting out of control.

"Let me take the flowers," she said, anxious to at least solve one problem and stop the steady stream of water that was spreading over the marble tiles.

The woman was too quick for her. She was making her way into the downstairs lounge and her eyes feasted on the opulent surroundings. Now the flowers were dripping onto one of the rich, blue silk Persian scatter rugs that accented the open space.

Standing beside one of the two six-seater white leather sectionals, she stroked a tasseled tapestry pillow that had a pink flamingo embroidered on it and the motto, "Think Pink, it's the Magic Link."

She forced Serena to do the polite thing and make a decision. "Can I sit down?" she asked.

Flustered, confused, and praying that her parents would show up, Serena twisted a strand of her lovely dark hair into a tight corkscrew around her index finger and bit the inside of her cheek.

"I have to go out," she said, hearing the weakness of the

argument even as she said the words. "Someone is waiting for me. Coming for me. Picking me up. I need to get ready. I'll tell my mother you stopped by, thank you, and I'll pass on the flowers."

The stranger had not waited for permission; she sat holding the flowers in her right hand, which she extended some distance from the couch, allowing the flowers to continue dripping on the floor.

"Please, let me take the flowers," said Serena, angry now that she was being held hostage in her own home. The front door was still ajar. "I'll show you out."

The woman reluctantly held out the flowers to Serena, but made no move to leave.

"Serena, it's a lovely name, suits you," she said. "Serena, my name is Kathleen. Have your parents ever mentioned me to you?"

Serena stared into the distance off to the right, searching her memory for mention of a Kathleen. "No, I don't think so," she answered. She could not put a name to the feeling she had when the woman looked directly at her, but she could not deny a familiarity and it made her feel decidedly uncomfortable.

Kathleen apparently took a decision to stop playing games. She took a deep breath. All the years when the emotions had been held painfully inside her and the hundreds of times she had imagined saying these words to her daughter, came out on one rush of breath. "I'm your mother," she declared and one tiny, baby tear ran down her cheek.

Serena stared at the woman who sat before her. A

stranger but also a mirror image. She had not aged well. Her face once beautiful now was ravaged and covered with too much makeup in an attempt to hide the lines and wrinkles and frowns. Dark eyes that surveyed the world from behind long heavily mascaraed lashes still held a hint of former sparkle, but they were suspicious and guarded. Her long dark hair was pulled into a messy ponytail and secured with a butterfly hair clip. The woman's hesitant smile did not reach her eyes and when she did open her mouth, her teeth looked too large behind the painted red lips. Probably not yet forty, she looked a decade older. The years had not been kind to Kathleen.

Her outfit was designed to hide some of the extra weight she carried: black loose-fitting pants and a frilly scarlet overblouse helped distract attention from her full figure. The high-heeled shoes had seen better days and the once smart business shoes were shabby and down at heel. Overall, the impression was of someone who had gone to a great deal of trouble to look presentable, but lacked the wherewithal to pull it off. She looked blowsy, unhealthy, and more a creature of the night than a sunny Florida day.

Serena thought of her mother, Maria. An exotic, black-haired, flashing-eyed Latin beauty, always immaculately groomed, stylish, confident, and radiating health, wealth, and glamour.

Not knowing which way to turn, Serena walked to the open doorway and gestured. "I think you better leave," she said with more authority than she felt. "Please just go. I don't know what's going on and I don't want to know."

It took all of Kathleen's resolve not to reach out and

hug Serena. She had longed for this day, dreamed of the day when she could see and touch her daughter. Her heart filled with longing and she despised the weakness in herself that made her pretend it was all about the money. She is my flesh and blood, she wanted to scream, do not deny me the chance for one magical moment to gaze upon my child.

*   *   *

Kathleen stood up and walked toward Serena but, instead of exiting, she tried to put her arms around the young girl. Serena pushed her away, let out an involuntary scream, and ran out of the doorway onto the mosaic-tiled pathway outside.

A loud mechanical sound caused both women to turn and stare toward the entranceway. The gates swung open and her father's sleek black Mercedes pulled into the driveway.

He struggled to assess the situation. Seeing Serena, the open door, and a shadowy figure in the hallway, Humberto stopped the car, jumped out of the driver's seat, and ran toward his daughter. Serena sobbed and clung to him; she was still in shock at the events that had transpired. Between sobs she tried to get the words out and tell her father what had happened.

Humberto already had his cell phone in his hand ready to call 911. "Get out of my house," he shouted to Kathleen who stood uncertainly, half inside and half outside the house. "Now. Out. I'm calling the police."

Kathleen lost her nerve. She had felt confident and empowered when she was dealing with a child, her child. Now she was scared. The police were no friends of hers.

She cursed under her breath; the effects of the drinks she had taken for Dutch courage had worn off, and she was beginning to experience the all-too-familiar symptoms of alcohol withdrawal.

* * *

The new boyfriend she had met in a downtown Miami bar close to the railroad station, where she had arrived on a train from New York, had refused to buy her any more liquor.

"Go and do your business first," he had told her, after hearing the story of why she was on a mission and needed a ride to Miami Beach.

"My daughter lives there, in a mansion," she had boasted, employing the well-known grandiosity of drunks when trying to elevate themselves above other no-hope drinkers and aiming to impress. "With this rich couple. They've got plenty of money and I need to go and collect my share."

Barroom tales rarely being what they seem, Kathleen's new drinking partner was not convinced but until proved wrong he agreed to go along for the ride.

Downing another beer, Scott, a redneck with dirty blond hair in his early thirties who hailed from upstate Florida and sometimes worked construction, had listened to the story.

"They owe me money," said Kathleen, warming to her theme. "I deserve it. They bought my baby and I never made a cent. Now I make them pay. They are so frightened of their precious daughter finding out the truth that when I threaten to tell her the Big Secret, they give me more money. It works every time.

"Drive me to the beach. I'll get my payoff and the drinks will be on me."

Scott was warming to the idea of a rich girlfriend and the more she talked up the money, the more attractive she looked. Truth was she was too old and past her prime for him, but in the dim light of a drinking den he could imagine the beautiful, fresh-faced young woman she must have been way back then when she was a teenager.

"My heart broke when I had to give away my darling baby girl," said Kathleen, who was wearing her Sunday best name, but also happy to answer to Kathie or Katie depending on who wanted to know.

A maudlin drunk was the last thing Scott had wanted to deal with, so he cheered her up by announcing, "Come on, I'll drive you there now. No time like the present."

* * *

Kathleen had never been so bold as to show up at the house before, though she had known the address for years.

The green post-it note from the desk of Sister M and M, on which she had written the address of the adoptive parents of her baby, was a prize possession. For almost sixteen years, it had been a precious secret she hugged to herself. That was before she started using the address to send requests for money.

Maria and Humberto had gotten into an argument the first time a letter arrived from Kathleen postmarked New York.

The cheap envelope with the scrawled ballpoint address had been placed on top of the pile of mail the maid had collected from the mailbox. Humberto was puzzled. It didn't look like the usual professional mail he received or even the carefully addressed charity requests that were sent to his household.

He sliced through the top of the envelope with a small paring knife as he sat at the kitchen counter drinking coffee and reading the *Miami Herald* before setting off for a day's business downtown.

On blue-lined notepaper, Kathleen had not wasted words.

> *"Please help me, I am in a very bad way and I need money. You can send the money to me at my friend's address. Cash please. I won't bother you again, but I know you are good people and would not want to see the mother of your child in such dire circumstances. With your help I can get medical attention and get myself back on my feet. I don't know where else to turn. Thank you.*
>
> *Yours sincerely, Kathleen O'Shaunessey."*

Humberto could not begin to fathom how Kathleen had got their address. The convent always assured them that it would be strictly confidential. Not just to prevent requests for money but to ensure the security of the adopted child and parents.

Humberto's first thought was to ignore the letter as he did with the dozens of letters suggesting that with all his money, he could pass on to other deserving and not so deserving causes.

Instead, he decided to share the contents of the letter with Maria. She did not hesitate, "Of course we must help," she said. "The woman has never asked before so she must be desperate. After all she is the mother of our child. We have a duty to help her."

Humberto tried to caution his kind-hearted wife. "You do know that you may well be opening the floodgates to constant demands?"

"Yes, and we may never hear another word," said Maria with compassion. "Either because she is too sick to get in touch—or because she gets better and doesn't need our help."

Humberto smiled with affection at his wife. Her response was typical of the beautiful generous spirit he had fallen in love with over twenty-five years earlier.

The letters, the requests, the excuses would continue, he had no doubt of that. In his wildest dreams he could not have envisioned just how bad things had got for Kathleen.

*   *   *

Scott drove his battered old pickup truck across the Venetian Causeway, the oldest bridge, opened in 1926, that connected downtown Miami to Miami Beach across the Biscayne Bay.

"This is truly paradise," said Kathie as they drove in the warmth of the joyful sunshine under a blessed bright blue sky, where pure white clouds played, and a caressing breeze bid welcome.

"On the Travel Channel they named this as one of the top ten most spectacular waterways in America," said state native Scott knowledgeably. He had pulled up his sleeve and leaned his left arm further out of the window to increase the sun's exposure on one forearm.

Air-conditioning was not a working feature in Scott's truck and they had driven with the windows down, thankfully experiencing the perfect weather conditions and stunning scenery. Meandering between the small white stucco-lined bridges that separated the islands, Scott and Kathie had delighted in pointing out the houses to each other: huge McMansions and discreet traditional 1920s haciendas on the series of manmade residential islands that jutted to the left and right off the causeway.

"That's mine. And I'll have that one. Ooh, I love that one," they had exclaimed excitedly.

"I never knew such places really existed," said Kathie. "My daughter was a very lucky girl to grow up here. I'm glad I gave her that chance. It might not have been the right decision for me but for her it certainly could not have been better."

Reading from the scrap of paper in her hand she had checked the road signs. "Here, here, turn right. This is her island. Just drive and I'll tell you when to stop."

Scott had obeyed the instructions and when they stopped, half a dozen houses up on the right, a waterfront property with tall gates, Kathie had checked the house name and number carved into a sandstone pillar on the roadside beside the mailbox.

"Leave me here," she had demanded. "I don't want to be seen in this old truck. No offense, but it's not the way I imagined arriving. Still I know, beggars can't be choosers.

Come back for me in an hour and wait at the end of the road. Don't drive down here."

Scott had waited and watched from a discreet distance until he saw a maid in white uniform come out of the gates and make as if to climb into a waiting car. She was obviously in a hurry and as Kathie approached her, holding aloft the flowers she had bought on a hasty grocery store stop, the maid had held the gate open and waved her inside.

Promising himself he'd check out the bikini beauties on Ocean Drive, Scott was anxious to be off.

Now that the father was home, Kathleen too was anxious to be off. But she would not leave without asking for what she considered her rightful due. Serena, still crying, ran past her into the house and headed for the stairs up to her bedroom.

Humberto confronted Kathleen. "How dare you come here? We have an arrangement. We keep our side of the bargain. Why would you do this to us, and more importantly to Serena? You agreed you would never try to see her. What on earth possessed to show up here? I've a good mind to call the police and have you arrested for trespassing."

In the face of his anger, Kathie lost her sense of self-righteousness. "I'm sorry," she said. "It was a spur of the minute thing. A gentleman friend invited me to travel to Miami with him on Amtrak; he works for the railroad and he got me a ticket.

"I'm only here overnight. We travel back tomorrow."

Kathie looked like the eager child Humberto remembered from his convent visits sixteen years previously.

"I wanted to see Miami just once. What a wonderful

place to live," said Kathie wistfully. "You have a beautiful home and I thought I'd died and gone to heaven when we drove over the causeway. I'm glad my daughter got to grow up here."

Humberto felt himself being seduced by her emotional blackmail. He had to make a conscious effort to stop himself from inviting his adversary into the home and showing her around as if to prove that he and his wife had indeed fulfilled their commitment to give their beloved daughter Serena the best upbringing love and money could buy.

"I cannot approve of what you have done," Humberto said in a stern tone. "You must leave immediately. Serena's mother will be home soon and I can't allow you to upset her."

Kathie felt the anger that had led to bitterness and resentment over the years arise, aided and abetted by the copious amounts of booze that she had poured down her throat to anesthetize the pain.

Boldly she stood her ground and challenged Humberto.

"Could you let me have some money for a hotel?"

With a look of disdain from him that she tried to avoid admitting was directed at her, she watched greedily as Humberto reached into his back pant pocket and pulled out a wad of dollar bills.

Without pride, Kathie held out her hand as casually as any street drunk asking for a handout. He peeled off tens and twenties and stopped when he reached $100. Silently Kathie stared and pointedly did not remove her open hand. He revised the dollar amount to $150.

A healthy bonus, he calculated on top of the regular

payments she received and the one-off extra payments when Kathie encountered "an emergency" or "a bit of bad luck" or "unexpected bills."

He regretted the day he had responded to a letter from this grasping money-hungry blackmailer. The letters had not started till Serena was in Junior High and Humberto and Maria had agreed to make the initial payments out of compassion. But like all blackmailers, her demands had grown rather than diminished and, determined not allow her to carry out her threat to confront Serena and tell her the truth of her birth, they agreed instead to pay up.

Now the Big Secret was out. Neither money nor truth had been able to protect Serena from the facts of her origins.

"You are not fit to call yourself her mother," Humberto told Kathleen. "Go and please God, do not let me ever have to see you again. If you show up at this house, I will have you forcibly removed." Sweat poured down his face, and his whole body trembled.

Kathie had got what she came for. She had seen her daughter and got some vacation drinking money.

Scuttling away from the house, she saw Scott's pickup parked in the road opposite. She ran toward him triumphantly.

"Let's go and party in Miami," she invited him, as she scrambled up into the grubby vehicle, waving her ill-gotten gains like a trophy.

Using an electronic device to activate the system and close the metal gate behind his unwanted visitor, Humberto felt the pain strike his heart.

He crashed to the ground on the tiled driveway, clutching his chest. Still with his cell phone glued to his hand, the window showed 911 on speed dial from when he had threatened Kathie with the police.

He hit the "call" button.

"Which emergency service do you require?" asked the call center operator. She got no reply. Humberto had already drawn his last breath.

His wife Maria found him spread-eagled on the mosaic tiles, dead, when she pulled into the driveway within minutes of his fatal heart attack.

She was already shaken up, having narrowly avoided being hit by a speeding gray pickup truck as she drove into the palm tree-lined waterfront paradise that she and her family called home.

CHAPTER TWENTY-ONE

Moving On, Moving Out

With all the precision of a military operation, Maria Perez commanded the troops from the moving company and issued orders in a no-nonsense, "my way or the highway" tone of voice.

She had long since accepted the need to move out of the home that she had shared so happily with her darling husband and beloved daughter. Now the two were to take up residence in one of the swanky new, full-service condominiums oceanside on Collins Avenue, Miami Beach.

The speed of forced change since Humberto's sudden death had taken Maria and Serena by surprise.

For one thing, it turned out the property was actually owned by the real estate and development company, and his long-time partner and best friend was being less cooperative than might have been expected.

"It's business," he had explained when Maria had tried to appeal to his better nature and request that she be allowed to stay in the family home, at least while she was going through the grieving process. "Humberto would have understood. It was his decision to put all assets into the corporation and now the shareholders have ownership of the property and finances.

"You will be offered a fair settlement of all affairs."

When she had tried to press him further, Carlos, the best friend and fellow revolutionary who had come from Havana to Miami with Humberto forty years previously, had suggested that rather than make appointments to see him in his downtown Brickell office, Maria should allow the lawyers to handle negotiations.

Maria was suffering. Life had taken on a surreal quality. She moved through days but often felt she was more a ghost than even her dead husband.

"I don't know who I am anymore," she had admitted to her own reflection in the mirror.

Only one close friend really seemed to understand. She too had lost her husband unexpectedly.

"When did I give the universe permission to steal my title of wife and make me a widow?" Maria had demanded, knowing there was no answer. "Every little thing makes me cry. I can't even listen to music in the car because when I hear certain favorite songs, I fall apart. The sense of loss is like being stabbed in the heart."

Humberto, her rock, the love of her life, the man she trusted implicitly and relied on for every major decision, was no longer alive. She felt like a limb had been removed. So closely were their lives and possessions and memories enmeshed that she could not identify the space where she ended and he had started.

One beneficial consequence of the major house move was

that it was mandatory to have a clear out of her husband's clothing and personal effects. The church thrift store at one point called and apologetically stated, "Grateful as we are for the money it will raise, we have no more room. Our shelves our now full of your late husband's belongings."

Planning the house move and directing the staff to pack, wrap, store, and sort the contents of a five-bedroom, four-bathroom house acquired over almost a quarter of a century kept Maria occupied and gave her a purpose, though not necessarily a welcome one.

When the grief completely overwhelmed her, Maria allowed herself the luxury of duvet diving.

Her meals were served and her needs met by the maid whom she had initially fired on the day of her husband's death. There was no question that she deserved to be held to account when she admitted neglecting her responsibility, opening the gate, and allowing unrestricted entry to a woman she did not even know.

Maria had relented a few days later and taken pity on her long-term employee. In her saner moments she had to admit that ChiChi, who had worked with the family for almost twenty years, could not seriously be considered an accessory to Humberto's heart attack.

Maria needed all the support she could gather around her. Following her husband's death, she had cried so much that it honestly felt at times as if life was not worth living. She was not surprised to read that fifty percent of long-time partners die within six months of the death of their husband or wife.

"Some days it's too much of an effort even to get out of

bed," Maria had admitted when Serena took her to task for staying in her lounging pajamas all day.

Refusing to take "no" for an answer, Serena had arranged for the hairstylist to take care of her mother's hair and the beautician to come to the house to give her mother a manicure and pedicure. The masseuse was also instructed to keep coming, though Maria had refused to work with her personal trainer. "I haven't got the energy or the desire," she had explained.

Father Christian, from the local Catholic Church was a frequent visitor to the strangely silent waterfront home and Maria allowed him to counsel and support her. Like a little girl lost, she seemed unable to comprehend how her world had changed so completely and without warning.

Serena had become the strong one for her mother, though the two had endured some disagreements when endeavoring to discuss the situation regarding her "other mother."

That she should have been told about the circumstances of her birth was a no-brainer for Serena, and one night as mother and daughter cataloged photo albums in the downstairs lounge, an emotional storm blew up that threatened to engulf both of them.

"I had the right to know," she challenged her mother. "You weren't protecting me, you were deceiving me. I may have had all kinds of questions about myself, my birth mother, and the reasons you chose to adopt me. I was denied the right to live the truth of who I was, the real me, all the DNA that makes up my psychological and physiological makeup. You were so determined that I would be like you, did it never occur to you that I wasn't allowed to be me?"

"Your father and I only ever wanted what was best for you," Maria said over and over again.

Raising her voice, Serena regretted making her mother cry, but she had to try to make her understand.

"You lied to me and I feel cheated."

Then dropping the ultimate bombshell, she declared, "You have yourself to blame for Papa's death. If I had been in on 'The Secret,'" she had emphasized the words, "then my birth mother showing up like she did would not have produced the same devastating effect. Everything would have been out in the open."

Serena's pain drove her on and she shouted at her mother, who huddled in the corner of the very couch where her biological mother Kathleen had sat dripping water from her wilted bunch of flowers onto the tiled floor.

Now her mother's tears threatened to overflow and splash onto the white-veined marble too.

Serena continued her relentless assault. "Perhaps I wanted to meet her. Were you afraid I would love her more than I love you?"

Maria flinched as if she had been hit.

The sharp points of Serena's words inflicted pain as surely as if they had been physical blows.

"I wish I had never been born, to either of you," Serena declared dramatically as she choked back heartfelt sobs.

Maria could stand it no longer. She jumped up and, though she knew she was likely to be rejected, rushed to comfort her darling daughter.

Refusing to be brushed aside, Maria assumed the role of parent and, taking charge, pulled Serena into her arms. She walked her gently to the couch and took her hand as the two sat side by side.

"Don't torture us like this, sweetheart," she said softly, her heart full of love for her chosen child.

"You are the only daughter your father and I could ever have wanted. We were blessed beyond measure when God sent you to us. Your own mother shared her precious gift with us knowing that we would love you completely. Mother Michael, the Mother Superior at St. Bernadette's Convent, rejoiced with us that we were to make you our own. Our relationship with you was always blessed with the power of prayer and that is what will get us through this horrible time.

"We have to believe that your father is in heaven and looking down on us. He will give us strength and one day the black clouds will lift and we will be happy again. In the meantime, we have each other."

Maria entwined her hands in those of her daughter and playfully encouraged her to join her in a favorite childhood game. Linking fingers they formed a flat base of joined knuckles to make "the church" and "there's the steeple" and turning over their hands, "open it up and there's the people."

Emotional crisis over for another day, together they laughed.

"I'm sorry, Mama," said Serena, leaning her head on her mother's shoulder and taking hold of the pink flamingo pillow with the "Think Pink, It's the Magic Link" motto and cuddling it for extra comfort.

"It's forgotten already," said her mother. "But you must promise me one thing. From now on there will be no more secrets. We need to trust each other, to know we can say whatever we need to, and the response will always be unconditional love.

"You are MY daughter and nothing will ever come between us."

Lifting a photographic album from the glass-topped coffee table where she had left the unfinished work of organizing and dating the photos, she said, "Now let's get back to these. Was ever a child more beloved? There must be a thousand photos of you here. They'll cover every wall in our new home."

CHAPTER TWENTY-TWO

Prom Queen

"I'm grounded," said Serena, adopting a tone of outrageous indignation. "Can you believe it? My mother has gone ballistic about the engagement story and I'm grounded till after graduation at the end of the month."

It didn't help that Karl laughed.

"No problem, I've got a really heavy schedule and you, my lovely, are too much of a distraction. Best let the dust settle and I'll plan an off-the-chart getaway for us after you finish school. Can't wait to see you in your cap and gown. Talk later, chow, keep in touch."

Serena was in full pout and she threw her pink sparkly phone petulantly onto the bed. Seconds later the sound of Karl's hit "Kick it Up" erupted from the phone and she eagerly answered the call.

The excited voice of her best friend, Monique burst into her ear. "I want to hear all the details about the wedding. Who, where, when? What will you wear? Who's going to design the gown?"

Serena knew that the engagement announcement made her the envy of all her friends. Though they were educated, independent, wealthy young women ready to graduate and take on the world, all they longed for was Prince Charming to sweep them off their feet.

"Mom's throwing a fit," said Serena putting the "poor little me tone" back into her voice. "Says I'm too young and Karl's too old. He's only twenty-six. I thought she was cool with our relationship. Seems I was wrong. I think she's menopausal," Serena concluded.

"And can you believe, she's grounded me till after graduation?"

Monique was suitably sympathetic and being an ace problem solver she saw a way out. "She can't stop you going to buy a prom dress. The girls are on retail alert this afternoon. Did you hear the style criteria from the school? No shoestring straps, no overly short skirts and, listen to this, you can't show the small of your back.

"Come with us, we're going to hit every store in Aventura Mall and then move on to Coral Gables. They have 'to die for' gowns on Miracle Mile. And the wedding dresses are out of this world."

Serena cheered up. "Okay, I'll get back to you. I might need a ride so she can keep tabs on my movements, unless she's planning to put an electronic tag on me."

Out with friends, Serena had devised various ways to avoid being recognized by fans. Hats, sunglasses, wigs, and geek frames all helped to deflect from her real identity. If she did get spotted her friends, who had all known her from kindergarten, knew how to surround and protect their famous friend.

Serena discovered early on in her pop career that when

she wanted to draw attention to herself she could easily project herself and pull focus. When she wanted to remain under the radar, it was not too difficult. Stardom was about image and she had read that many famous actors in New York walked around unrecognized because they were not deliberately making themselves appear larger than life.

"Act normally," her mother never tired of telling her. "You're just one of the crowd. On stage that's different. Your star quality shines through under the spotlights, but you'll soon burn out if you keep acting the big star all day long. Feet on ground, head in the clouds. That's the way to live."

Maria lifted the curfew to allow Serena to go shopping for a prom dress. Karl was not on the guest list; the rules stated, "No dates over twenty-one years of age."

She had hoped that her daughter would invite her along, but no doubt she would receive photos from the "shop till you drop" session. "Bring the girls back and I'll order in food," Maria told her.

They enjoyed hanging out at the luxury condominium complex on Millionaire's Row that Maria and Serena had moved into after leaving their Venetian Island home.

A towering block of glass and steel, their luxurious ultra-modern home in the sky, on the twentieth floor, overlooked the ocean and the beach. Recreational facilities were those of a high-class resort: Olympic-size lagoon swimming pool, Jacuzzis, gyms, saunas, hair salons, nail bars, restaurants, bars, and community and media rooms.

Maria had given the decorator a simple instruction for the three-bed three-bath apartment. All white walls, marble floors, leather furnishings with sky blue and turquoise accents.

Splashes of color in a carefully selected modern art collection delivered high visual impact and originals of the Miami artist Romeo Britto's vibrant geometric work featured prominently. Maria had been determined to make a fresh start when she had left her beloved family home and, apart from a few treasured pieces lovingly preserved in their new home, she had donated rooms full of her household belongings.

"Pass it on" was her default mentality.

Two years on she no longer thought of herself as a widow. Now she was a single woman for the first time in her life. There had been huge adjustments to make, but many aspects of her new life suited her very well.

She did not like to date but did have many close male friends, most of them gay men, who escorted her to concerts, the theater, and charity events. Arts and culture had always been her passion and as an enthusiastic fundraiser, generous benefactor, and sought-after committee member, she had a rich and diverse social life.

Carefully choosing her favorite charities, she was particularly active in the Copper Bridge Foundation, an organization that specialized in fostering art and cultural connections between Cuba and Miami. Her husband Humberto had been an early supporter and Maria enjoyed continuing the tradition.

Her husband's wealth supported a privileged and prosperous lifestyle but still she harbored resentment against the former trusted business partner who so blatantly stole the firm after her husband's death. All the legal advice she received at the time suggested that she could have sued and won. However, her heart was too broken to put herself and Serena through an extensive legal case.

Much as she would have been inspired to fight for the principle, she did not need the money.

"What goes around, comes around," she reminded herself.

Since those early days after her husband's sudden death Maria had not given too much thought to Serena's birth mother, who could not be absolved of at least some responsibility for what had happened on that fateful day.

The lawyers had paid her off, yet again, and threatened they would be forced to take legal action if she ever showed up again.

Serena raised the question from time to time and had even outraged Maria on one occasion when she suggested they invite her to visit and get to know her. Hear her side of the story. Maria was adamant. She did not intend to have Kathleen anywhere near her or her daughter.

*   *   *

Graduation Day at Miami Beach High School was a red-letter day in the school calendar. Hundreds of graduates with their families and friends celebrated the end of school life and entry into the adult world.

The day was divided into two distinct segments. The cap 'n' gown events held at the school grounds were the preserve of the teaching faculty, speeches and scrolls marking academic achievements; the prom, a couple of weeks earlier, showcased the social aspects of high school life: music, dancing, parties, friends, fashion statements, dates, and outdoing the competition in showing up in the biggest and best limo.

Serena's classmates had imaginatively and gleefully planned a mode of transport that they were sure could not be beat. They planned to show up in a fleet of pink Cadillacs, crazily decorated with hundreds of balloons and banners and driven by chauffeurs in white tuxedos.

The boys in the class had teased the squeamish girls that they had hired the distinctive and brash amphibious craft of the Miami Pirate Boat Tour. A bright blue land and water vehicle garishly decorated with pirates, treasure chests, parrots, skulls, and crossbows.

Expectations for the night had reached fever pitch and the talk among the classmates was constantly of dresses, shoes, bags, and jewelry.

Walk-in closets full of clothes were all ignored in favor of the up-to-the-minute latest celebrity fashion, the hottest color, the must-have outfit.

Hours upon hours and days upon days were blocked out of the calendar to undertake shopping trips, dress fittings, spa treatments, beauty parlor appointments, elaborate hairdos, customized nail services, and professional makeup makeovers. Restaurants, photographers, and limos were chosen and bragging rights established by those who had enough foresight to book the best and most glamorous locations well in advance.

Hollywood had its Oscars and Golden Globes; in Miami Beach, in June the hottest ticket in town was prom night and Serena Perez was the undisputed Prom Queen.

Graduation Day for some seven hundred students in their white gowns and caps was held in the Convention Center. The day started as usual on Miami Beach with a pink cloud-filled sky. Another day in paradise.

Kathleen was staying in a cheap motel on Biscayne Boulevard.

The desk clerk was disinterested as she showed him the tatty and torn front page of an entertainment magazine.

"Look at that," she urged. "Exclusive: Engagement announced. Karl gets his Girl. That's my daughter. Isn't she beautiful? And she's famous."

Unable to speak English, unlikely to be able to read English, and unwilling to engage any further than absolutely necessary with overexcitable clients, the clerk refused even to feign interest.

"You pay for another night?" he asked.

The shabby motel rented rooms by the hour but the management always pressured staff to encourage nightly occupancy. Drug dealers, prostitutes, and all manner of common street criminals frequented the motels along the Biscayne corridor and it was a decidedly unsafe place at night. But good times were coming. The city promised that money would be made available to regenerate one of Miami's major downtown thoroughfares and the Art Deco hotels now fallen into disrepair would be renovated and restored to a brand new architectural glory. In the meantime, The Sinbad, the Vagabond, The Seven Seas, and a sprinkling of others, plied their trade to whichever customers pushed their cash across the counter.

Kathleen had no cash left. She'd spent what little she had

on a bus ticket from New York and a few medicinal bottles of booze.

Accepting that further interaction with the desk clerk would be a waste of time and energy, she adopted an attitude of indifference and returned the scruffy cutting to her faux black leather overstuffed purse.

One last stop at the restroom and she'd be on her way.

Kathleen still looked attractive to a certain type of barroom gentleman and it was this ability to pick up strangers that convinced her she still had something to offer the opposite sex.

Like Blanche de Bois in *Streetcar Named Desire,* she was often forced to rely on the kindness of strangers.

Peering through bloodshot eyes she stared deep into the grimy mirror above the chipped porcelain washbasin. She scrunched up her shoulders, leaned forward until her head rested on the glass, and confronted herself.

"It's time you pulled yourself together, my girl," she said in a stern voice. "You deserve better than this. You know better than this. I'm going to give you one last chance."

On the verge of tears she instead smashed her hand into the mirror. "Don't turn the waterworks on with me," she shouted. The mirror was intact, not even made of glass; instead a shiny reflective metallic material that more than one customer over the years had tried to damage.

In the metal mirror Kathleen saw the restroom door open and the manager appear, his scowling face backing up his implied threat. "Okay, lady, time to move on."

Out on the street, Kathleen tried to get her bearings. Only one thing for it, find a bar and ask for directions.

Her pocketbook was empty but Kathleen managed to inveigle a sympathetic customer into buying her a small beer. One drink led to another and soon she'd made friends and was able to share the story of her rich and famous daughter. The engagement story had also carried the information that Serena was to be in the class graduating from Miami Beach High that weekend.

"Is anyone going to Miami Beach?" asked Kathleen, now already something of a celebrity herself being a visitor from New York with a celebrated daughter.

"I need to get to the High School, my daughter is graduating today." Checking herself she furrowed her brow. "I think it's today. If this is Thursday then I've got the right day."

A delivery driver on his way across the causeway agreed to give the proud mother a ride. On the way she pointed out to him a car with a bumper sticker, "Proud parent of a Miami Dade student."

Kathleen stared out of the passenger window, hurt and ashamed. He didn't need to know that she had never seen her daughter in a school uniform, attended a PTA meeting, or baked a fundraiser cookie; today she felt the loss as surely as if her child had been stillborn.

The pale green Art Deco building of the Fillmore Theater claimed a prominent position on the intersection of Washington Avenue and 17th. "Here, I'll check out for you what's happening," he said and promptly jumped from the cab of the auto parts delivery van.

"Over there at the Convention Center half a block away," he pointed when he returned from asking directions of the parking marshal at the gate. "They're finishing up, so you better hurry."

The ceremony was almost at its end and, being conscious of Kathleen's slightly bedraggled appearance and agitated manner, the marshal took pity on her. Many students and parents had left so although the theater had originally been filled to capacity, there were now some empty places.

Kathleen walked across the foyer and followed his directions to a higher tier of the auditorium. Slipping into a seat near to the back and at the end of the aisle, she furtively watched the proceedings from upstairs. Hundreds of students in caps and gowns sat on the stage awaiting presentation of their diploma folders.

A Graduation Day banner decorated the stage and the members of the teaching facility ushered students forward to the podium, where they met the mayor and local dignitaries. There followed a handshake and congratulations from the principal and an official photograph.

The principal was making closing remarks and thanked everyone for their attendance.

"We are extraordinarily proud of every one of our students," she said, her voice breaking slightly, "but I am sure you will indulge me if I ask one special young lady to return to center stage. Let's give a big round of applause to one of our star pupils. Voted Girl Most Likely to Succeed and, I am sure you will agree, she has already done that, Graduate Serena Perez."

Serena acknowledged the cheers and applause of her fellow High School class; she smiled to her mother who was sitting in the parents' section in the orchestra stalls of the packed hall. Back on stage she walked to the podium and thanked the principal and her teachers.

"You are an inspiration, Serena," the principal told her, "And I am sure we will be hearing lots more of you in years to come."

Serena waved her diploma, acknowledged her fellow students, and called out proudly, "Thank you Miami Beach High."

Her mother Maria shed a tear and sent out a silent prayer. Thank you, God, for the gift of my special daughter. If only her father could have been here today. He would have been so proud of his little girl.

Hiding in the shadows, Kathleen thanked God that she had been able to see her daughter graduate. She wiped a tear from her cheek and made a promise.

One day she will know me and I will make my daughter proud.

CHAPTER TWENTY-THREE

Star Power

Serena projected the full force of her dynamic personality across the stage lights into the capacity audience. She was rewarded with the adulation of her adoring fans who joyfully turned the theater into a holy shrine.

They cheered and applauded their goddess. Serena was an inspiration to teenage girls and a fantasy figure for high school boys. One thousand pairs of eyes gazed on her perfect form and mentally imagined being her, or possessing her. The chosen one in the spotlight reflecting the current popular ideal. Dish of the day. An Icon. A Star.

Dressed all in white, her stage costume exaggerated her statuesque persona and perfect size two figure. She strutted and prowled the stage in superskinny jeans that looked as if they had been sprayed on; a cleavage revealing, micro crop top showed off a sculpted body, tiny waist, and killer abdominal muscles.

Dazzling white, sky-high, thigh boots appliquéd with Swarovski crystals drew attention to her choreographed dance steps and projected star bursts of light from the brightness of the stage into the darkness of the auditorium.

Waist skimming, glossy coal-black hair fell like a water-fall of midnight waves and the curls danced and shone, even without the wind machine that blew her hair wildly and seductively.

Serena was a pop sensation. The success that had started while she was still at high school went into the stratosphere after she left. Resisting all her mother's entreaties that she should attend college, Serena had dedicated herself to a full-time performing career and been rewarded with the glittering prizes of smash hits and multimillion dollar video sales.

The technical team running the sound and light console that looked like the flight deck of a jet liner flashed giant images of Serena on to stage screens. She was surrounded with ephemeral visuals, chandeliers, candles, and sparkling moonbeams which added the magic and mystery to transform a human being into a phenomena.

Music industry experts predicted that Serena could emulate the global dominance of Madonna, Britney Spears and Beyoncé. But Serena Perez took success in her stride. It was her default position. Brought up to believe that she could do or be anything—she willingly accepted challenges and was programmed to overcome. Nothing defeated her. "What doesn't kill you, makes you stronger," was her mantra.

As she approached her twentieth birthday, her latest release "Love Spells" was riding high in the charts and tonight was the culmination of a national tour of concerts and appearances.

The much-hyped triumphant hometown return to Miami Beach was proving all she'd hoped for and imagined.

Not least because there to share her showstopping victory was her fabulous boyfriend, Latin singing sensation, Karl Valero.

The golden couple had captured the imagination and the front pages of the celebrity magazines. They had elevated posing on the red carpet together to an art form. A publicist's dream team.

"Thank you, Miami." Serena acknowledged the wild applause of her fans and told them, "I love you. I love Miami. Viva Miami."

Karl was backstage; Serena had caught sight of him moving to the beat in the wings earlier in her performance. Now she invited him to join her on stage.

The crowd was ecstatic. Serena really did have it all. Fame, fortune, beauty, and one of the hottest men in town.

"If you've got it flaunt it," she smiled, and accepted his extravagant greeting, as he kissed her hand.

They had a deal: neither would upstage their partner but always be there to love and support the other's career. Karl had deliberately not been invited to perform at Serena's concert; he was there to add even more icing to her cake and deliver extra eye candy for the girls—and the boys.

Dressed casually in black pants and a white shirt with his long dark hair curling on the collar of his shirt and wearing one tiny discreet diamond earring, Karl had been ranked fourth on the annual list of Most Handsome Men in the Latin World by a celebrity magazine.

In photo shoots and real life, he knew exactly how to exploit the currency of his smoldering good looks, toned body, and an overtly tactile demeanor. He had a way of caressing his limbs, a hand on the thigh, a subtle stroke on his forearm, or a fingertip on his forehead. He also knew how to push the volume on the charm meter to the max. Twinkling chocolate brown eyes with diamond bright flashes of gold, a full-mouthed seductive smile, and amused grin that played around his lips, and devastating dimples that suggested a secret.

Serena teased him that he reminded her of the Mona Lisa—no one could quite fathom what he was thinking. But they all hoped that maybe they figured in his thoughts.

However, the attraction was more than his magnetic good looks: he had charisma. Star quality that radiated and lit up a room.

Oh yes, this one is a real asset, a keeper, Serena told herself constantly. Do the math. What do you get if you combine a beautiful girl, a gorgeous man, two talented award-winning stars, and the fairy tale of love, romance, and glamour? The perfect package. Cinderella meets the Prince and they all live happily ever after.

Over two thousand hopelessly romantic hearts watched Karl present Serena with a long-stemmed red rose, and in a collective heartfelt breath, they suspended belief and bought into the dream.

Careful not to overstay his welcome, Karl walked off the stage and as he exited, blew one last kiss to the special lady in the spotlight.

Serena launched into her last number and, clapping her hands over her head, brought to an end the intimate interlude and encouraged the audience back up on their feet to rock out the concert.

Even after two encores, the audience continued to give her a standing ovation and demand more. "Leave them wanting more" was an old show-business adage and Serena's creative team had finely honed the thin line between the delivery of a high-quality stellar performance and ensuring that the audience would crave more, especially when it came time to open their wallets at the merchandising booth. Music downloads, signed photographs, posters, books, programs, T-shirts, hats, jewelry, all were on sale for those who desired to take home a reminder of the evening and a personal memento of their idol.

Serena ran off stage and into the arms of Karl.

"I'm all hot and sweaty," said Serena.

"Just the way I like it," said Karl.

Serena slapped him playfully, "Beast. Give me ten to shower and change and we can leave."

"Mick Jagger runs straight to the waiting limo with the sweat of the stage dripping off his body."

"Too much information," replied Serena. "There's a difference. In case you hadn't noticed, I'm female."

"I noticed alright," said Karl, as he treated her to one of his trademark seductive smiles. "Want me to show you?"

With a laugh, Serena ran in the opposite direction from his outstretched arms toward her dressing room.

* * *

Miami Beach's famous Jackie Gleason Theater had been a permanent fixture in the living rooms of the America television audience in the fifties and sixties, when the famous comedian had broadcast his highly rated variety show from

Miami Beach. Popular myth had it that on vacation with his family in the Oceanside city, he loved it so much he refused to return to a cold New York studio. The whole show and production team had transferred to the beach. Over the decades and following several name changes, the Art Deco theater retained its attraction as a popular venue for theatrical events and pop concerts. However, despite renovations, facilities remained far from the state-of-the-art arenas, such as the triple AAA home of the champion basketball team Miami Heat, situated across the causeway in downtown Miami.

"I heard Madonna has a Jacuzzi installed and the walls painted pink at every place she performs. All I ask is a shower that works," Serena complained as she stood in the stall soaping her svelte body and shampooing her long hair.

"I need to act more like a diva," Serena called over the sound of the running water to her personal assistant who was busy packing up the designer stage costumes, dozens of pairs of shoes, mountains of accessories, and boxes of makeup and hair products.

"Don't even think about it," was the reply from her mother who watched the concert from a VIP box and had now made her way through the shrieking fans and burly security guards to the inner sanctum, backstage.

"Hi, Mama," Serena responded and silently she mimicked the next sentence. "You should get an early night. Don't forget, you have a dawn call tomorrow for the filming of your new video."

"You should get an early night," said Maria. "Don't forget ..."

Serena cut her off. "I'm not six years old," she said, and struggled to keep the annoyance out of her voice. "I'm sleeping over at Karl's tonight. You don't mind, do you?"

Maria had to admit that the "sleepovers" at Karl's were the very thing that made her determined to continue to impose some discipline. If her husband, Serena's father Humberto, were alive he would certainly put his foot down and refuse to allow what he would undoubtedly see as unacceptable behavior?

To get back into her mother's good books, Serena added. "I'll have you know I have a reputation for always being on time—not like some performers who turn up hours late."

Maria felt old-fashioned and out of her depth. She couldn't deny the fact that her little girl had grown into a woman, and a hugely successful one. To impose a curfew seemed impossibly outdated.

Still, she did adhere to rules that made her comfortable and, despite strong opposition, refused to let Karl share Serena's bed when they stayed at her home. Maria chose to ignore sights or sounds that would suggest that the couple adjusted sleeping arrangements when she was safely out of the way. What the eye doesn't see, the heart doesn't grieve over, she reminded herself.

In the Latin tradition, parents still believed they had the right to enforce strict codes of behavior and most expected daughters to live at home until they married. Culture and tradition clashed and in a modern world, the majority of parents and children learned to compromise while respecting diverse worldviews.

Serena emerged from the shower, a fresh-faced young

girl, devoid of makeup, stripped of hairpieces, and looking more like a regular teenager, if only for a few more weeks.

Maria joyfully embraced her darling daughter.

"You were wonderful," she said. "I am so proud of you. You really gave it your all out there. I don't know where you get it from. Heaven knows, neither your father nor I were ever performers. You're a natural."

If she had been pressed to provide an explanation, Serena might have come to the conclusion that all the hours of dance classes, singing lessons, and drama workshops had done their job and provided her with the skills to develop her natural talent.

Maria, and her father while he was alive, had given her every opportunity and resource to be trained in the theater arts by first-class professionals who encouraged, supported, and allowed her to pursue her performance dreams. Their dedication and hers had paid off handsomely. But if truth be known, Serena's talent had its roots in the genes she inherited from her birth mother, Kathleen.

"So it's okay if I stay at Karl's?" Serena asked, hopping on one leg as she slipped and slid her way, inches at a time, into skinny jeans. "We're off to dinner first and it might be late when we get home. Lots of our friends are in town and you wouldn't deny me the chance to do a little partying now that I've finished work."

Maria smiled, knowing that the argument was lost before it started. "Just remember..."

"I know. Early start. Don't be late."

They laughed together and as Serena stepped up onto

her strappy five-inch high-heeled shoes, she asked, "Do you want us to drop you off at home?"

"No need," said Maria, "I have my own driver. I told him to come back for me. Give me a kiss goodnight and I'll be off. I'll forgo the pleasure of forcing my way through the crowds, trying to keep up with you, and being ignored by your adoring fans."

Serena gave her mother a kiss on the cheek and reminded her, "You were once asked to sign an autograph as 'Serena's Mom.'"

"Oh, yes, my moment of fame," Maria laughed.

"Goodnight, my lovely, and well done again."

Karl entered the dressing room as Maria exited. "Nothing personal," said Maria and offered Karl an affectionate hug and kisses on both cheeks. "I'm already on my way. Look after my little girl."

While it was already taken for granted that they were a perfect match and Serena and Karl would very likely go onto marry, Maria hoped it would not be for a long time yet.

Fortunately, Maria was still an innocent abroad. Never in her wildest dreams would she have guessed the secret that had been kept from her. Not even her daughter knew the devastating reality hidden behind Karl's enigmatic grin.

Karl Valero already had a wife. He'd conveniently left her in Buenos Aires, having enthusiastically depleted much of her family fortune. He figured that her being so much older, his need was greater than hers.

Someone had to fund his meteoric rise to fame. The expensive professional demo-recording sessions, promotional videos that cost upward of a quarter of a million dollars, top PR companies, commission hungry agents, and fancy, expensive managers. It took money to become an overnight sensation complete with new name, new identity, and a stable of hangers-on.

Karl liked to compare himself to the legendary Frank Sinatra: everyone knew his success was attributable and in a large degree dependent on "help from the boys." Of course no one could deny his phenomenal talent, but a financial investment was what put the wheels on the star vehicle.

The acquisition of a rich wife and benefactor had propelled Karl from a modest singing career in a seedy nightclub to being able to scale the heights and compete in the ferociously competitive world of popular music. His songwriting abilities had won him Grammies and brought lucrative record deals, endorsements, and advertisements.

Karl flew high, private jets whisked him to engagements all over the world, and he preferred to travel solo. A wife no longer figured in his plans. Truth was she had never been more than a convenience, a means to an end. Being a married man wasn't good for business or his carefully cultivated image. On the other hand, being the lover of a gorgeous twenty-year-old American superstar ticked all the boxes.

Karl knew it was time to change his profile to single.

CHAPTER TWENTY-FOUR

Spider's Web

Karl stretched out his naked arm from under the silky black Egyptian cotton sheet and attempted to pull the disheveled flight attendant back into the supersize bed. Mile-high club activity on a private jet had distinct advantages over the cramped conditions available on regular commercial airlines; however, Karl would not deny that he had satisfying memories of many such erotic encounters. His motto was, *when the desire arises, so will the opportunity.*

The pretty platinum blonde with pouty, full lips and a knowing smile shook her head. "We'll be there in about half an hour. I have to prepare the cabin to land—and make myself look presentable—but you still have time for a nap."

Karl agreed that sounded like a good idea. He was exhausted, mentally, physically, and emotionally. Before arrival in Buenos Aires he would take a shower and change clothes. The silence that surrounded him in the silk-lined walls of the private jet placed him in a seductive cocoon. He closed his eyes, drifted into a pleasant postcoital meditative state. Unbidden thoughts took him back in time. He remembered the first night he had met Madame Bianca—his wife.

*   *   *

No one dared use the strategically placed front row table, the one closest to the stage in the dark, smoky nightclub, directly in front of the microphone. A permanent *Reserved* sign put it out of action, unless the woman who claimed ownership was in attendance.

Madame Bianca, it was claimed, had men killed for lesser crimes than stealing her table.

"Tango d'Fantasia" nightclub was one of Buenos Aires' best kept secrets. An intoxicating theater of surreal entertainment, on stage and off, ignited by passion, intrigue, money, influence, power, and corruption. For the right price, it was apparently possible to hire everything from a princess to a dancing elephant. Popular myth claimed that in a magical cloud of smoke and mirrors, arrangements could be made to make people, places, and things disappear.

Madame Bianca was the ringmaster of this constantly revolving three-ring circus. A myth, a legend, and one of the most powerful women in the city, she knew all the tricks of the trade, and religiously, as any sworn member of the Magic Circle, kept her secrets.

Wild tales circulated that her famous conjuring box held everything from ivory-handled knives and guns with silver bullets to trunks where people were sawn in half and not put back together again; to cabinets with secret compartments where money, jewelry, contraband, and drugs disappeared.

Night after dark night, the ominous presence of Madame Bianca dominated the drinking den. Like a black widow spider she sat and held court, attended by her henchmen; she watched everything and weighed up all possible scenarios as she stalked and selected her prey.

With opulently bejeweled hands she elegantly held the cocktail glass containing her favored vodka and Kahlua drink, known as a Black Russian. Enveloped in a cloud of smoke, she continuously smoked one of the oldest brands in the world, the colorful Sobranie Cocktail cigarettes with gold tips upon which she invariably left the unmistakable mark of ruby red lipstick.

Madame Bianca had armed herself with unmistakable signature trademarks long before personal branding became popular. Her attention-grabbing appearance was carefully contrived. To disguise her small stature and less than perfect proportions, she wore corsets that forced her cleavage to push up and overspill, and high-heeled lace-up boots produced the appearance that she was balanced on the tips of her toes and always constantly in motion.

Her expensive clothes were exquisitely fashioned in extravagant velvets and satins, painstakingly detailed and carefully chosen in vibrant shades of red, purple, and black that refused to be ignored and deflected from her figure imperfections.

A feathered plume in her hair provided the crowning glory for her outfits. A throwback to a more stylized and elaborate time, she may have modeled herself on a Wild West saloon singer, a New Orleans brothel keeper, a Parisian can-can dancer, or a Spanish courtesan.

Whatever the inspiration for her creation, there was no denying the impact. Dyed blonde hair, piled high with curls or rolled into a French pleat gave light relief to all the darkness; outsize diamonds flashing at her ears and throat lit up her surprisingly pretty features. Aged somewhere between forty and fifty, or even a whispered sixty, rumor had it that she had taken a photograph of Marilyn Monroe to show the plastic surgeon how she wanted her face to look.

Money was no object. Madame Bianca d'Ella Signati Campelletto claimed to be the illegitimate daughter of a European aristocratic.

The story she liked to reiterate but few believed, was that her father was a swashbuckling adventurer who had arrived in Argentina at the invitation of President Peron and his wife Eva Peron to reclaim his family's lost fortunes and had discovered a lucrative trade in piracy and smuggling. Most of her history was perceived as a figment of her imagination and the reality was that her father was a powerful crime boss.

Whatever the source of their wealth, the family fortunes put them in the superrich category of the one percent of the one percent. A thousand-acre estate was located in the countryside outside of Buenos Aires. Madame Bianca lived alone in a magnificent mansion, waited on hand and foot by servants, and surrounded by security fences, bodyguards, and dog partols. The true nature of the family business was shrouded in mystery, but there was no doubt that Madame Bianca had claimed her inheritance and followed in her dead father's illustrious footsteps to run his wide-ranging, highly profitable enterprises.

Madame Bianca chose to think of herself as an entrepreneur.

A highly intuitive businesswoman, she never missed an opportunity to make money or forge alliances. She commanded a vast network of employees and advisers. Madame Bianca guarded her privacy and business interests compulsively and while, on occasion, drink might loosen her tongue, she still played her cards close to her chest.

Just one man had her complete trust, her lifelong friend and lawyer, Enrique Baroque. He was her right-hand man and confidant but, if it were possible, Enrique was even more tight-lipped than his boss Bianca.

She lived a vampire-like existence. Slept all day and came alive on her nightly chauffeur-driven outings to the Tango d' Fantasia. In all probability, she was the owner not just a customer of the nightclub, but she did not choose to disclose that information and no one who had a modicum of sense would dream to ask the question.

"You have been summoned," the manager told Karl on his third night as a guest singer at the club. "Finish your act and then go and join Madame Bianca at her table. Good luck. You'll need it. She'll eat you for breakfast."

Handsome young men came and went regularly in the life of the insatiable cougar. She tired easily of new conquests, but the perceived wisdom was that payoffs were generous enough to maintain loyalty and discretion.

Other methods to enforce the contract of confidentiality were available but in matters of the heart, a ladylike Bianca chose to think she acted with her heart not her head.

Karl was fascinated by Madame Bianca and thrilled to be issued with the summons to join her table.

Under cover of the stage lights, he had discreetly watched her nightly as he stood directly in her line of vision on stage. The consummate performer, he endeavored not to be too obvious about his intentions. He pretended to spread his love and attention to every woman in the room, but he had known and she had known there were really only two players in the game. He had sung to her, made love to her through the lyrics, and kept his gaze fixed firmly on her.

Sitting at her spinning table, Madame Bianca wove a web to entrap him and Karl crawled in greedily, eyes wide open, he expected to be devoured but was also determined to pursue his own agenda.

The dangerous game was on.

Karl, who was still known by his birth name of Ricky, was just half the age of his opponent but he figured that, like a prizefighter, he had the advantage of youth while she could claim experience. He had grown up on the tough streets of Buenos Aires and run with the gangs, though his friends joked that, as a pretty boy, he definitely made a better lover than a fighter.

Ricky's "Get Out of Jail Card" had always been his good looks, his endless charm, and a low animal cunning. He was more cat than dog, being programmed to lap up to the one who fed him, not naturally inclined to remain loyal to any one master.

Coming from a large boisterous family in the bottom three of a dozen kids, worn-out mother, and absent father, he had grown up knowing how to take care of himself and how to manipulate to get what he wanted.

If Madame Bianca thought she was dealing with a no-clue impressionable youngster, she underestimated her opponent. Ricky saw himself as a match for her and he knew exactly how to gain his advantage. It always worked like a charm.

As he surveyed himself in the mirror, Ricky ran his fingers through his hair and made sure it appeared to be effortlessly casual. He called it his "join me in bed" look. He turned up the collar of his classic white shirt and discarded the dark jacket he had worn on stage. He debated whether to leave two or three buttons undone.

Women were attracted to the visibility of dark, curly chest hair but he insisted that his display should not look contrived. The leather belt at his waist had a gold buckle and the leather loafers he wore were carefully designed to project an image of money and class. Classic not casual was his style and even though the reality was that he had just one suit and half a dozen white shirts to call his own and hang in a tiny closet space in a bedroom he shared with three brothers, he still managed to look immaculate.

Mentally he was prepared for Madame Bianca. Like a sweet-talking gigolo, though he despised the label, he would convince her that he found her to be the most exciting woman on the planet.

She did not acknowledge him as he walked across the small dance floor, but he knew she was watching his every move. Employing a trick of tango etiquette, Ricky placed himself in her line of vision and made a tiny gesture of eye contact to ask permission to approach.

Two henchmen were seated with her. They watched and waited.

Bianca nodded imperceptibly. He made his move as stealthily as if plotting on a chessboard. "May I join you?" Ricky asked and without waiting for a reply, pulled out a chair from the table. He turned the seat to face him, sat down legs astride and rested his arms on the back of the chair. He reached out as if to shake Bianca's hand, but instead held her hand in his and gallantly kissed her fingertips. He caressed her hand and did not let go.

Such a bold approach toward her was most unusual, and coming from one so young, she was highly impressed. *The kid has balls,* she decided.

"Drink?" she asked.

"Same as you," he answered.

Lights in the main room dimmed, the audience turned expectantly, all eyes focused on the tiny performance space. The stage was plunged into darkness and further conversation, even if desirable, was impossible.

Faces reflected in the front row round black lacquered table, the electricity and sexual chemistry passing between Ricky and Bianca threatened to light a fire. In the dark they sat, joined at the fingertips, and silently breathed in each other's force field.

The nightly tango floorshow began. A dance of passion and power, erotic and hypnotic, the couple on stage strutted arrogantly through their stylized moves of love, hate, rejection, and reconciliation. The male was dressed all in black and as an opener threw his hat across the floor to signal the start of the ballet. The girl was dressed provocatively in a high-waisted, fitted black skirt, red, low-cut ruffled blouse, and cruel stiletto-heeled shoes.

Her slim, muscled legs were the stars of the show. Encased in black fishnet tights, the seams studded with rhinestones, the intricate patterns of the dance burst into life as the rhinestones flashed and she pivoted, stepped out seductively, traversed backward across the floor, and flicked her legs aggressively between the man's legs. All the time responding to an unspoken signal from him that she was free to take her place center stage, he allowed her to show-case her movements and revel in her femininity. The woman made not one move without permission. Without a word, the man controlled the entire dance, every step of the way. Locked in a passionate embrace, their eyes were transfixed on the object of their desire; the presence of the audience bordered on voyeuristic.

In a final dramatic gesture, the male dancer dismissively threw his partner away from him and left her in a heap, arms and legs outstretched on the bare floor. Hopelessly, helplessly ravaged. Ricky watched and observed the look of rapture and wonder on Bianca's face, as she lost herself in the tango being performed on stage. He knew the secret— every woman longs to be tangoed.

The dance on stage ended, the dance between Ricky and Bianca began. There was no discussion about what should happen next; it was a foregone conclusion that Ricky would accompany her. In the back of the limousine, as the chauffeur discreetly closed the partition and drew the privacy blind, Ricky made his first move.

Draped across the voluminous layers of her elaborate outfit, he cupped her face tenderly between his strong hands, pulled her toward him and, with eyes wide open, forced her lips apart as he thrust his tongue into her mouth.

Breathing through the nose, he maintained the embrace but made no move to touch any other part of her body. Without question, she acquiesced and accepted his dominance. It had been a very long time since any man had dared to put her under his control.

"Buckle your seat belt," he whispered in her ear, "you are in for the ride of your life."

Doors opened as if by magic at the mansion. The chauffer held open the car door and a manservant held open the reinforced wooden front door of her home. Bianca walked straight through without a glance at either of them and headed for the gilded staircase.

At the top of the white marble stairs she threw the door to the master bedroom wide open and allowed Ricky to follow her inside. The room was as over-furnished and well-upholstered as its owner.

Every piece of furniture came with its own built-in hug factor, seeming designed to reach out and comfort the occupant: stuffed pillows, plumped-up cushions, elongated bolsters, warmth-giving throws, and slippery silky covers.

Ricky mentally threw his hat into the ring and commenced to dance. Without hesitation, he lifted the mighty

Madame Bianca and laid her full length on the custom-made king-size bed. With infinite care he undressed her and, as each item littered the floor where he discarded it, Bianca's breath began to escape in deep relief from her ample chest as she anticipated what was to come.

Catching her off guard, Ricky told her, "I don't want to have sex with you. We will create the dance of love."

When she was naked, he nodded his appreciation and slowly peeled off his own clothes. Naked and erect, he lay beside her, gazed into her eyes, and smiled. "Now we can get to know each other. I promised you the ride of your life.

"The journey begins here. Prepare to be tangoed."

*   *   *

Ricky made a sacred pact with himself. While he lived in her house, slept in her bed, spent her money, and used her fortune to give his musical career the rocket launch it needed to take him global, he would not dishonor her. She craved love and he would open his heart to fulfill his side of the bargain.

Madame Bianca was feared and loathed and vilified even by those closest to her. Ricky did not want to believe the gruesome stories he had heard about her cruel streak and how she maintained the ferocious control that he knew she exerted over an international crime syndicate.

Like the passive wife of a mafia boss, content to enjoy the rewards but not willing to acknowledge the facts, Ricky decided that the less he knew, the better for his survival. For as long as he could avoid it and play dumb, Ricky would not "join the organization."

Madame Bianca had other ideas. While she allowed him to exert control in bed, in all other matters, she held the upper hand.

Power, the ultimate aphrodisiac, was the fuel for their passion. Neither was willing to relinquish control. They locked horns and hearts in a battle of love and destructive rivalry.

A fight to the death was inevitable.

CHAPTER TWENTY-FIVE

Dangerous Love

Madame Bianca's scream pierced the eerie silence of the mansion. "Bring him to me. I will kill him with my own bare hands," she yelled, intent on ensuring that every person in the vicinity heard her cry of anguish.

The cat that everyone around her had tried to keep in the bag was well and truly out.

A front-page story showed his fiancée sporting a huge diamond ring on the third finger of her left hand; the number one celebrity gossip magazine carried an exclusive: *Karl Gets His Girl,* Latin chart topper Karl Valero is engaged to be married to the all-American girl, singing sensation Serena Perez.

Talk of proposals, engagements, and weddings created excitement and generated huge publicity for the media and the fans, but this was one announcement that Karl would have rather kept under wraps.

A private agreement between him and the current girl of his dreams.

In truth, she was the girl of almost every man's dreams—but Karl was all too aware that after the bliss of nighttime fantasies, a wake-up call was never far behind. The grand gesture had been made in a totally spontaneous moment without consideration that daylight would intrude on the magic of his romantic proposal.

Even the purchase of the ring had been on the spur of the moment—to be used as and when the time was to his best advantage. Serena was part of a strategic investment in his carefully plotted climb to the top of the charts and into the hearts of millions of music fans. Although he would deny it strenuously, even to himself, she had been a carefully interlocked piece of the career jigsaw as he maneuvered himself to the top professionally and personally.

From the day that Ricky had become Karl, he closely guarded the details of his dual existence. Madame Bianca was happy to collude and she had been more than willing to provide all the resources he needed to make the journey from club singer to superstar. Being the power behind the throne held great appeal and, more than that, she truly believed in her protégé and lover.

"You are the number one singer in the world," she told him. "I know. I made you. From the first day I saw you singing at the Tango d'Fantasia, I knew you were destined to be a big, big star."

Madame Bianca did not need a contact book. She already knew how to make connections with everyone who was anyone in whatever area of business she was currently dealing.

Her lawyer Enrique, who was on speed dial to her twenty-four hours a day, picked up the phone and delivered the demands. The word went out to supply all the creative resources, publicity, and marketing that Karl required to make the leap to the top of the fame game.

"How long will it take to make him an overnight sensation?" Enrique asked the top media marketing company in Latin America.

"One year with the right backing," they had calculated.

"Put twice as many people on it, we'll double your fees, make it happen in half the time," he told them. "If you can't deliver, we'll hire someone who can."

Even for one of the largest international media teams in the business, it was a huge challenge, but with the backing of serious money and an ever open bank account, they could gain access to top producers, video makers, photographers, and personal stylists; they could book recording studios, musicians, performance venues, advertising space in all the celebrity and music magazines, and call in favors on the top talk shows and diary programs.

A London firm with Belgravia offices, impeccable credentials, and a knight of the realm as their head were the chosen media specialists. Experts in the projection and management of the image and global brand of entire countries and blue chip corporations.

Thanks to them, Karl Valero soon had as much brand and name recognition as BP. And should a little damage limitation be needed when leaks and disasters occurred, the firm were up to speed in handling that too.

Mimicking the modus operandi of many other internationally known individuals, Karl phoned his publicist first and lawyer second. First, he needed to plot a strategy, then London would do the fire fighting.

From the safety of his penthouse in Miami, Karl read the tabloids and knew that he was in serious trouble. Bianca was not the forgiving type. He had awakened a roaring lion and provoked the wrath of his protector. All publicity was not good publicity.

Karl had meticulously kept her informed about Serena while he made his moves and used the younger woman to build his image and raise his profile. First he took the role of escort, then good friend, he soon upgraded to boyfriend then to attending premiers, charity events, and walking the red carpet. "Taking care of business," as Elvis would have described it. The hype, the hoopla, the publicity, the awards; all designed by the music business to make itself ever more important among the movers and shakers of the entertainment industry and find the next new sensation, the huge grossing money spinner, the performer who could cross over into movies, endorsements, and lucrative franchises.

Bianca agreed reluctantly that Karl was required to play out the game as suggested by their respective publicists and record companies to generate world attention for the inspirational combination of Karl and Serena. "Karlena" had a celebrity ring to it, kind of like Brangalina.

"She's a kid, a nice girl," Karl assured Bianca as they lay naked in bed. "Strict Latin family, probably a virgin, though I personally have no plans to check it out.

"Now you, my darling, you are a w-o-m-a-n." He had spelled out each letter and it had sounded like a song. "You look like a w-o-m-a-n, you smell, like a w-o-m-a-n, you feel like a w-o-m-a-n. The w-o-m-a-n I love."

To prove his point he squeezed her prominent love handles, before he took possession of both her arms and pinned them above her head. With a pair of silver handcuffs, a permanent fixture of the leather-quilted headboard, locked securely in place, he reached up and unfurled a red chiffon scarf to tie around his lover's eyes.

"Now let me remind you," he threatened, "What happens when you question my love for you?"

Bianca did not resist. Never before had a man made her feel so totally feminine, completely loved, truly wanted, and perfectly protected. She had learned to trust and would allow nothing and no one to ever come between her and the love of her life.

Karl loved Bianca, in his own way. To cause her pain or humiliation would not serve his long-term purpose or conform to his admittedly individualistic criteria for the rules of relationship.

When he desired a younger, sleeker, more adventurous model, ultimate discretion was his watchword. He paid a high price for his required services. One-night stands with professionals provided by an agency with a track record and top rank clientele ensured that all his demands were satisfied. And what happened in Vegas or any other city in the world, stayed there.

Except for the tricky situation in which he now found himself. It was not meant to happen that his love life was splashed all over the front pages of a dozen magazines, leading the news on *Entertainment Tonight* and going viral on YouTube and Twitter.

He needed to go and see Bianca and persuade her that it

was in neither of their interests that their private business should become public. His big fear was that to deflect from what she would perceive as a betrayal and humiliation, she would take it into her head to break the agreement they had about their own secret wedding, and make a dramatic announcement.

Only Karl, Bianca, and the lawyer Enrique knew that they were married. In a small informal ceremony in the den at their home months previously, they had signed paperwork that legally made them man and wife and put in place a prenuptial agreement.

Bianca had no family, no blood relations, no next of kin, but she wanted Karl as her husband, less for romantic reasons than to protect her from the danger that one day he might find it expedient to testify against her citing criminal activities he had witnessed.

Bianca had a fearsome reputation as an enforcer who had no mercy for those who betrayed or double-crossed her in business.

"If they think they are dealing with some feeble-minded woman," she explained, "my enemies will exploit me, steal my money, corrupt my best men, betray me to my enemies. I need to keep strong. To teach them a lesson, I don't just order an execution, I watch them die."

Karl had no stomach for violence but he had always been careful not to show weakness when Bianca extolled the virtues of bloodshed in worker management.

Fortunately for her there were many others who reveled in the punishment of perceived wrongdoers. Even Bianca had to agree that it would not be good for Karl's image to be seen as a killer, criminal, or even accessory to some gruesome murder.

"Leave me out of your business, Bianca," he pleaded. But Bianca already knew that she had all the evidence she needed of his complicity in the tapes, photographs, and video recordings she had ordered when, even if he were not actually present, he was party to information and conversations about her underworld dealings.

By the marriage she lost the advantage of being able to testify against her new husband, but more important was the fact that Karl could not testify against her.

Nor could he walk away from her, which she feared more than anything else.

The public announcement of his engagement to some stupid girl singer was not in her game plan.

The stakes had been ramped up sky high for both of them.

Karl made his mind up before he boarded the private jet from Miami on his early-morning flight to Buenos Aires, Argentina. Stretched out, feet up, in the plush beige leather recliner, Karl was the only passenger on board. He gulped down his third glass of champagne and ignored the flirty female attendant who offered warmed nuts and mini pretzels; it did not escape his notice that she was also offering much more but he would get around to that later.

For now, he had to concentrate. He stared out of the window and reviewed the most dangerous decision of his life. The ultimate betrayal. An irreversible solution. He planned to kill his wife. All he had to do was make sure he stayed alive long enough to see the plan through. He had carefully weighed all his options.

If he turned her in to the authorities she would go to jail and so would he. He would lose everything, her money, his career.

If he turned himself in, besides jail time, he would lose his reputation and international status. Being killed in jail was also a very real possibility to stop him talking.

If he asked for a divorce, he would be cut off from Bianca's power, money, and protection. Not that she would ever agree.

No, he was a rat caught in a trap. Whichever way he turned he faced disaster and ruin, financially, personally, and professionally.

Bianca's death would make him a free man and, not to be completely mercenary about it, a fabulously rich one.

CHAPTER TWENTY-SIX

Fight or Flight

Till Death Do Us Part. The words tortured Karl. Ever since making his decision to kill her, he had endured, awake and asleep, disturbing images of Bianca lying majestically in a scarlet satin-lined coffin. With coal black eyes wide open, she stared at him accusingly.

Although it may have been an exaggeration, a deliberate device to add fuel to the fire of how wicked she was, and intimidate those who would try to challenge her, the body count on Bianca's watch was said to be in excess of one hundred victims.

Life was cheap in the deadly world of international criminals. Entire cities in South America had become no-go zones because of the level of violence. Decent citizens needed bodyguards and high-level security firms to keep them safe; criminals used guns for their own protection. Lawlessness had turned the streets into Wild West frontier towns.

But how could one man murder his own wife?

Karl wrestled with his conscience but he was still that rat caught in the trap. He could see no other way out. He had to be rid of Bianca once and for all and, although he wasn't the only person who wanted her dead, he was the only one who could get close enough to take her life.

"Kick it Up," a high-volume fast-paced version of his latest hit, exploded from the cell phone in his top jacket pocket.

Bianca growled, "What time you arriving?"

"Just about to land," he told her. "Give me an hour."

"Better use the time to pray," she said in a voice chillingly stiff with ill will. "You've got some explaining to do. Better make it good."

Without waiting for a goodbye, she disconnected.

Karl felt like a schoolboy summoned to the principal's office, or the altar boy caught drinking wine and forced to answer to the priest.

Settled in the back of the stretch limo his feet up on the footrest, on the familiar journey back to the opulent mansion he called home, Karl reflected that his life was destined to change forever. The open champagne bottle was in reach, already on ice; he poured himself a glass.

Sure, he knew he'd had way too many already today, but that wasn't about to stop him. If alcohol gave Dutch courage then he'd drink to Holland.

Karl was scared to death. Every nerve and cell in his body vibrated with a deadly anticipation of what was to come next. Certain that he was about to throw up, he opened the electronically controlled window by his seat, and stuck his head out of the vehicle.

Just his bad luck. A passing fan in the nondescript vehicle alongside recognized him and excitedly shouted his name. Likely she had already been studying the tinted windows of the limo as it raced down the road from the airport, and wondered who was inside. Now she was rewarded with a close-up of her idol, Karl Verona. Before he could recover his composure, she snapped a picture.

Within seconds the close encounter was over but the chauffeur had spotted what happened and increased his speed to overtake and pull ahead of the other car. Back inside, Karl closed the window.

He shook his head in an effort to clear the fuzziness and wiped his mouth with a tissue. Not for the first time, he had to accept that the price of fame for celebrities was that you couldn't even throw up without someone putting it on YouTube.

He rummaged on the narrow shelves of the mini bar for a mint. There were none, but in an open package he found a couple of sticks of chewing gum. He unwrapped one, popped it in his mouth, and put one in his top pocket in case he needed it later.

Irrationally, he felt a rising anger about the lack of mints. Noisily he pushed aside the privacy partition and asked the driver, "Does no one ever replenish supplies around here?"

"There's another fresh bottle of champagne, if you need it, sir," he replied.

"Not champagne," said Karl, "mints."

The driver turned around, momentarily taking his eyes off the road, and looked perplexed before realization dawned and he answered.

"Must have been Senor Xavier."

Now it was Karl's turn to look perplexed. "Senor Xavier?" he asked for clarification. "*The* Senor Xavier?"

The driver hesitated. He did not know the right answer to the question and strongly suspected that whatever answer he gave was going to be the wrong one, for somebody.

Karl caught the merest glimmer of triumph in the driver's eyes.

He wanted Karl to know but did not want to be the one to tell him.

Bad luck, there was no one else in the car, and he suspected that the messenger might be about to be shot for delivering the news.

At that moment, a speeding police car turned on its wailing siren and flashing lights; the driver pulled across the traffic to let it pass and managed to disengage his eyes from Karl's steely gaze.

Karl angrily banged the partition closed and slumped into his seat. Thoughts and fears crowded into his panicked mind.

So, Senor Xavier was back on the scene. This was worse than he could have dared imagine. *When did he get out? What business did he have in the back of Bianca's car, eating mints?* But Karl already knew. Senor Xavier was the real Numero Uno, the Godfather. The man for whom Bianca kept the light on and the bed warm. He had been in jail for a decade and now he was out, no doubt he would settle a few debts.

Karl's thoughts raced. They were almost at the mansion but he signaled to the driver to open the privacy glass.

"Change of plan, I need to go back to town," he said in as casual a tone as he could manage.

"Madam Bianca asked me to drive you straight home." The triumphant look of a few minutes before was now one of open defiance.

"And I said I'm going back to town," said Karl. "There is a special gift for her I forgot to collect."

The driver did not believe him for a second.

"She expects you. Shall I call and ask what she wants me to do?" he asked.

"No, that will spoil the surprise." Karl was aware they were rapidly running out of time and miles to the final destination. He had no desire to engage in a battle of wills.

As the car pulled up at a traffic light, Karl acted fast. "I'll make my own way," he said and grabbed the door handle. A split second later he saw the driver reach for the central lock but he had left it too late. Karl threw open the door and narrowly missed crashing the door into the adjacent vehicle in the inside lane.

He hit the sidewalk running and left the passenger door open as he headed for an alley and ran to find a place to hide. Ducking and diving through the narrow streets, as he had done as a child, constantly on the run from police, brothers, or other gang members, instinct took him through the winding alleys and out into a parallel thoroughfare.

Sweat ran from every pore, he leaned up against a wall to catch his breath. Water, he needed water. He checked his back pocket and was relieved to find his wallet containing ID, a few US dollars, and credit cards, including a treasured

ELLEN FRAZER-JAMESON

no-limit Black American Express card. Just the thing with which to buy a bottle of water in the slums of Buenos Aires.

Inside a small convenience store he asked for a large bottle of water and the owner excitedly pointed him to a refrigerator, waved away payment and demanded instead an autograph. He handed Karl a scruffy piece of paper torn from the top of a newspaper. A small price to pay.

Next he needed to make a phone call. As he exited the store Karl fumbled in his back pocket and located his emergency phone; small and slim as a credit card it had a GPS that tracked his movements. His manager insisted he carry it at all times.

"You could be a kidnapping risk," he told Karl. "You'll be glad of it one day."

Fortunately, the network was linked to his manager's office, not Bianca's home. She had not, as far as he knew, ever found the need to track him.

Karl pressed the digits of her number into his mini phone.

She answered almost before it rang. "And?" was all she said.

"Last-minute change of plan," he told her. "On my way now."

"Wait," she demanded. "Meet me at Tango d'Fantasia. I have business there."

Karl pressed the off key. Passing taxicabs indicated "For Hire" and he stepped into the roadway and hailed one. Before the words, "Tango d'Fantasia" were out of his mouth, the driver asked, "Aren't you that singer?"

"No," said Karl. "But I wish I had his money."

223

The driver was not impressed by his smart-aleck passenger and did not attempt further conversation.

As he pulled up at the entrance to Tango d'Fantasia, he tried just once more. "Well you certainly look like him."

"Not me," said Karl. "I'm younger and better looking."

The driver didn't like that answer any better than the previous one; he drove off with a sour look on his face after he unceremoniously threw what he obviously considered a pitifully small tip, even though it was American dollars, into his money box.

Karl laughed; he enjoyed winding people up once in a while, and being recognized a hundred times a day soon lost its attraction.

"Have a nice day," he called after the surly driver.

A moment's light relief had taken some of the paralyzing fear out of his body and he walked into the club ready to face his foe. But first he called a friend.

A career criminal, they had grown up together on the streets. This man specialized in contract killing. He was the one who was to supply the present for Bianca. A silver bullet.

Karl had already discussed his requirements with him on the phone while he was still in Miami, but no firm plans had been set in place. All he'd known was that he wanted to be rid of Bianca. Now the appearance of Senor Xavier introduced urgency to the situation.

"It's kill or be killed," he told the hired gun. "How soon can you take care of it?"

Bianca was already on her way to Tango d'Fantasia. Karl calculated he had an hour at most. He swaggered into the club with a bravado he did not feel. Fortunately, the manager still had fond memories of when the then unknown Ricky Rosen sang at the club.

Karl's profile had been written and rewritten until it barely resembled his life story at all, but the publicist's version always focused on the romance of a rags-to-riches story and Karl's humble beginnings. Poor boy makes good.

Bianca had played her part but not many people knew that story. In private to her confidants she liked to boast about her famous conquest and her part in his meteoric rise to fame.

"I discovered him. I made him," she claimed.

Only a few chosen people, one of them being the manager of the club who had seen Karl perhaps only half a dozen times in the intervening couple of years, knew the full story.

"It's good to see you, my friend," he told Karl, with genuine affection and shook his hand vigorously and hugged him.

"Bianca's on her way," Karl told him. "I'm to meet her here."

The manager nodded his head toward the back room. "She's already here. Senor Xavier is with her."

In the grand scheme of things, Karl had figured he might be able to sweet talk Bianca thereby buying himself time to formulate his ultimate plan.

The appearance of Senor Xavier on the scene had changed everything. He was definitely not going to respond to sweet nothings being whispered in his ear.

Karl knew when he was beat. Only a fool would walk into the lion's den unarmed.

Karl needed a Plan B. Fast. The manager indicated that there was no one in the gent's restroom. Karl entered cautiously as he checked for himself and locked the door securely behind him.

"How long before you get here?" he whispered frantically when the hit man answered the phone. "I am in big trouble. You need to do the job NOW."

"It's not a pizza delivery service," his friend responded angrily. "I need a little more time. You should not be anywhere near the scene when the work is in progress."

"Too late for that now, I'm on the premises," said Karl. "Just help me out here, for God's sake."

"Okay, wait for me outside. And remind me never ever again to do a job for a friend. This has all the potential to go horribly wrong."

Karl hung up even as he heard the gunman complain that his professionalism was being compromised. This was not the time or place to try to reassure him.

Karl peered around the door of the restroom, scared rigid that at any moment he would be discovered. He called the manager over and put his arm companionably around his shoulder as he told him, "Don't tell them I'm here yet. I'll be back real soon."

Outside the club Karl quickly crossed the road and took up a position where he could observe the entrance and check out all vehicles as they arrived and left.

The minutes felt like hours as he waited for the cavalry to arrive. Desperate not to draw attention to himself, he pressed deeper into a crevice between two buildings, terrified that Bianca and Xavier would appear and he would have no means to stop them from leaving.

An insistent beep on the horn from a newly arrived car acted as a signal. Karl nodded in recognition and ran across the road, as the front passenger door opened to allow him to enter. The hit man did not undertake the job alone; he had an accomplice who acted as getaway driver. The professional with the shooter was in the back curbside with the window wound down.

"Get down on the floor in front of the seat," his friend commanded. "It's going to get lively around here."

Karl felt the familiar adrenaline surge through his body, fear and excitement, a powerful combination that demanded fight or flight. His palms were sweaty, his mouth dry, and his heart pounded. The fight was about to start and the subsequent flight couldn't come fast enough for him.

The wait was not long. Bianca and Xavier had obviously come to the conclusion that Karl was not about to accept their invitation to meet up, especially not in the privacy of the backroom.

As they exited the club, Bianca resembled a galleon in full flow; an extravagant black satin cape acted like a sail and she propelled herself on her high-heeled boots right into the line of fire.

The gunman emptied the chamber of his gun into her overblown body. She was dead before she hit the sidewalk. Too late, Senor Xavier attempted to push her out of harm's way. She did not stand a chance. Her husband concealed in the assassin's car did not see her die.

Senor Xavier, much to his surprise, was unhurt. His name was not on the contract and he was not a target. The bodyguard, initially in a protective position in front of the couple, had made a bad decision and walked on ahead to open the car door. There was no time to draw his gun before the car that carried the gunman sped away, tires screeching, from the scene of the crime.

The fight was over. Karl was on his way to catch a flight back to Miami. Anxious to be safely out of the country, he had ordered that his private jet be fueled and ready to go as soon as he arrived. This time he refused the champagne; he had already thrown up the contents of his stomach in the restroom at the airport.

Being a single man didn't feel as good as he had anticipated.

CHAPTER TWENTY-SEVEN

Pay Back Time

Serena squealed with childlike delight as the spray hit her face and she wrapped her lithe suntanned limbs tighter around the strong, muscled body of her fiancé, Karl, as he manfully maneuvered the bucking jet-ski through the azure blue Caribbean Sea.

"I love you," she shouted above the noise and the sensory disorientation caused by the waves and the playful breeze.

"Love you more," he called back, taking one hand off the controls to stroke her leg and stop just before he reached the top of her inner thigh and the point where her barely-there thong struggled to cover the intimate area between her legs.

As Karl had promised at the time of their engagement, he had whisked her away to a secret destination for an "out of this world" luxury vacation on a private island. The palm-tree-fringed island with a rocky shoreline was reachable only by motor launch and, apart from an army of servants on hand to cater to their every need, and a high-level security team, Serena and Karl were the only castaways.

An hour by air from Miami, the tropical paradise had once been the home of a European princess and was now owned by a British media mogul.

Royalty, aristocrats, Hollywood movie stars, celebrities, world-famous recording artists and fashion designers, captains of industry, rulers of countries, and sporting superstars treasured invites to the ultimate vacation destination. For honored guests, no expense was ever spared and every imaginable luxury was provided.

Karl and Serena felt they were in seventh heaven. The beachfront cottages were tastefully but simply furnished to blend into the environment and complement the natural beauty of the seascape. Designed with wood, polished stone, bamboo, shells, and coral, the spacious rooms had removable walls that were open to the elements and brought the outside into the room with plants, grasses, and seaweed sculptures. A natural stream filled the swimming pool that bubbled down through a waterfall in the rocks.

The party-size Jacuzzi in the bathroom could easily accommodate a dozen guests and the silk-covered king-size bed had room for at least that number.

Steps from the patio and its swinging hammocks and cushioned lounge chairs was a playground full of water-sports equipment. A speedboat, half a dozen jet-skis, and a collection of plastic-shaped floating beds designed like boats, pianos, and fast cars. There were skis, water boards, flippers, masks, snorkels, fishing equipment, balls, bats, and even a wild contraption, which when hoisted into the air by the speedboat, allowed the seated passenger to fly through the sky.

Karl loved boy's toys. Serena loved to lounge.

"Want me to take you for a ride in the sky?" he asked, desperate to get her attention away from the notebook in which she was writing.

"No, thanks," she told him. "I'm determined to write a song and you're to blame for me not being able to do it."

"How come?" said Karl, as he lifted a freshly prepared piña colada from the tray the maid had just delivered and took a long, hard swallow through the straw. He moved pineapples and cherries out of the way and stirred the mixture with a glass swivel stick.

"Do you want one of these?" he asked her. "I can ask the maid for a virgin cocktail, no alcohol for my child bride-to-be."

Serena pouted. "I'm twenty-one," she said. "And we have been engaged for a whole year." In response to his question she added, "A soda will do fine, thanks."

He carefully removed the decorative colored umbrella from the drink and walked across to where Serena lay on her front and kicked her legs in the air, pen and notebook in hand. He cheekily tucked the paper umbrella into the back of her white bikini bottoms. She smiled indulgently at him.

"So, I'm to blame for what?" he asked.

"Well, everyone knows that the best love songs are about broken hearts. I'm too happy with you. I only want to write about hearts and flowers and romance. Perhaps you need to break my heart then I can write lyrics that are deep and meaningful."

Karl frowned at her, "Don't tempt fate," he said.

"I know, it was silly of me," said Serena. "Mom always

warns me, 'God is listening. From your lips to his ears. Be careful what you pray for.'"

"Speaking of your mother," Karl said, as he sat down alongside her on the lounger. He took the umbrella from where he had tucked it into her bikini and placed it behind her ear.

"Does she still insisting that you are way too young to get married?"

Serena sighed. "She won't change her mind. The only question is whether I decide to go against her wishes. She won't give in easily, but I'll work on her."

Karl would never have admitted it to Serena, but the fact was that her mother's opposition suited him perfectly. It saved him from making big explanations about a certain Madame in Buenos Aires.

Serena still basked in the personal and media excitement of a wedding on the horizon and flashed her six-carat, square-cut diamond ring at every opportunity. Karl was able to persuade her that an extended engagement would allow her to plan the event and maximize the ongoing publicity. "Keep them guessing for as long as we can," he told her. "It's all good for our star status."

* * *

Serena had no idea that besides a reluctance to commit to a high-profile wedding, Karl had other legal matters on his mind; he was in touch with a lawyer who took care of his interests in Buenos Aires. He had no intention to return to the country, but he did want to try to maximize whatever financial benefits would come to him from the death of his wife.

Gangland vendetta—Godmother of crime gunned down, the national news headlines in Argentina and America had declared. "We *will* find the killers," declared the police chief. However, the search for killers of international criminals never did figure high on the list of crime-solving priorities. No one had been arrested and there were still no credible suspects twelve months on.

Sympathy was in short supply for the victims and obstructed by the code of the streets, the difficulty to gain evidence, and track down witnesses, which compelled the authorities to let the criminals deal with their own internal battles and power struggles.

Karl was aware of all the conspiracy theories through the lawyer he had engaged to act in his interest, but he was determined not to incriminate himself in any way.

"Senor Xavier is convinced the gunman meant to kill him," the lawyer confided. "He even thinks that Bianca may have played a part in the conspiracy because she would have had to relinquish control now that he is out of prison."

Karl listened intently, alert to any indication that his name might be on a list of suspects. Still, he remained confident that he was safe. He was sure that only his friend the hired hit man could point the finger at him.

He was prepared to wait and bide his time before he pushed ahead with making claims on Bianca's estate, but he did want confirmation from Enrique that he was a beneficiary.

Deep down he knew that Bianca's reasons for marriage had been to fulfill her own agenda. She did not really intend him to inherit all that she owned. Certainly not once Senor Xavier was back on the scene. He would not put it past them to try and write him off—but at least he would try to make sure that he received a payoff. And a substantial one at that.

For all his global success, the financial outlay involved in an organization like his was enormous and without Bianca around to foot the bills, he already realised that he needed to act to ensure his financial security.

"I have to make a couple of phone calls," he told Serena, as she began to slip into a leisurely sleep by the gently lapping ocean.

"Are you sure you don't want to come for another ride with me on the jet-skis?"

"You go," she said dreamily, and added seductively, "I'm saving my energy for later."

"Okay, I'll go and make those calls and then go out on the water. Love you," he called.

Karl pressed the keys to connect to Bianca's lawyer and right-hand man, Enrique.

The response was chilling. "Hello, Ricky," he said, to remind him where he came from and putting him back to where it all began. "What can I do for you? We were disappointed that your performance schedule meant you could not attend the funeral of Madame Bianca."

"You know I would have got there if I could have, Enrique. I mean, it's not as if I wanted to miss my own wife's funeral." Karl waited for the reaction.

There was silence.

"Enrique, are you there? I said it's not as if I wanted to..."

"I heard what you said, but I am afraid I don't understand. I don't know what you mean."

"You signed the papers, Enrique; you witnessed the ceremony, in the den at the house. Bianca insisted that if I was her husband I would not be able to testify against her." Karl knew he was already fighting a losing battle.

"Enrique," he shouted into the phone. "She was my wife."

"I have no knowledge of that," said Enrique, icy contempt in every word.

"You'll hear from my lawyers, you won't get away with this. I'll fight it in court," Karl said, desperately trying to make his point. He felt like he was drowning, and all his life was passing before him.

Enrique stood his ground. "There is no paperwork, I would have remembered if you had married Madame Bianca. You are not her husband or her beneficiary. We have no business to discuss with you."

Karl tried one last time. "What financial settlement do you intend to make for me?"

Enrique laughed. "Ask Senor Xavier, he still regrets that he did not have opportunity to meet you at Tango d'Fantasia. Goodbye, Ricky."

Karl hurled his phone down on the sand and stamped on it. The screen cracked.

In frustration he picked it and threw it into the sea. Beside himself with rage and humiliation, Karl kicked at the sand and then sat down at the water's edge and cried.

When the hot tears of shame and pain abated, he stood up and stalked toward the jet-ski that he had left pulled up on the sand earlier that afternoon.

He pushed the vehicle into the swell of the frisky late-afternoon ocean foam and climbed into the driver's seat. He kicked the engine into life.

The spray pounded at his face and covered the salty tears that refused to stop overflowing. The all-too-familiar taste of adrenaline in his mouth mingled with fear and the rage inside threatened to explode. Like a cowboy on a bucking bronco, he shouted at the top of his voice. "Goddam them, Goddam them." He stood up on the seat of the jet-ski and screamed into the waves. "Faster, faster, faster."

Speed met speed as a powerboat tried to swerve to avoid the jet-ski as it entered the wrong side of the shipping lane and bucked out of control. Later, the other driver reported he saw Karl stand up on the seat and appear to shout a warning. Perhaps he knew that the cable on his brakes had been cut.

* * *

Serena dreamed sweet dreams until she was shocked into wakefulness by the sound of an explosion out on the ocean.

The manager of the complex was the first on the scene. He called the emergency services—and his boss. "We'll put out a statement immediately. First on our own network, of course. The others can catch up with the news after that."

"Stay calm," Maria urged Serena. "I'm on my way. I will take care of everything. Stay calm."

Serena shrieked into the phone, "Come and get me now."

"I will. I will," said her distraught mother. "Arrangements are being made even as we speak to fly me out there. I'll bring you home. We'll get you off the island at the first opportunity."

Fox News and CNN reported the tragedy. "Breaking News. We have received reports that the international singing star Karl Valero has been fatally injured in a jet-ski accident while on vacation at a private island in the Caribbean.

"Mr. Valero was engaged to the teenage chart-topper Serena Perez. The happy couple was due to be married in a lavish ceremony at a secret location later this year."

CHAPTER TWENTY-EIGHT

No Way to Treat a Lady

Blackness enveloped the oceanfront home where Maria and Serena spent their sad and lonely days. Her daughter was in mourning and Maria Perez rarely left her side during the weeks and months that followed Serena's fiancé's tragic accidental death.

Maria remembered all too clearly how desperately she had struggled to retain the hold on reality that followed the death of her husband, Humberto, Serena's father.

"There are no rules," she told Serena. "You feel as you feel and you are free to do whatever you choose. No one else's opinions matter. Not even mine. There are days when you will feel almost normal and others when you are convinced your heart will break and you will fall into a deep well of depression.

"A dark hole opens up in your soul and you are completely bereft. Without your father, I saw no reason to go on living. He was my life, he made my very existence worthwhile, gave it meaning.

"Only because I still had you did I force myself to put

one foot in front of the other and keep doing the next right thing."

Maria shuddered at the memory of the bleakness she had experienced after her darling husband died. She tried to console Serena and let her know that everything she was going through was a normal part of the grieving process. Maria believed there was a set of symptoms, a formula that those left behind endured, though there was no real rhyme or reason to the when and how. In the words of the country singer John Denver, "Some days are diamonds, some days are stones."

Maria gently described how it had been for her. "It can feel that a healing process is underway and then out of the blue, a song, a TV program, a memory, plunges you right back into the depths."

Serena stayed in her room with the blinds closed.

She played Karl's albums and watched his music videos constantly. Since the early days after the funeral, which had turned into a three-ring circus thanks to the oppressive attention of the media, Serena had refused to go out of the apartment.

Friends continued to call to ask how she was, but only her best friend Monique ever had a personal conversation with Serena. Maria worried that even she would lose patience soon.

As she knew only too well, much as they were sympathetic and wanted to be supportive, life moved on and everyone had their own agenda to pursue.

Maria devoted herself to supporting her daughter and treated her like an invalid, she allowed her to sleep when she chose and wake when she wanted. She instructed the maid to prepare Serena's favorite meals and come up with suggestions for tasty snacks to tempt her.

Serena's bedroom had previously been a joyful and noisy place, a hive of manic activity with clothes strewn around and the happy laughter of teenage girls. They tried on clothes, applied makeup, checked out new hairstyles, and created a lively center of fun and laughter and gossip. Now Maria knocked at the door cautiously and spoke in a whisper, eager not to upset or disturb her grieving daughter.

The morose atmosphere weighed like a dark cloud as Serena, dressed in black like a Victorian widow, mourned her fiancé.

Maria made a decision that all she could do was be available and wait for a breakthrough. She walked on eggshells, chose her words carefully and came to accept that Serena did not want to be reminded that one day she would be able to contemplate a future without the man of her dreams.

Maria gently shared her experience in those uncertain days after her loved one passed.

"Strange as it seems, at times you will momentarily forget that Karl has gone, until you lift up a phone to ring him and realize you will never talk to him again. The finality of death is so cruel.

"I lived with an expectation that one day I would wake up and everything would be back to normal. I expected your father to just walk through the door and we would all resume our lives.

"Just one more day, I used to pray, if only I could have one more day, or an hour, or a minute to say goodbye. Even now, two years later, I am convinced that it is not really final. He wouldn't have just left me without a farewell. He never even left a room without saying where he was going."

Serena listened and she was truly grateful for her mother's insights, but there were times she wanted to explode. Much as she tried to hold on to her emotions, the anger erupted and she lost control. Face flushed, tear-stained eyes red rimmed with constant crying, at the top of her voice she screamed at her mother.

"Karl was too young; he had his whole life ahead of him. He was riding high and we were going to be married. You had a whole lifetime with Dad. You've got years of memories. My future has been stolen from me."

With his death, the legacy of musical superstar Karl Valero had taken on a life of its own. His record company released compilations of past hits and put out albums of new material and never before seen video footage to promote the music.

Questions about his meteoric rise to fame and rumors of criminal connections, never diminished his appeal; instead they served to add further excitement and glamour to the myth. Karl Valero was legend.

Serena was approached and asked to do a "ghost" version of one of his hits, where she would sing alongside his version. She refused.

She had her reasons.

Lying snuggled up alongside her mother as they watched television in the large comfortable bed where she sometimes ended up in the middle of the night when she couldn't sleep, Serena sadly confided her fears.

"I've lost my voice," she admitted.

"Each time I try to sing, I start to cry. The pain is so deep and the voice seems to release it. I don't want to feel. I want to close down all that emotion. The lyrics tap into a deep place inside my heart that hurts so badly. A dark hole in my soul. Does that make sense?"

Maria felt a lump rise in her throat. All her life, singing had been a joy for her daughter. She was a natural. Now it seemed that her great gift had been taken from her along with the love of the man she had hoped to marry.

"Time heals," said Maria as she stroked her little girl's hand. "Give it time. God will guide you to know when the time is right for you to be able to feel those emotions again. Don't worry, you will one day be able to create the beautiful music that we all love."

Serena began to cry. "I wrote a new song, the day Karl died. I want to share it with you."

Maria thanked God for the powerful bond she and her daughter shared and answered, "I'm listening, Princess."

Maria hardly recognized the whispered, dreamy voice, so unlike Serena's usual powerful, confident delivery.

The lyrics she had written sounded like a prayer.

"Be careful what you wish for; God answers every prayer,
He grants your dreams; permits your schemes,
Fulfills your heart's desire,
Don't ask God for heartache, the broken pain won't heal,
Be careful, what you wish for, your one true love
  he'll steal.
Be careful what you wish for, God answers every prayer."

Mother and daughter held close together, each suffering their own hurt and pain and loss.

"One day, the joy will return to your life, you will experience happiness and you will learn to smile again and your lovely voice will be heard loud and clear," Maria promised her daughter.

"God will answer our prayers."

*   *   *

Maria continued to administer tender loving care and, to her relief, a day at a time, Serena began to recover from the worst excesses of her grief.

There were hopeful small signs at first. Serena allowed the blinds to be opened and let the sunshine in. Then one day she suggested that Maria ask the maid to set lunch up on the table outside on the balcony that overlooked the ocean.

Like all mothers, Maria was convinced she would see the progress she longed for quicker if she let Serena take the lead and believe that everything that happened was her decision.

Maria had no intention of rushing her, but she did have a plan. One that she would introduce when she judged the time was right.

Together the two became avid fans of the early morning magazine program live from Rockefeller Center.

"I'd love to do that job," Serena commented out of the blue one day, as she watched the bubbly blonde host interview a member of a British pop band. Serena had shared a concert bill with The Spiders when she was on tour promoting one of her records.

"I know all those guys and I used to love to host the promo videos we did for our shows," she explained.

Maria seized her chance. "I've got an idea. Why don't we relocate to New York for a while?' she said excitedly. "We have so many contacts in the entertainment business. I'm sure we could get you a start on the career ladder."

To her surprise, Serena readily agreed. "Yes, I need a change of scene." She didn't need to add, "And to get far away from all the tragic memories."

Maria was anxious to press her advantage. "Remember how you used to love to ice skate at Rockefeller Plaza under the giant Christmas tree; we can go see the Rockettes Show at Radio City and shop till we drop."

"Oh, yes, Mama, what a great suggestion," said Serena, happily she turned to concentrate on her musician friend being interviewed on the popular television show. "Where will we stay?"

"How about we become Park Avenue ladies? I know the perfect location, a furnished apartment that we can rent on Park and 66th in a fully serviced luxury building. It will be an adventure. We'll close up the condo here for a few months, but if it gets too cold we'll still be able to come back home to Miami Beach."

For the first time in way too long, Serena was filled with enthusiasm and anticipation.

That afternoon, Maria overheard her on the phone to her friend Monique, telling her all about the New York plans.

Maria lost no time in pressing home her advantage; she didn't intend to give Serena the chance to change her mind.

In a flurry of activity, she called a meeting of her house-keepers and told them to prepare to close up the condo. In Maria's five-star building it was far from unusual to have whole floors of apartments closed and shuttered for months on end while the owners enjoyed the luxury of traveling to homes in different parts of the world.

Snowbirds, New Yorkers, and people from up north who relocated to Miami to escape the cold winters, generally arrived as hurricane season ended on November 30, after spending Thanksgiving with their families, and stayed till the end of May and left before hurricane season started on June 1.

Maria planned to make the expedition the other way around. She and Serena would have Thanksgiving dinner on the beach and then leave for New York.

She signed the lease for a year on a swanky New York apartment. Maria reached out and made phone calls to friends and checked out opportunities in the field of tele-vision for Serena.

"You'll have to be prepared to start at the bottom," she warned Serena. "Don't think they are going to give you a prime-time spot straight off when you don't have any expe-rience."

Serena accepted the offer of an internship at the national award-winning television station she already dreamed of conquering, Serena admitted her high-flying ambitions only to herself.

"Six months, till I learn the ropes and have the top job," she calculated. "With hard work, luck, and the special help of my beloved in heaven, I'll be on my way."

CHAPTER TWENTY-NINE

Reach for the Stars

Chaos reigned in her ear as Serena tried to distinguish the voice of the director from the voice of the producer, and cut out the background noise of the other technical team member's in the television channel's control box.

"Turn toward camera two," said one voice.

"Ask about their new record," said another.

"Get ready to go to autocue," instructed another.

"Counting down," called yet another disembodied voice.

Serena was aware of the need to not blink her eyes as she faced the auto cue and attempted to match her words to the speed of the rolling words.

"I'll follow you," the auto cue operator explained patiently. "Read the scrolling words at the pace that works to hit your clock."

"After the break, sorry, after the breakfast news, we meet a real life hero, a mother, no, not mother, another in our Hero for the Day series. We'll be right back."

Serena had been thrown in at the deep end of live television, she was unexpectedly called upon to host when one of the regular presenters was taken ill and pulled out of the show at the last minute.

Eager to curry favor with the big boss of the network and show that he was a man of vision, the assistant producer had decided to take the chance and give Serena her big break.

Affecting an attitude of importance, he had called her into his private cubicle, which was tacked on like an afterthought to the larger open-plan production office. It looked like an out of control storage space. Paperwork ran riot: scripts, files, letters, requisition orders, invoices, and memos. There were towering edifices of books, disks, videos, and products of every imaginable shape and size that people hoped to be able to promote on the show.

"Sit down," he had said, though there was not a spare inch of floor or chair space in the office. He did not even attempt to sit, he preferred instead to walk to his window on the world, high above Rockefeller Plaza where crowds had already gathered for that day's live show.

"This is your big break," he told her. "The regular anchor will carry the show, and you will fill in for some short links, sit on the couch and look pretty."

The producer was probably no more than thirty, but he looked much older, being careworn and suffering from the constant affects of jet lag that assailed all participants in the live morning-show schedule.

Getting up at 3 a.m. played havoc with the body clock, the pressures of the job were immense; competition for viewers was fierce and the jockeying to get from assistant producer to producer, to senior producer to executive producer, would make any eager young man go bald.

"Here's a script. You already know the running order and

guests for this morning's show; study your segments while you're in makeup," he told her.

"We'll try to persuade the director to give you a quick run through, but don't bet on it. He's never at his most amenable this time of the morning.

"Miss. R's P.A. will help out. I already ordered coffee for you, use her dressing room, wardrobe will meet you there to fix you up with an outfit."

He walked across the cluttered room quickly and straight out of the door.

"Good luck," he called over his shoulder. "I'll buy you brunch when it's all over."

Serena's head was reeling. *A star is born.* She felt like the chorus girl about to step into the lead role. *Understudy steals the show.*

Of course, she was not totally unprepared, she reminded herself.

For months she had worked at the studios every day, happily helping out wherever she was needed and all the time she watched, learned, eager to seize opportunities when they were presented.

So far she had been allowed to do a couple of guest presenting spots and the network executives had been complimentary about her interviewing skills and performance.

Previous star status and the public sympathy vote that followed the tragic death of her fiancé gave her huge viewer credibility, and the audience were fascinated by the glamorous Serena Perez.

Her name inside a hand-drawn star had been hastily scribbled and stuck on the door of the number-one dressing room. Although referred to as the "star" dressing room, the small unit was surprisingly modest. As broadcast hour approached, the area became jam packed with all the technical and creative crew who required her attention or needed to impart information before the show. Two senior producers held a conference in her dressing room even as she changed into her colorful camera-friendly outfit, and there was a steady succession of script supervisors, auto cue operators, a sound man to mike her up, makeup artists to refresh the face job they had finished just half an hour before, hair stylist, wardrobe, gofers.

The production team proclaimed their importance as they bustled around wearing earpieces, carried clipboards, and transmitted instructions via walkie-talkies.

"Thirty minutes to show time," called a runner as he scurried down the narrow studio corridor singing out his time check like a town crier.

It felt like only two minutes later when the word had changed to, "Miss. Perez wanted on set. Top of show. Fifteen minutes."

Three hours of live television flew by and Serena used her familiar performance trick of converting the adrenaline and nerves into total concentration, she focused only on the here and now.

Be present, Serena reminded herself. This is a gift, that's why it's called the present.

As the closing credits appeared and the music signaled the end of another live show, Serena smiled and gave a small wave to the audience. "Hope you enjoyed today's show. I'm

Serena Perez. Thank you for having me. Goodbye and have a wonderful day."

Most technical crews are jaded and not easy to impress, but on her first day Serena was treated to a spontaneous outburst of applause from everyone in the studio.

Her mother was already on the phone, "Good job, congratulations," she told Serena proudly.

After her celebration brunch with the assistant producer, two senior producers, the director, and a studio executive, Serena felt confident that she had exceeded their expectations.

"Today you've earned the star treatment. Let me walk you to the limo," said the program executive as he rose from the table when they finished brunch, and he proceeded to escort her toward the elevator outside the double doors of the studio restaurant.

Admiring eyes followed their progress across the restaurant. The word was out. Watch this space. Although young and relatively inexperienced, Serena had passed her baptism of fire with flying colors. Her star was in the ascendant.

Serena exited the sky-scraping Rockefeller Center and stopped to sign autographs and have photographs taken with a small crowd of fans and well-wishers who congratulated her on her first show.

The studio doorman held open the door of the limousine as Serena stepped into the back of the sleek vehicle and settled gratefully into her seat. As she sank into the earthy leather upholstery and kicked off her shoes, in that moment, her attention was drawn to one particular fan.

Their eyes locked for a second. The woman was shabbily dressed and looked like a down-and-out but she was smiling at Serena. As the limo pulled away she gave a shy wave. Serena thought there was something familiar about the woman. Involuntarily, she admitted that the knowing look on the woman's face stirred up an uncomfortable cocktail of fear and anxiety.

Day one as an anchor on prime time television and looks like I just acquired my first celebrity stalker.

Better get used to it. Serena forced herself to smile, the rocket ship had launched. "Serena Perez reporting for the Entertainment Channel—fasten your seat belts."

*   *   *

The morning show viewers loved Serena. Her natural ability to connect with the audience and her youthful exuberance, coupled with a solid work ethic, ensured she was an instant hit. Most national presenters start on regional stations and work their way up. Serena started at the top and consolidated her position from there.

As with everything else she had undertaken in her life— schoolwork, sports, performance arts, pop stardom—she was a natural. Gifted, gracious, and endlessly hard working.

Living the life of Park Avenue Ladies gave Serena and her mother a new enthusiasm for artistic experiences and the wonderful cultural life of New York. The popular pair were members of the Metropolitan Museum, the Museum of Modern Art, Lincoln Center, New York City Ballet, and regulars at Broadway and off-Broadway shows.

Serena experienced a surreal sensation of living a make-believe life in an up-scale movie. Not able to properly identify or describe the feeling, she watched from outside herself as she pulled up in her studio limo or yellow New York taxi-cab and walked the short distance on a carpeted sidewalk under a navy blue and gold canopy to the gilded entrance where a liveried doorman held open the door to the prestigious Park and 66th building.

Watched over protectively, she glided passed the polished wood security desk and entered the shiny bronze elevator as it rose to her sumptuous and elegantly furnished sixth floor apartment.

"We are well blessed," said Maria at least a dozen times a day, as she reflected on the wonderful transformation that had taken place in her daughter following the move to New York.

Serena's career was on an ever-upward trajectory and she loved the job of presenting a live, national morning television program, and the other opportunities that it brought for promotion, appearances, and the ability to embrace and support good causes.

Maria sat on the board of several charitable organizations and used her considerable experience and expertise to head up fundraising committees and organize high-profile events.

Mother and daughter were working ladies who lunched and embraced their abundant socialite lifestyles. Together they shopped in the high-end 5th Avenue designer stores and looked for quirky boutique finds in The Village.

"The perfect day is one that combines work, retail therapy, and entertainment," Maria often observed. "And if I can share part of that day with my darling daughter, what more could I ask."

Serena smiled and outwardly agreed with her mother, but she deliberately hid inner turmoil that she knew would disturb her mother's idyllic if sometimes unrealistic life view.

Maria had always been an uncomplicated and optimistic individual. She saw the best in everyone and wanted to believe that good motives and honorable intentions would lead to a better world.

To practice forgiveness came with her religious beliefs and she refused to hold bitterness even toward her dead husband's business partner who had behaved in such an unethical and unscrupulous manner after Humberto's death.

"Only God can judge a person's heart," she told her daughter.

Serena never told Maria about the shadowy figure who watched her silently from a distance, almost every day after she signed off her appearance on the morning show and entered her company car at Rockefeller Plaza.

Most fans wanted autographs, photographs, or at least to exchange a few words with the star they had watched on the screen or on the set as a member of the studio audience.

The mystery woman never approached Serena or asked for anything. She appeared content to wait and watch. Serena knew who she was.

Although a handful of years had passed and the woman had aged dramatically, Serena recognized her from the one time she had shown up at the family house on the Venetian Island in Miami Beach. The day her father had died of a heart attack on his own doorstep. To whatever degree, it could not be denied that the woman had contributed significantly to his distress, agitation, and ultimate heart-stopping demise. Serena was filled with a toxic cocktail of emotions when she relived the tragic events of the day that changed her life.

Battling to hide her fear and slow her breathing to a normal rate so she would not be in danger of hyperventilating, on the day when she could stand her brooding presence no longer, Serena walked purposefully across the Plaza and asked, "What do you want?"

Before the woman could make a move to scurry away, Serena blocked her path, looked her in her pale, watery green eyes and said, "I know who you are, or who you claim to be. What do you want from me?"

Confronted, the woman seemed unsure whether to answer or not. She looked about as if wondering whether someone, anyone would intervene.

The limo driver stood by the sidewalk, ready to spring into action and open the door for Serena, but the encounter with a strange woman on the Plaza had not attracted his attention. There were always fans dancing attendance on the exiting television stars, including the lovely young Miss Serena Perez.

Serena asked again, "What do you want? Why are you here every day?" The anger and insecurity began to rise. She raised her voice. "Tell me, what do you expect of me? What do you want me to say? You're harassing me, just by being here. Is it money you want?"

The woman still did not say a word, just stared. Without taking her eyes off Serena, she reached a hand out. Serena jumped back in fear.

The woman spoke in a surprisingly strong and articulate voice. The words rushed out, tripping over each other.

"Don't worry. I wouldn't hurt you for the world. I love you.

"Can you ever forgive me for what I did? God knows, I can't forgive myself."

Serena had not expected that reaction and was at a loss to know what to say. She attempted to weigh up the woman's intentions; they seemed genuine enough.

Serena avoided having to commit to an opinion, caught as she had been so unawares. Instead she used the philosophy that her mother Maria had taught her: "It's not for me to forgive. Only God can judge what is in someone's heart."

Seeing the disappointment in her birth mother's face, she relented. "Thank you for telling me. I know it must be very painful but you have done a brave thing. I hope it brings you some release."

The woman smiled, and said, "You're a lovely well-brought up girl. Thank you."

Serena smiled back and tentatively took the woman's hand, she repeated, "Thank you. Now I must go. Please take care of yourself."

She walked quickly to the waiting car and when she turned around to look, her birth mother had already disappeared.

Reflecting on the encounter, Serena had to admit that it had given her a sense of satisfaction. A piece of unfinished business laid to rest. And there was something else. She realized that she was fascinated by what she saw as physical similarities between herself and her biological mother. She found herself wishing that she would one day see those sparkling green eyes shining and happy.

Leaving the studio each day, she checked out the place where her mother had been accustomed to taking up her solitary vigil. She did not appear.

Days passed into weeks and Serena forced herself to stop looking.

She had almost given up hope of seeing her again when she was approached on the Plaza by an older woman who said she had a message for Serena.

"Kathleen asked me to come," she said. "She wanted you to know that she's gone into rehab."

Serena looked at her and waited for more information. "I'm Kathleen's friend, Concepta. We've been friends for over twenty years," said her new confidant. "She's a good person and she talks about you all the time. She is so proud of you."

Serena was beginning to feel uncomfortable. She turned to go. The friend sensed that further explanation was required.

"Kathleen is a little overfond of the bottle. She's got the disease and it forces her to behave in ways that are way out of character. But she's decided that this time she is going to beat it. She's going to get sober. She asked me to let you know, in case you wondered where she'd got to these days."

Serena thanked her, still reluctant to be drawn too far into the obviously dysfunctional world of her mother.

The friend was determined to make sure that Serena was aware of the situation; she wanted to be able to report to Kathleen that she had passed on the message in full.

"Poor Kathleen, she has a dark hole in her soul but this time she promises to make a real effort to get sober. You can be sure that I'll stay close and keep an eye on her."

Serena relented. "Thank you," she said, with a genuine feeling that this was an important development and her support just might help make a difference.

"Does she need money?" Serena asked.

"No, thanks for asking," said her mother's caring friend. "She's in a city facility where they will detox her and try to set her back on the straight and narrow. Recovery is possible for those who want it."

"Tell her I'm pleased to hear she's sought out help and I will send out loving thoughts." Serena felt a real desire to be helpful.

"Your mom was right," said her friend. "You *are* a lovely girl. And you look so much like her. She was a beautiful girl when she was young and a wonderful entertainer. I know she's still inside there. I just pray we can get back the real Kathleen.

"By the way, we love watching you on the TV. It's one of our favorite shows. That's how your mom knew where to find you; we're real fans. Anyway, I won't keep you any longer. If it's alright, I'll let you know how the treatment goes on. Goodbye, see you again."

Serena's heart felt light and she sent out a silent prayer that her birth mom would get well.

When the time was right, she would tell the full story to her mother, Maria. But not yet. A sober Kathleen would surely get a better reaction from Maria than a drunken one.

Doctor Feel-good

"Bath salts?" Serena shouted into the phone. "What the hell do you mean 'bath salts'? My best friend died from inhaling bath salts?"

Serena and Monique had an enduring special relationship. The women led completely separate lives and often there were months or even years between them meeting up, but they shared a deep bond and always considered each other, in the words of the socialite Paris Hilton, best friends forever.

Serena could not believe what she was hearing. Bubbly, full-of-life Monique had died and the cause of her death was being blamed on her use of a type of synthetic stimulant known as "bath salts" or "gravel."

Other fatalities from the drug had occurred in the Miami party scene and the trauma was known as "acute alpha PVP toxicity."

Monique was a party girl. She had not graduated from the young scene where kids spent their lives attending music festivals, drinking free cocktails in bars and clubs, and hanging out at the faux glamorous settings of the entertainment scene of celebrities, music moguls, models, rappers, and reality TV shows.

Miami Beach born and bred, she knew everyone who was anyone and could get a party started just with her far-reaching social-networking connections and light a fire of publicity by her association with a new club, restaurant, or store.

Serena hung up the phone. She was alone in her New York apartment. She lived alone but her mother lived only a dozen blocks away in the apartment they had moved to when they first came to the city. Maria now owned the property and also the apartment where Serena lived.

She needed to clear her head and she decided to walk over to her mother's building. It wouldn't be right to tell her the news about Monique on the phone.

Serena's balcony apartment was modern and high tech, while her mother still preferred a more traditional setting.

Living close but not together suited mother and daughter, who shared many common interests especially their passion for charities and giving back to the community.

"To whom much is given, much is expected," Maria liked to quote, Serena's father's words.

The two shared a work ethic and Serena credited her family with her ambition and drive to pursue excellence.

When asked why she continued to work so hard despite all her successes, Serena always answered, "I need a reason to get out of bed in the morning and I think I would lose my mind if I didn't. We all have the ability to change a life, whether we volunteer at a soup kitchen or work with children with special needs. When you give back you leave the world a better place."

Quoted by one of her charities, Maria had said, "It is the responsibility of every human being to provide for others and make a difference."

The two women were a formidable force in the world of philanthropic foundations and with Maria's dynamic fundraising capabilities and her daughter's ability to raise the ticket price of an event tenfold just by her presence, mother and daughter were highly valued by charitable institutions. Their genuine desire to help and make a positive impact marked the two socialites as powerful and hugely effective board and committee members.

Charity work within the arts offered high-profile participation in spectacular events at the landmark cultural institutions and other smaller arts events, but one of Serena's favorite outings was to a local soup kitchen. There she rolled up her sleeves, tucked her lovely ringlets inside a baseball cap, and from behind the counter, served homeless men and women.

She searched every face. Always looking for her birth mother, hopeful that she was now sober, clean, and enjoying a happy and productive life. That was her fervent wish, but she was fearful that instead she had slid further down the social scale to a place where she was powerless to claw her way back to some kind of normalcy.

"Please God, let my birth mother, Kathleen, be okay. Give me a sign that she is alive and well."

With a silent prayer, Serena blessed every woman she served across the counter. She stared deep into their eyes and, even though they often snatched their dirty hands away, as she handed over the hot bowl of soup, she would offer a small brush of her hand to signify a kinship.

"You are someone's mother, or daughter, or sister or wife," she would remind them in a soft voice filled with love. "Please know that those loved ones are very likely sending out prayers and lighting candles for you. You are not forgotten."

Serena walked at a brisk pace through the streets of New York. She found a rhythm and paced her footsteps to match the words of her favorite prayer. She had found the words on a pamphlet from Alcoholics Anonymous when she researched information on ways an alcoholic person could begin to recover.

"God, grant me the serenity to accept the things I cannot change, courage to change the things I can, and the wisdom to know the difference."

Serena had never identified her friend Monique as one with a drink or drug problem. Monique did not live on the streets and she never went to jail, thanks to her parents who had got her the best lawyer money could buy when she got her second traffic violation for driving under the influence. She had not lost jobs or homes and did not show up as a patient on a regular basis at hospital emergency departments.

Except on the night of her death. Monique had been taken unwell at a nightclub and friends placed her in their car while they went onto another club. She was unconscious when they returned hours later.

Serena wondered whether Monique could have been saved if she had a more purposeful lifestyle. She had never had a "proper" job or pursued any career. Her parents funded her and her boyfriends were usually other rich trust fund babies, who had no responsibilities and no real purpose except to party and dress in the latest fashions and be seen in the right places.

Monique's family clamed that she didn't do drugs. At this early stage, with her body not yet buried, they did not know or want to admit that she drank too much, used cocaine, and relied on diet pills to keep her weight down.

By the time she reached her mother's apartment, Serena had allowed herself to process some of the grief she felt for her friend and to see with a fresh eye signs that she had ignored for years.

Maria, who had treated Monique like a second daughter, immediately telephoned the family and offered her services to do anything they required in the midst of their tragedy. As soon as the date and time was set for the funeral, she and Serena would travel to Miami.

Serena's career had taken her from the highly popular morning television show to an anchor position on the highest rated evening magazine program, and because her fans could not get enough of her, the network additionally periodically scheduled series of high-profile interviews with celebrity guests. With each promotion came more money, more fame, and more exposure.

Serena Perez was acknowledged to be one of the highest paid women ever in national television and when another powerhouse woman presenter opened her own television network, Serena was offered an executive consultant title and on-screen specials.

Having it all still appeared to come easy to Serena, but as she liked to say, "The harder I work, the luckier I get," but there was no doubting the phenomenal success of her career and the effortless grace with which she was perceived to accept her role in the spotlight.

The publicity machine reveled in her charmed upbringing with rich parents, a Miami Beach lifestyle, and her teenage career as a pop sensation.

Her star-crossed love affair with Karl and his fatal accident at the height of their engagement still endowed her with the persona of a tragic heroine, especially as she had never publicly had another relationship in the decade since his death.

Serena was a beautiful and passionate female, but despite the occasional one-night stand and a couple of brief flings since Karl died, there were no relationships though many men would have liked to claim her for their own. Privately she admonished herself for a morbid compulsion to wait at the altar for the love of her life to return from the dead.

No real man could measure up to the memory of her beloved.

"Better to have loved and lost than never have to have loved at all," she believed.

*   *   *

Monique's funeral was held at the historic Gesu Catholic Church in downtown Miami, a French Empire domed building opened in 1896, resplendent with gilt statues, colorful paintings, and glittering chandeliers.

In recognition of her family's impressive connections in

local politics and business ventures where they participated in the restoration of the downtown area and helped establish the city as a world-class arts and cultural destination, over five hundred people attended the ceremony, led by the mayor and local dignitaries.

After the funeral mass, a breakfast was held at the gloriously restored First National Building, with its bronze flamingo, palm tree elevators, and vaults; a popular wedding and events venue that had previously been a banking house.

There was still an old black and white photograph of the then Bank President who stood with a wheelbarrow full of money offering funds back to customers who were panicked during the crash of 1929. Like a scene from the classic James Stewart movie, *It's a Wonderful Life,* he had promised that the doors would not close until everyone had withdrawn what they wanted from their accounts. The bank was the only one in the city to survive the crisis.

Serena and her mother Maria had places of honor alongside the family members and although a limousine was offered, they chose to walk the few streets to the famed Banking Hall.

Many people came to pay their respects to Maria and offer condolences to Serena, who had lost her best childhood friend.

"May I introduce you to Dr. Eduardo Vasquez?" said one of the other guests, who noticed that Serena was standing alone.

Serena took a deep breath; it was foolish of her to think she could get any peace or privacy in this crowded environment. Even in the somber surroundings of a funeral break-fast, there were still people whose primary purpose was to make business and social connections.

She raised her eyes and extended her hand. Serena was ready to politely acknowledge the individual before her and then flee.

Dr. Eduardo Vasquez, a well-known doctor from the island of Cuba, was a poster boy for doctors and it was no surprise to learn that he had featured in a reality television series about celebrity doctors.

Devastatingly handsome, he was a silver fox, old enough to be her father, but he exuded style, refinement, and afflu-ence from the immaculately styled steel gray hair to the dark, well-defined eyebrows, well-proportioned nose, laugh-ter lines, and a smile full of reassurance. His clear brown eyes were fearless.

He was dressed in a midnight blue suit, so well-tailored its angles were almost architectural, a white stiffened cut-away collar, and sky blue silk tie with gold and white stripes, and a perfectly proportioned medium knot at the neck. White cuffs showed below his jacket sleeves and his shoes were black patent.

Serena observed his hands, long pianist fingers, shaped and manicured nails.

Embarrassed, she looked away, she blushed at the thought that she had actually, in the very first moment of meeting, imagined herself in a passionate kiss with this stranger. Dr. Eduardo Vasquez sure had perfected his bed-side manner.

Don't dare go there, Serena told herself, you are moving

way too fast. Not since she had met Karl had she felt such instant attraction.

"May I call you, Serena?" asked the doctor, "I feel as if I already know you. But of course I suppose everyone says that."

So lost in wonder was she as she gazed at the beautiful stranger, she did not notice that they had been joined by another funeral attendee, a family member of Monique's.

"Do you know Dr. Vasquez?" asked Serena, glad of a moment to collect her thoughts and aware of being seen to do the right thing in introducing the pair.

With a venom she had not expected, Monique's relative looked contemptuously at Dr. Vasquez.

"I know him alright, she said, and stressed every syllable. "D-o-c-t-o-r Eduardo Vazquez. One of Miami's notorious 'drug dealers in white coats.'"

CHAPTER THIRTY-ONE

Heart Wide Open

The smile was fixed on Dr. Vasquez's beautifully sculpted face but it disappeared from his eyes.

"My condolences," he said with a bow of his head to Monique's aunt and turned to Serena as he enquired, "May I call you?"

Serena wanted desperately to say "yes," but was also conscious that she did not wish to be disloyal to her dead friend, or to appear too eager. She indicated her acquiescence with a slight nod of her head and the doctor turned on his heel and walked away across the packed function room.

Monique's aunt was unrepentant. "People like him should be in jail," she told Serena as she launched into a tirade.

"They peddle their prescription pills to vulnerable people: pain medication, stimulants, diet pills, sleeping pills, antidepression drugs. Just because they call them 'patients' doesn't mean these doctors provide medical services. They sell the prescription drugs right out of their fancy offices and don't care what harm they are doing. They destroy lives and users and abusers like Monique die all the time.

"Just because doctors with letters after their names don't stand on a street corner peddling drugs, doesn't make them better than regular pushers. They should call their patients by their real name; they are 'victims' and the doctors who prey on them are 'drug dealers in white coats.'"

In her years of growing up in Miami Beach, Serena had largely allied herself with the glamorous image of high-profile celebrities, free-spending millionaires, Art Deco-style, waterfront mansions, hot fashion, model photo shoots, and the vacation destination that called itself "the coolest sixteen blocks on the planet."

It was no secret that Monique ran with a faster crowd; the club kids who drove speed-freak cars, partied all night, and lived on the edge of the seedy, degenerate, a little out of control, a little dangerous, tropical, "anything goes" culture.

Now she was dead, and although her family had previously claimed that Monique was not a drug user, if her aunt was to be believed, the cause of her death should rest at the door of prescription drugs; albeit without taking into consideration the large amounts of a cocktail of recreational drugs which included cocaine and alcohol, mainly champagne, she had consumed on the day of her death. All of that and now in addition they had learned about the chemical stimulant *"bath salts."*

"I am very sorry about Monique," Serena said. "She was a wonderful person, a very important part of my life. We had a lot of fun together. Please let me know if there is anything I can do to help."

Monique's aunt shrugged and her eyes filled with tears. "She leaves a dark hole in my soul," she said, swallowing a sob.

"A light has gone out in our lives."

Serena reached out and hugged the distraught woman. There were no words to console her. "Stay in touch, please," Serena told her, knowing it would not happen. "Don't be a stranger."

Helpless and at a loss to alleviate the deep pain of grief, Serena took her leave.

For a moment she experienced déjà vu as she remembered the troubled faces of concerned, uncomfortable people in the receiving line at Karl's funeral. Although words were inadequate, they had so wanted to express their sadness and share feelings of sympathy and empathy.

Serena smoothed down the skirt of her black Armani two-piece suit and moved quickly through the crowd, she averted her eyes so as not to attract attention or invite interruption to her selected exit path.

She sought out her mother who was engaged in conversation with a small group of women Serena vaguely recognized as Miami Beach "Ladies who Lunch"; she acknowledged all of them with one dazzling celebrity smile and quietly told her mother, "I need to get out of here. Now, please."

"Not a problem," said Maria. "The driver is outside, ready whenever you need him."

"Please excuse us, ladies," said Maria to her friends. "So good to see you all—hopefully next time we will meet under happier circumstances."

Monique's family were stationed at the large double doorway that led out of the function room. Serena and Maria respectfully said their goodbyes. As she walked away,

Monique's aunt called after her, "Don't forget what I told you. Do not be fooled."

Maria gave her a quizzical look and Serena explained, "Later. I'll tell you later."

Arm in arm they walked down the carved staircase, and outside to the downtown street where the chauffeur held open the rear passenger door of the hired limousine. The driver, Carlos, was an old faithful who had driven the family for years; he had been her husband Humberto's private chauffeur.

Since Maria's full-time move to New York, he had taken a job on the staff of a limo service, but was always more than ready to respond to a call from his favorite clients. Maria kept her custom-painted ice-blue BMW with the personalized number plate at her luxury condo building on Collins Avenue and Carlos took care of her car. He drove and serviced it to ensure it stayed in good condition.

Maria instructed Carlos, "We are going home, thank you. I will let you know whether we require you to take us to the airport for our return trip to New York."

In the car, Serena told her mother, "I'd like to stay in Miami Beach for a few days, if that's okay with you. Sun and sand appeal right now. I can always stay alone if your schedule doesn't allow you to take time out."

Maria was in no hurry to return to New York; she had checked the weather reports that morning: Miami 84 degrees sunny, New York 54 degrees rain. No contest.

"We can stay together," said Maria. "The housekeeper has opened up the house. I'm happy to stay. I can make a few phone calls when I get home. Always remember, no one is indispensible. If I'm not there, they will soon get someone to take my place. What about you?"

Serena shecked her diary and answered, "I pretty much cleared the decks. I didn't know how long I would want to stay or if I might be needed, not that I can help Monique in any way."

Maria challenged her daughter, "*What* was all that about with her aunt? '*Do not be fooled.*' It sounded like a warning."

As best she could, Serena attempted to explain: "The whole family is desperate to come to terms with their loss and determined to find someone to blame for Monique's death. They crave closure. Truth is they do not want to believe that she took the substances that killed her. She always was a bit of a risk taker. Not like me. I was the scaredy-cat. Too frightened of the consequences."

Maria patted her daughter's hand. "You were always a good girl."

"Well, I can't imagine me taking '*bath salts*' to get high."

The two did not want to make a joke out of the circumstances of Monique's death, but they were so unfamiliar with the drug scene that the whole idea did sound pretty unbelievable.

"Addiction is a terrible disease," Serena said and then quickly closed the subject before being tempted to make any comments about her own biological mother or the effects of alcoholism and addiction on that sad life.

Silently she sent out her constant prayer, "Please, God, let her be okay."

On the journey through afternoon rush-hour traffic from downtown, Maria leaned forward to speak to Carlos,

"Take the Venetian Causeway across the Bay, and drive past the old house."

Serena looked at her mother, "Are you sure?"

"Yes, it's no bad thing to be reminded. We must never forget all the good memories as well as the sad ones," said Maria. "Life goes on. We know that. I still miss your father and it's no surprise that I've never been able to find myself another husband who could replace him, but it doesn't hurt anymore. Well, not too much. Time does heal."

Serena blinked away a tear and turned her attention to concentrate as she looked out of the car window. "I know," she said with a heartfelt sigh that seemed to reverberate right through her body. "Time does heal."

* * *

Serena set to work and made a series of beauty appointments at her favorite spa, The Standard on Venetian Causeway. With time to spend and money no object, Serena loved to indulge in the signature hot stones massage, the exotic Hassam room baths, the outdoor mud baths, and the invigorating hot waterfall splash pool.

In New York her beauty maintenance regime was always conducted at top speed because she had so many time constraints, but now on her last-minute mini vacation, she had promised herself time to enjoy all the pampering and special treatments. She particularly wanted to experience the hot stone massage in the Haman hot and cold therapy room and the blue body detox and sea clay mineral soak.

"I'm going to spend the day at the Standard Spa," Serena called out to her mother who was stretched out in a recliner on the balcony overlooking the ocean, reading a book.

"Can I drive your car or do you want me to take a taxi?"

"Take the car," said Maria, "but don't forget to validate the ticket otherwise it costs a fortune to valet park."

Serena drove to the spa, a waterfront hotel on Biscayne Bay in sight of the drawbridge which opened every fifteen minutes to allow boats and water traffic to pass. She made a right into the driveway of what had been the old Lido Spa, a Miami Beach landmark hotel for over fifty years, now called The Standard, with its quirky marketing gimmick of printing the name of the hotel upside down.

She handed the keys of her mother's BMW to the valet and walked through the lobby of the hotel toward the elevator that went directly to the treatment suite. Before she followed directions and turned it off for the duration of her spa experience, Serena checked her phone for messages.

Doctor Eduardo Vasquez had called and left a voicemail.

Serena had expected the call.

In a small city like Miami Beach, she had known it would not be long before he tracked her down. Both high profile, they had many mutual friends and acquaintances.

The message was precise and polite, his voice attractive and yet professional.

Serena replayed it. "Dr. Vasquez here, Serena. It was a pleasure to meet you yesterday. I have long admired your television appearances and your mother is a generous donor to one of the hospitals where I am on the staff.

"You indicated it would be in order for me to contact you and I have an invitation that I hope you will choose to accept. The Miami City Ballet open their season tomorrow with a performance of *West Side Story*. Despite the short notice, I hope you will agree to join myself and my other guests at the welcoming cocktail party. If you are available, please let me know and I will arrange to have you collected and brought to the event by my driver.

"Of course, we would be delighted also to welcome your mother, so please let me know whether you can make it.

"Bye, have a great day."

One more time, Serena played the message. The sound of his voice was seductive and she felt a powerful attraction, just as she had at their first meeting.

She certainly could make it. No, she did not need mother as a chaperone but it was a sweet thought. If a little calculated.

Excited and eager to call back immediately, Serena instead played it cool.

She clicked the phone to "off," she walked into the elevator.

Ahead lay the serious business of luxurious beauty preparations and a meditation on what to wear for the event she thought of as their first date.

Serena smiled. Dr. Eduardo Vasquez certainly knew how to attract a girl's attention. *One meeting, one phone call, not to mention one dead friend, and I am hooked.*

The white-coated spa attendant, a tall beautiful Asian girl with a long black braid, showed Serena to the changing area. As she emerged, the ever-watchful attendant indicated that she should leave her robe and step into the bubbling hot tub.

"You will love today's special aqua healing experience,"

she told Serena. "Give yourself over to the wonderful combination of detoxifying bitter orange, ginger, and the purification of perfumed sweet vine roses in our exclusive blend of health giving *bath salts.*"

CHAPTER THIRTY-TWO

Feels Like Love

"Mother, PLEASE, help me," Serena called out, her hysterical high-pitched tone, full of drama and angst and a demand for immediate attention. "I'm going mad. You need to help me NOW."

Maria turned down the volume on the early-evening news, gently lifted her white Bichon Frise puppy, Carmen, from her lap and laid her beside her equally snow white and fluffy brother, Hortez. The two immediately snuggled up together on the squashy couch in the all-white lounge of the Miami Beach Oceanside apartment. She was glad she had heeded popular wisdom and bought two of the lively, sociable little dogs; they were best friends and did keep each other company.

"Sorry, babies," she said, "closet emergency."

Serena had been acting as excitable as a teenager ever since she had returned the call that confirmed she would be the guest of Eduardo Vasquez at the exclusive black-tie gala event at the world-class Miami Center for the Performing Arts.

Festivities were to include the elegant cocktail reception

at the start of the evening and dinner and dancing after the performance.

The fact that the top tickets would cost Dr. Vasquez at least a thousand dollars per guest did not faze Serena. High-profile events and charity fundraisers were a well-practiced part of the public relations of her job.

As a national television celebrity, Serena's appearance at red carpet events and glittering social occasions assured the host organizations of a higher capacity attendance and more money-raising opportunities. Gold-embossed invitation cards lined the shelves of her office bookcase at the studio in New York City, and her personal assistant was polite but firm, as at least once every day she turned down a request for Serena's attendance at charitable events. She had to cherry pick those she was able to attend and carefully choose the organizations she supported. Charities generally held auctions and to help raise money, Serena's office sent network-merchandising items: complimentary tickets to TV shows, T-shirts, mugs, books, videos, or autographed photographs to be raffled.

A professional "meet and greet" she could do effortlessly, but this situation was different. This was personal. Initially, Serena had felt reassured by the invitation to attend the gala as just another guest of a rich man who bought influence and social status with extravagant public gestures. After all, he had invited her mother too, though Maria had enough black-tie events in her own diary to ensure she would decline.

Serena had even begun to doubt herself and ask herself if it was a date. Perhaps she had read more into the invitation than was intended. There was nothing to suggest he was not the same as so many other movers and shakers who constantly social climb and make an art form of collecting celebrities to enhance their own professional and personal standing.

"MOTHER," she called out again, "I'm almost out of time."

Maria entered the master bedroom with floor to ceiling windows and sleek white furnishings that Serena had claimed for her own on the day they moved into the two-bed, two-and-a-half-bath high-rise Seacoast condominium on Collins Avenue.

Serena appeared to have unloaded the entire contents of the mirrored wall-to-wall closets onto her king-size bed. The bed had disappeared under an unruly pile of dresses, long, short, and in between; dozens of pairs of shoes were scattered haphazardly across the floor and handbags and jewelry formed a crazy accessory tower.

"Has there been a robbery?" Maria asked, "Doesn't look like they took much but they made one helluva mess."

Serena rolled her eyes. "Very funny, but this is serious. What am I going to wear? I've already changed twice. I just can't find the right outfit. All my best evening clothes are in New York."

"Lucky the thieves left you some spares," Maria laughed.

"A little black dress is too safe." Serena looked to her mother for approval. "Red is too bold and glittery and feels too stand-out. White is totally out, it will look as if I've leap-frogged from first date to the wedding in one evening."

Maria was amused by her daughter's obvious panic, but

careful not to smile or be dismissive. Serena was usually totally accomplished in social settings and, although she loved clothes, her main object was to look good and be appropriately dressed for the occasion.

This lack of confidence obviously betrayed a deeper anxiety about the entire situation. Since Karl, she had shown little interest in having any serious relationship and Maria worried that her own acceptance of her single status after the death of her husband had given Serena the justification for not trying to find someone with whom to share her life.

"You're a young woman, and a beautiful and talented one," Maria told her daughter. "You have so much to offer and a loving relationship could enhance your life. Don't dismiss men before you've even got to know them. Give them a chance. It's doesn't always have to be love at first sight."

Serena gave her mother an amused look and teased her, "Oh, yes, that's rich coming from you. A teenage violet seller in the local carnival when you fell in love with the ringmaster in his top hat—even though he was nearly twenty years older than you."

The memory even now nearly forty years later always brought a smile to Maria's face and she could not deny that she'd had a monumental crush on her handsome husband from the day she first laid eyes on him.

"How old did you say this doctor is?" Maria asked.

"About fifty," laughed Serena.

"Ancient," said Maria. "Perhaps I should go on the date instead of you."

"Hands off," Serena warned. "If he doesn't live up to expectations, I might throw him in your direction but for now I'll check him out. And if it all leads to a happy ever after, you can join your boastful female friends and brag about, 'my son-in-law, the doctor.'"

Maria was shocked to hear her daughter so obviously enamored by a man she had only just met and, at that, a much older one. She worried whether in the absence of any suitable men of her own age, Serena had decided to settle for the perceived security of a father figure.

However, this was not the time for deep psychological discussions about motivations and desires; the car coming to collect Serena would be here soon, and the immediate decision was what dress to wear.

"Did you consider the beige vintage Halston?" Maria asked, in an effort to be helpful and talking to her daughter's back as she stared into a wall mirror, where she critically examined her hair and makeup; both had been professionally done that afternoon by a friend of Serena's, a well-known makeup artist from the Glam Squad who had been happy to make a house call to her famous client and work her magic.

"I was suggesting the vintage Halston," Maria reiterated.

Serena was dismissive. She shook her head. "Too safe. I need the 'wow factor' and I know just how to get it. Cavalli, silk animal print."

Maria zipped her daughter into the figure-hugging strapless goddess gown; her size two figure and shining healthy eyes, teeth, and complexion showed off the dress to perfection. Her statuesque beauty and a pair of towering bronze high heels ensured she would stand head and shoulders above most women, and many of the men.

To dazzle but not overpower, she kept her jewelry classy but real—gold diamond-studded hooped earrings twinkled through her shiny long black curly hair and on her wrist a slim diamond bracelet. Serena still wore the supersize diamond engagement ring that Karl had given her a decade ago but Maria noted that tonight she was wearing it on her right hand. A small gold clutch held her phone, lipstick, mirror, and a credit card.

"You are gorgeous," Maria told her proudly.

"You always say that, Mother," Serena laughed, "but you're biased."

"Do you think I would have chosen anyone other than the most beautiful baby in the nursery?" asked Maria in a rare private joke about Serena's origins.

"No, because you planned to pass me off as your own," Serena retorted a little sharply, but there was only love in the look she gave her mother.

The house phone rang and Maria walked toward the small console table by the front door to answer it. The two dogs who had been asleep in the lounge jumped up and barked at the phone.

"Car for Miss Serena, main entrance," said the concierge.

"Thank you, she'll be right down," Maria told him.

Maria shooed the dogs away, as they attempted to weave their way around Serena's floor-length dress.

Maria could not resist one last compliment to her beloved daughter.

"You certainly know how to dress to impress," she said.

"I just hope he proves to be worthy of you. Remember, not everything is what it seems."

*   *   *

A chauffeur-driven, gleaming red Bentley Continental convertible, list price over $200,000, awaited Serena and she was relieved to note that the top was up. Much as she loved the breeze in her hair while driving on the causeway between Miami Beach and Miami, she had not spent all afternoon creating the picture-perfect effect with her hair and makeup to arrive at the black tie event windswept.

Eduardo had been at the top of the stairs as he greeted guests, but he swiftly made his way down the polished marble staircase as Serena arrived. A feeling of pure delight came over her when she saw him and her heart leapt with excitement. *Was this how her teenage mother had felt when she saw her father, the ringmaster, in his top hat?* She smiled.

Even the most ordinary-looking men enhance their appearance when they wear a tuxedo, but Eduardo in a tuxedo looked like a movie star.

He opened her door before the driver could exit and make his way around the vehicle.

Eduardo extended his hand to Serena and helped her from the car. Their eyes locked and held. Their smiles mirrored each other and both knew they already shared a secret.

Eduardo escorted Serena up the staircase and together they walked the red carpet hand in hand into the exquisitely decorated ballroom.

Invited guests, beautiful, expensively attired people,

completely at home in the luxurious surroundings, shared an evening shimmering with glitz and glamour. The spectacular affair included a stylish cocktail party, first-class entertainment, and the finest selection of gourmet food and wine from a star-studded cast of Miami celebrity chefs.

As always, Serena chose the vegetarian option and was glad to note that Eduardo did the same. They sipped sparkling champagne from crystal flutes and nibbled on bitter black chocolate petit fours.

The official opening of the cultural season was declared a "dazzling success."

With perfect ease, Serena charmed Eduardo's other VIP guests as they sat at the glittering table settings, bathed in candlelight, and enchanted by the sky-high table decorations. Members of the audience discreetly acknowledged that they had a star in their midst, and went so far as to give Miss Perez a round of applause when the Master of Ceremonies thanked her for gracing them with her presence.

It came as no surprise that her celebrity status attracted attention, but tonight Serena felt a new vitality and vibrancy as she sparkled in the spotlight.

Eduardo beamed at her and she shone even brighter. Not since her concert-rocking days with Karl by her side had she felt so complete. Serena felt joy in her heart and, with a sudden realization, she admitted what she had denied for so long. "Karl died and I refused to live. I went through the motions. Now I have come back to life. I am ready to love. I am ready to love Eduardo."

The heady pleasure of the evening worked its magic and bathed Eduardo and Serena in a mysterious light of love.

Before the night was over, they appeared to have transformed into a couple. Treading sedately down the marble staircase on their way out of the concert hall, Serena almost expected to hear the clock strike midnight. Be careful you don't lose your shoe, she warned herself silently.

The red Bentley was waiting curbside and Eduardo indicated to the driver that he should settle Serena in the car.

He excused himself and walked purposefully in the direction of a fellow guest who beckoned to him. The two conducted a low level but apparently heated discussion.

Eduardo came back to the car and, as he eased into the rear seat alongside Serena, the man in the tuxedo approached, and placed his hands on the half-raised window. He leaned into the car.

His manner was menacing and his voice angry as he told Eduardo, "Call yourself a doctor? You won't get away with it. You killed that girl."

CHAPTER THIRTY-THREE

Eyes Wide Open

"Take me home, immediately," Serena demanded of Eduardo.

Deliberately distancing herself, she moved away to the far side of the cream leather seat and silently stared out of the window, she held tightly onto the clutch bag on her lap as if he might steal it.

"Don't touch me," she said in a quiet but firm tone, as he reached out to hold her hand. "That man accused you of being a murderer. My friend Monique's aunt called you a 'drug dealer in a white coat.' Please don't underestimate my intelligence and attempt to fob me off with some vapid explanation. I won't be made a fool of at yours or anyone else's expense."

Eduardo turned his whole body toward her, but was careful to maintain the no-go zone. He addressed her profile as she stared straight ahead and he asked, "Please, this is extremely important to me. Will you at least give me the benefit of the doubt for just a few days until I am able to tell you the whole story?"

Serena allowed herself a quick sideways glance to see if she could judge his sincerity. Why should she trust him? She didn't know him from Adam. She owed him no loyalty—that belonged to her childhood friend Monique—and yet she wanted to believe him, she wanted to allow him his explanation. How could she be so conflicted? On the one hand she truly thought she had fallen in love at first sight with this mature, charming, and handsome man. On the other she sensed dangerous intent in the charges that were being leveled against him.

Shivering in the cool air conditioning of the car interior, Serena wished she had brought more than a flimsy silk scarf to cover her shoulders. A deep icy uncertainty threatened to overwhelm her and she was embarrassed that she might begin to cry.

"Just take me home," she said. "Let me think it over. I can't make sense of it now. I'm too tired."

Serena was shocked to find that she wanted nothing more than to rest her head on Eduardo's shoulder and to be held until all the bad feelings and doubts and fears faded away.

She was determined to resist what she knew would be a totally inappropriate reaction. The drive home was mercifully short, midnight traffic was light even on the tourist thoroughfare of Collins Avenue.

The Bentley came to a sleek stop by the valet station at her building, the driver jumped out of his seat at double-quick speed and opened Eduardo's door first, he then walked quickly around behind the vehicle to open Serena's door. Eduardo helped her out and, although she allowed him to take her hand, the spark had cooled.

"My friend is not staying," she pointedly told the valet who waited to direct the driver of the car to a parking space.

The doorman held the door open, inward to the lobby of the building, as Serena walked up the short flight of steps, Eduardo a step behind her. He did not rush to keep up but was obviously not used to being left behind.

At the door she turned and said politely, "Thank you for a lovely evening. Goodnight."

Eduardo leaned toward her and managed to brush her cheek with his lips before he said. "My pleasure entirely. Do I have your permission to call you in a couple of days?"

Serena nodded an almost imperceptible "Yes."

"Thank you, I am most relieved," he said with a smile.

One last look passed between them as Serena acknowledged the doorman who still held open the door and she walked quickly across the marble lobby toward the elevators. Her heels click-clacked, and her long skirt swished the floor.

Eduardo watched her go, even as the doorman closed the glass screen to indicate that it was time for him to leave. Relieved, he bounded down the stairs and jumped into the front passenger seat of his car. The driver had already activated the mechanics and opened up the convertible top.

Eduardo made himself comfortable; he unknotted the necktie, left it loose under the collar and undid a couple of buttons on his shirt. He relaxed back in the seat and stretched out his long legs.

"Home to the Island so I can change out of the waiter outfit," he laughingly told the driver who was a close friend as well as being an employee. "Then leave the car, I'll drive myself."

The summertime tropical temperature was still in the seventies and Eduardo was far from ready to finish the night.

"Doctor's orders," he said with a wink. "I need some action. Drugs, sex, and rock 'n' roll. Bring it on, I'm ready to party."

He reclined with a satisfied smile on his face, Dr. Vasquez congratulated himself: his grand plan for the gorgeous television star Miss Serena Perez was underway and, despite two unfortunate confrontations, he was confident he could complete the mission.

His professional reputation was desperately in need of a rebrand and being the husband of an A-list celebrity was just what the doctor ordered.

Maria was waiting up for Serena, anxious to hear all about the event. She had a list of questions. Who was there? What did they wear? What did you eat? Did anyone ask for me?

"I promise to tell you all about it," Serena told her. "Just let me get out of my glad rags. And yes, the dress was a sensation."

Serena slipped out of her glamorous clothing and laid everything she had been wearing on a small table at the entrance to the changing room in her en-suite bathroom. Thankfully, the maid had cleared the closet disaster of earlier in the evening and all items had been returned to hangers, with shoes, bags, and accessories stored in their see-through boxes which featured color photographs showing the contents.

Tonight's outfit would be checked and cleaned before being put away by the maid; dresses and wraps would be examined for tears, stains, marks, unstitched seams, loose buttons, or stray threads; shoes scrutinized for scuffs; bags looked over for scratches or marks on the lining. Serena's jewelry would be returned to the mini safe in her mother's bedroom.

"I'm in the bath Mama," Serena called out as she turned on the faucets. "Won't be long. I'll come and tell you all about my wonderful evening. You should have come. You would have enjoyed it. The ballet was breathtaking. Since the current Artistic Director took over, they've acquired some excellent young dancers."

"Serena," her mother replied, "how many times do I have to tell you that I can't hear what you are saying when the water is running?"

As she removed her makeup and brushed her hair, Serena heard the click as her phone rang and went straight to voicemail.

Not able to resist the temptation to listen, Serena closed the bathroom door and checked the message. Just as she thought: Dr. Eduardo Vasquez.

His deep, cultured voice made Serena quiver inside.

"Please forgive me," he said apologetically. "Two days is far too long. I can't get you out of my mind. I can't sleep. When I lie down and close my eyes I see a picture of you.

"Thank you for this evening. You have bedazzled me, Miss Serena, I am under your spell. Please say you feel it, too. Please say we can meet again, soon. Goodnight, sleep tight."

Serena wanted to play the message again but decided to wait till she too was in bed.

For a mad moment she considered whether to let her mother hear it, but thought better of it. It was the kind of girly experience that she could have shared with Monique, but not with her mother. No, she would need to be very careful what she told her mother. Edited highlights only.

Loving the long-forgotten giddy experience of a new romance, Serena longed to luxuriate in her steaming hot bath.

Selecting a pretty butterfly clip to anchor her long hair on the top of her head, she exposed her naked body as she dropped her fluffy white towel onto the Italian marble floor and stretched across to reach the multicolored glass jars, perfectly arranged and spaced on the tiered mirrored shelving.

Releasing the free-flowing perfumed powder into the misty water, Serena stepped into a sweet-smelling sea of foaming bath salts.

Light-filled bubbles covered her body and she lay back, eyes closed, lost in a dream.

How did this happen? she wondered. My life was wonderful. I was happy and content, which I never thought I could be after Karl's death. I had everything I desired: a stellar career, enormous success, fame, fortune, friends, good works to keep me occupied, and the freedom to go wherever I wanted whenever I wanted. Even if half the time there was a television crew in tow filming the experience.

Now I am in over my head. Drowning in a sea of dancing bubbles, slipping below the waves, floating in the ocean, below the water, sinking, sinking, sinking....

CHAPTER THIRTY-FOUR

Tell It Like It Is

Serena was under the influence of a powerful drug. A love drug. She refused to eat, was having difficulty sleeping, and planned her whole day around the times when she could indulge in her newfound passion. The object of her desire had priority over all other areas of her life.

Maria was forced to stand by and watch helplessly as Serena fell more and more under the spell of Dr. Eduardo Vasquez.

Alerted on the night of that first date, when she had followed her intuition that something was wrong and found Serena almost totally submerged in the rapidly cooling bath water, Maria had been standing by to rescue Serena.

Serena had refused to accept that there was a problem.

"I thought you would be happy for me," she had said petulantly, behaving more like a teenager than she ever had even when she was one. "We are in love."

Eduardo, it was claimed, could sweet talk an alligator into donating his skin to make a pair of handmade shoes. His easy charm and flirtatious manner ensured that well-heeled patients returned again and again to his luxurious medical suite in one of the high-rise oceanfront buildings close to the exclusive designer shopping enclave at Bal Harbour.

Before she agreed to embark on a relationship with Eduardo, Serena insisted that he tell her what could have possessed two individuals to suggest that he was guilty of killing his patients.

Serena stated her position. "If you care anything for me, you will not drag me into anything illegal, sordid, or life threatening,"

To honor Monique's memory she must know what provoked the venom against him. For her own peace of mind, Serena demanded that Eduardo provide her with an explanation for the accusations that had been leveled at him. However, she had to admit that she was more than willing to hear what he wanted her to hear.

Their "serious discussion" comprised primarily of Eduardo's insistence that he had done nothing wrong; there was an ongoing investigation with the Drug Enforcement Agency cracking down on unscrupulous doctors who provided patients with prescription drugs sold direct from their offices; the DEA had switched their area of interest from the South American drug cartels to home-grown doctors but no charges had been brought against Eduardo.

Voice raised in indignation, Eduardo defended himself.

"The cartels who sell cocaine and crystal meth are so powerful that the enforcement agencies, who have lost the war against drugs coming into the country, are now going after soft targets like primary-care doctors who are trying to alleviate the suffering of their patients.

"We're talking prescription drugs—not illegal drugs. I'm no pusher. I am a doctor. I honor the Hippocratic Oath, 'Do No Harm.'"

Serena felt herself in sympathy with him.

"Patients do misuse prescription pills," he admitted. "The doctor prescribes to treat the symptoms, but we can't be there every minute to ensure that medications are taken responsibly in accordance with instructions. Many patients use multiple doctors to ensure they get extra supplies of their drug of choice."

Serena interrupted him, "What happened to Monique? Did you prescribe deadly bath salts for her?"

Eduardo looked as if he were about to laugh and Serena promised herself that if he did, she would walk out.

"No, I assure you, I did not prescribe 'bath salts' for your friend. They are 'club drugs.' I don't know where she obtained it, but I can tell you that she had a cocktail of drugs in her body when she was taken to the hospital unconscious and died.

"Please understand that because of patient confidentiality, even though she is now dead, I cannot tell you what I did prescribe," he said in a serious voice.

"Of course her family are distraught," he continued, "They want to blame someone. Families never want to believe that the dead person took actions that led directly to such tragic consequences."

Serena and Eduardo sat close together at the small breakfast table beside the infinity pool at his Flame Island mansion. On the western horizon a spectacular sunset played out its nightly ritual as it sprayed blood red splashes across the magenta sky.

Eduardo ran a manicured hand through his perfectly styled steel gray hairstyle. He looked like a male fashion model in an up-scale catalog, selling cruises or outrageously expensive time shares.

Casually dressed, he still turned heads. Especially Serena's. His white shirt and beige slacks were pressed to within an inch of their lives; he wore tan-colored Gucci loafers without socks and a matching leather belt with the entwined gold double GG.

An ostentatious Patek Philippe watch was his only jewelry apart from a discreet signet ring with a diamond, which he wore on the little finger of his right hand.

Serena studied the new man for whom she already felt such affinity. She endeavored to judge his sincerity and form an opinion as to whether he had done enough to win her trust.

Eduardo preempted her. "You have just come into my life and I don't want to lose you," he said, "but I will not have my integrity challenged. I've been a doctor for almost as long as you have been alive. My profession is sacred to me, I am proud of the good I have been able to achieve in the world.

"If you doubt me, then this relationship is over, before it has begun. We cannot operate from a place of mistrust. My reputation is my most valuable possession.

"Serena, if we are to go forward, you need to make a decision."

Serena was taken aback at the finality in his voice; she fiddled self-consciously with the skirt of the light yellow summer dress she was wearing over her white two-piece bathing suit. She twisted her hair and left it hanging in a single braid over her left shoulder.

His appeal moved her; she chose to believe that he was a good man. "I want to go forward," she said, and refused to hold back as she felt herself getting lost in the deep brown pools of his eyes.

Eduardo let out a sigh and angled his body toward hers. They fell into a deep passionate kiss. The deal was sealed.

*   *   *

"No one could blame you for wanting to stay in the Sunshine State, especially with the brutal weather up here, but you are missed. When will you be back?" the station manager asked Serena.

His tone was jovial and polite; after all, she was one of the biggest stars the network had produced, but many others were also asking the question and they expected him to have an answer.

"Difficult to say," Serena admitted. "I just need a little more time. Say one more week then I'll come back to the show."

Her mother had returned full time to New York months before, but Serena refused to be parted from Eduardo for more than a few days at a time. She had cut back on her on screen appearances so she could stay in Miami with him. Not that she had admitted that when confronted by the only female vice-president who ran a major network. Carlita, a beautiful blonde South American in her midthirties, had been hugely successful at the network, she had dramatically increased audience figures and advertiser ratings.

Carlita and Serena got along well and enjoyed tremendous mutual respect, but Serena knew that the longer she was not "on air," the more likely her hard won popularity would lose ground and the audience loyalty would transfer to another presenter—or, more dangerously, another television station.

Carlita would swim naked in shark-infested waters before she would relinquish her power position and the ratings war for her flagship evening magazine program on the fastest-growing television network in America.

"Don't apologize for making me fly all the way to Miami, I love it here," said Carlita graciously, as she and Serena settled themselves for lunch at the famous Fontainebleau Hotel restaurant, which had been immortalized in the opening credits of the James Bond movie *Goldfinger* and was the hangout of fifties rat-packers Frank Sinatra, Dean Martin, and Sammy Davis; more recently it had undergone a multimillion-dollar renovation and the hottest stars of stage, screen, and television still enjoyed seeing and being seen at the poolside.

Serena made Carlita laugh as she told her the story of the first owner, Ben Novack, who when his architect, Morris Lapidus, asked for guidance on the design of the hotel and particularly the lobby had told him, "Give me GLAMOUR, and lots of it. Make sure it reeks of luxury."

Lapidus had lived up to that instruction and had followed his own philosophy when he told his clients, "If you create a stage and it is grand, everyone who enters will play their part."

Carlita also enjoyed the story of the "grudge wall" built

by the owner of the next-door hotel, the Eden Roc. Just as he had planned with spiteful glee, the multistory windowless wall overshadowed the Fontainebleau's pool and terrace area.

"Miami never disappoints," said Carlita, "No wonder they call it a sunny place for shady people."

Serena smiled. "I thought that was Monte Carlo on the French Riviera, but it certainly applies to the wild cast of maverick characters in this city."

"Speaking of which," said Carlita, and before she could finish, Serena interrupted her and said, "Dr. Vasquez is not a maverick."

"No, I meant cast of characters," Carlita quickly countered. "What was the name of that television reality show he appeared in?"

"*Bedside Manor*," said Serena. "He's not in it anymore, didn't think it was good for his image."

Carlita risked a dig. "I heard it was unofficially known as '*The Pill Mill*.'"

Serena pursed her lips, "I never heard that, but you know what this business is like, someone is always out to undermine you. Shall we order?"

They sipped sparkling water and nibbled on minimal amounts of delicious food, over a gossipy girly lunch conducted half in English and half in Spanish, Vice President Carlita Nareiaga offered her star presenter, Serena Perez, an enticing solution to her location dilemma. Fact: her job was in New York, and the man she loved and had already set her sights on as a future husband, had his medical practice in Miami.

To fly backward and forward every week was not an option for Serena. She had tried that at an earlier stage before taking vacation time from her on-screen job. Serena was adamant that she did not want to be away from Eduardo all week.

Truth was New York had become a place of deep sadness for her. She constantly searched the faces of the women on Rockefeller Plaza and prayed that one day her birth mother would appear. She was filled with regret that she had no idea what had become of her and her pain was made all the more unbearable because there was no one to confide in. She was not able to share her personal loss with anyone. Least of all the head of the network.

The superslim, elegantly groomed, and always self-assured Carlita looked pleased with herself. "You might remember that the great sixties television star Jackie Gleason visited Miami Beach with his family and then refused to return to New York to present his national entertainment show.

"The network relocated the TV show, creative team, and entire production crew to Miami."

Serena was not slow to grasp where the conversation was going.

"If Mohammed won't come to the mountain, then the mountain will come to Mohammed.

"The President of the network has agreed—he likes to think it was all his own idea—to offer you a brand-new nationwide show, based here in Miami. *The Serena Perez Show* will have a first-class production team and a coveted spot on the evening schedule. You can work with your own creative people, some of whom have expressed an interest in coming down from New York to set up the new show and formulate an exciting new television platform for you. We ran the idea by a few people and we got a huge amount of positive feedback.

"How do you like the sound of it so far?"

"Carlita, I love it," said Serena enthusiastically. "I thought you had come down here to fire me."

Serena had spent sleepless nights as she wrestled with the dilemma of relationship versus career. On the one hand she missed the excitement of her glamorous television job and that feeling of being at the center of the action in national and world news events. On the other, she was not prepared to risk the loss of the one man she believed was a worthy replacement for her beloved Karl.

Unable to choose, she had delayed a decision as long as possible. Now the solution had been presented to her. The best of both worlds.

Bless her, Carlita was a true friend—and a shrewd operator.

The two women embraced as they waited for the limousine to take Carlita on to her next appointment and ultimately back to Miami International airport. Filled with excitement about their forthcoming plans, they shared the corporate joke, "Okay, my people will talk to your people. But let's push for an agreement here. It's a win-win situation."

The proposal surpassed any solution Serena could have hoped for and she couldn't wait to tell Eduardo.

Repeated calls to his cell phone went unanswered and Eduardo did not respond to her voicemail message for several hours. When finally they spoke, his reaction surprised and disappointed Serena.

"I was rather looking forward to a long-distance relationship," he commented. "You in New York and me 1,300 miles away in Miami." Serena remained silent. With a good-natured laugh, he added, "Only kidding. You know I can't get enough of you. You're my drug of choice."

CHAPTER THIRTY-FIVE

With This Ring

Serena needed an escort to lead her through the crowd of well-wishers as she left the New York television studios after her last scheduled appearance. Photographers and fans were out in force; they jostled for position on the famous Rockefeller Plaza.

"Thank you, thank you," Serena waved and acknowledged the loyal viewers who had turned out to wish her well. "Thank you for coming by today, I appreciate it, thank you, thank you."

Happily she signed autographs, posed for photos, and accepted gifts of flowers, cards, and cuddly toys. As she juggled with her trophies, an assistant came back and relieved her of the possibility that the gifts would drop from her overladen arms.

A camera crew filmed her exit and the on-air reporter asked for Serena's thoughts as she said goodbye to the massively popular show that had made her a national celebrity over the past decade.

Ever the professional, Serena spoke in sound bites. "It's been a fantastic journey," she said. "I had the time of my life but I don't look back with sadness, only forward with excitement. To film my new show in the Magic City, Miami, will be a challenge and I look forward to earning the degree of love and respect I have achieved on the evening show.

"I'll look out for every one of you," she said and gave one of the dazzling smiles that made her such a television favorite and, despite her huge success, portrayed her as a friendly, approachable, and caring human being. Girl next-door, high achiever, cheerleader, a deserved success. Serena addressed the camera directly and managed to make her special brand of connection with the millions of viewers of the network's highest-rated evening television show and make each one of them feel special.

"Watch out for *The Serena Perez Show* from Miami, coming soon," she said, plugging her new show and then attempted to sign off with a cheery goodbye.

The reporter wasn't finished with her questions.

"Serena, before you go, we want to congratulate you on your engagement and the upcoming wedding. Events appear to have moved at a fast pace. Why the hurry? Are your plans all in place?"

Laughing happily, Serena told the reporter and the television audience, "When you find the man you want to spend the rest of your life with—why wait? Everything is proceeding smoothly. Well, according to the wedding organizer.

"This really is my dream wedding. I feel like the luckiest girl in the world."

In a moment of unrehearsed but perfectly staged television theatrics, Serena asked, "Do you want to meet the man who has stolen my heart?"

A roar of approval went up from the crowd and Serena gestured to Eduardo, who had stood unobtrusively on the sidelines as he watched his fiancé's triumphant departure on her final show.

He didn't need to pretend to be embarrassed. He was. He had had no idea that Serena would ask him to join her in front of the camera.

Mercifully for him, his appearance was extremely brief, as the reporter was already receiving wind-up signals in her earpiece from the producer back inside the building.

Closing credits were rolling and play-out music signaled that the end of the show was over. The last shot was of Serena and Eduardo arm in arm as they waved happily to the audience in the Plaza and the viewers at home.

Out of the corner of her eye, Serena saw her. Her birth mother. Maria would be proudly watching at home, she was not likely to turn up at Rockefeller Plaza.

"Bear with me," Serena urged Eduardo. "There is someone I have to see."

Kathleen stood away from the main body of well-wishers, but her face was radiant as Serena walked toward her.

Serena also had a broad smile on her face and she immediately remarked to the woman who figured in her daily prayers and dreams, "You look well. You've had your teeth fixed."

Kathleen smiled. "Thanks for noticing."

Both women laughed. "It makes a wonderful difference," said Serena kindly. "How have you been? I've thought of you often."

Resisting an urge to reach out and stroke her face, Kathleen told her daughter, "Clean and sober six months. I have you to thank for that. You inspired me."

At that, Serena did reach out and take her mother's hand. "Well done, well done," she said. "I am so happy for you."

They stood face to face, strangers who owed each other their lives. Words were unnecessary; something of momentous importance had taken place, and both knew it.

Eduardo sent an assistant over to ask her to speed up her conversation.

"How can I get in touch with you?" Serena asked.

"I wrote down Concepta's address and her phone number, she always keeps tabs on me," Kathleen laughed and handed Serena a piece of page torn out of a mini diary.

"She meant to give you this when she came to see you, but she forgot. I think she was star struck, though she would never admit it."

Serena knew that most people got nervous and even tongue-tied when in close proximity to those who they were more used to seeing on the television screen.

"I got star struck when I met my heroine Hillary Clinton for the first time," admitted Serena. "I felt shy and my mind went blank. Not a good look when I had to interview her."

The assistant was on her way over again. "I'll be in touch," said Serena, and impulsively she leaned forward and kissed her mother on the cheek. "I am so proud of you. Keep up the good work."

Serena turned and with tears in her eyes, moved swiftly to rejoin her fiancé. Not wishing to rain on her parade,

Serena sensed that Eduardo was making a real effort to keep the irritation from his voice.

"What was all that about?" he asked.

"It's a long story and I need to tell you, but now is not the time or place. Tonight over dinner, I will tell all."

Holding firmly onto his hand, she teased, "You are going to learn a few secrets about your wife-to-be. Hope we don't shock you."

Eduardo laughed and kissed her. "I can't wait. A woman of mystery suits me fine. I may be persuaded to tell you a few secrets of my own."

*   *   *

Dinner was a quiet, intimate affair in the exquisite dining room of the Plaza Hotel. Serena had already had enough excitement for one day. The maître d' escorted the pair of lovebirds to a discreet table away from the higher traffic areas and curious but, admiring eyes of other diners.

Over dinner, Serena took her time and told her story. Weaving the publicly accepted details of her charmed upbringing and the reality of her true origins along with the dramatic discovery of her adoption, she told her husband-to-be all about the woman he was planning to marry. That included the truth about the woman in the Plaza that morning.

Serena had done nothing wrong and had nothing for which to reproach herself, but still she felt a huge sense of relief after the confession.

"My mother and father thought they were protecting me by not telling me the true story," Serena accepted. "They acted at all times out of love, but unfortunately the consequences were terrible."

Serena shuddered at the shocking memory of the life-changing day when Kathleen had appeared at their home and shattered the perfect world so carefully created by Humberto and Maria.

She made as if to pick up the wrap draped on the back of the red velvet-covered gilt chair and pull it over her bare shoulders. Eduardo stood up, ready to assist, but the maître d' did not miss a beat. He crossed the room and held in place the tasseled silk shawl for Serena to find comfort in its warmth.

"It was the worst day of my life, eclipsed only by the death of Karl," Serena said poignantly.

Eduardo knew the story of Karl and was mature enough to realize that while her dead fiancé would always hold a special place in Serena's heart, and quite rightly so, time had healed and she was now totally committed to him.

Realistic regarding the inevitability of death, Eduardo was not a sentimentalist. He assumed a caring but noncommittal demeanor, alert to react if Serena became emotional but otherwise resigned to sitting back and listen. He did not comment on the deaths of Serena's father, whom he had met from time to time as both pursued their interests in Miami's professional Cuban community, or Karl, whom he knew only by reputation.

Serena composed herself. "My birth mother Kathleen told me most of the story that day; well, she was anxious to be allowed to put her side of the story and Maria filled in the gaps."

Still unaware of the financial arrangements Humberto had put in place to prevent Kathleen's threat to expose the truth, Serena did not realize she had been party to only half the story.

Eduardo was curious. "How did you find her again, here in New York City?"

"She found me," said Serena. "Way back when I first started to present the television program. She would show up then disappear—sometimes for years. She appeared just where you saw me talking to her today on the Plaza. She used to show up from time to time and after a while we got talking. By that time I had guessed who she was."

Recalling the fragile details of their relationship, Serena stared off into the distance. "I hadn't seen her for a long time, though I often thought about her, until one day a friend of hers was there instead. She told me, Kathleen, that's her name, had gone into treatment. I hadn't heard from her for months, then today there she was, looking good, better than I've seen her before."

Proudly Serena reiterated what her birth mother had told her. "Six months clean and sober."

Eduardo smiled indulgently. "That's great news," he said, then he added, "Just don't get your hopes up. The numbers of alcoholics and addicts who sustain recovery is very small, about five percent. Many of them go through treatment programs many times and still relapse."

"Don't use the relapse word," said Serena angrily. Her eyes flashed and there was ice in her manner as she told him, "I've read a lot about alcoholism and addiction. I even went to a couple of open meetings of Alcoholics Anonymous.

"Relapse is not inevitable. I won't allow you to undermine what she has achieved by being clean and sober for six months."

Taken aback by her rigorous defense of the mother she hardly knew, Eduardo modified his tone.

"I'm sorry," he said. "My only concern is for you. I just don't want you to get your hopes up."

"Well, one day at a time, it's working," said Serena. "Everyone deserves the benefit of the doubt."

In a rare deliberate attempt to provoke a confrontation, Serena stared straight at him. "I gave YOU the benefit of the doubt. Do me the courtesy of extending that same grace to my birth mother."

Eduardo was not inclined to argue the point. He smiled. The girl had real fire in her soul and he loved her for it. When first he had set his sights on her and began to formulate his grand plan, he had been somewhat misled by her on-screen persona: always smiling, charming, a skilled but unfailingly polite interviewer.

She had all those qualities but she was also the tiger girl who had appeared in a daring Roberto Cavalli animal print for their first date. Married life would not be boring with his chosen bride.

Eduardo nodded for the check and it arrived already printed out and ready to be signed; he always saved time by presenting his black steel American Express card on arrival at a restaurant or other establishment. Eduardo was a man in a hurry.

*   *   *

"Forty-eight, forty-nine, fifty, and onward to infinity," Eduardo and Serena watched the floor indicator, counted and laughed together. Beyond the eighty-sixth floor observation platform and ever onward, the superspeed elevator powered to the top of the Empire State building. All one hundred and three floors of the tower.

In a romantic finale to the evening, one of the last they would spend as single people, the wedding being only a few weeks away, Eduardo took Serena's hand and led her to a secluded corner of the small platform that overlooked the iconic New York nighttime skyline.

He rescued from his inside jacket pocket a half bottle of Veuve Clicquot, one of the few champagnes named after a woman, two crystal champagne flutes wrapped in Plaza Hotel white linen napkins with the distinctive gold logo, and a small jar of finest black Russian beluga caviar with a matching gold spoon.

Drinking in the nighttime fairy-tale scene, the lovers gazed into each other's eyes, toasted each other in sparkling champagne, and enjoyed the taste sensation of dozens of tiny caviar bubbles as they burst on the tongue. "To happily ever after." They raised glasses.

As Eduardo and Serena kissed, it happened.

They experienced the uniquely romantic phenomena that up on the one hundred and third floor observation platform the electric static was so strong, couples literally saw sparks fly as they kissed.

"May the sparks fly all through our marriage," Eduardo toasted.

Ceremony over, Serena was amused and delighted as

Eduardo wrapped the glasses in the napkins and returned them, along with the spoon and empty caviar jar, to his pockets.

The happiness of the moment, and a sense that she could trust the universe to deliver anything she requested, made Serena bold enough to propose an intention she had not even been aware of until the words sailed on the sea of champagne and caviar bubbles and popped right out of her mouth.

"I plan to invite my birth mother to the wedding," she said joyfully.

Eduardo looked aghast. "I don't think that is a good idea," he said with determination in his voice.

The magic of a few moments earlier burst like a fragile floating bubble.

"A newly sober alcoholic at a wedding is a recipe for disaster. I don't want her there, the occasion will overwhelm her," he declared.

Serena was hurt and strangely embarrassed for her birth mother. "What about what I want?" she asked. "She's my mother."

Eduardo shook his head and that one gesture, whereby he implied that his wishes would naturally overrule hers, outraged Serena.

Face flushed with anger, heart palpitating, even as she felt her emotions spin out of control, she reacted and then acted.

Almost before she realized what she was about to do, she pulled her diamond emerald-cut five-carat engagement ring from the third finger of her left hand.

The scene transitioned in slow motion. Now Serena had Eduardo's attention.

She held the precious ring in her right hand and glared at him.

"Please don't do anything silly, Serena," Eduardo made a passionate please. "That ring is a symbol of my love for you."

Serena had a ludicrous image of herself in an old black and white movie playing the part of a woman wronged.

"You don't love me enough to understand how important it is to have my birth mother at my wedding. She has never been there for any of the great events of my life. I owe it to her."

Eduardo kept his eye fixed on the clenched right hand where she held firmly onto the engagement ring.

"Serena, let's talk about this," he said, in a voice designed to placate.

Too late. He watched horrified as she ducked under the safety railing, positioned herself as close to the edge as possible, raised her hand, and as if to cast a spell over all New York, with an extravagant sweep of her arm threw the ring into the blackness of the night.

Serena deflated on the spot like a balloon. All anger evaporated, the moment of insanity passed. Now there were the consequences to face. Her face crumpled as she turned nervously to look at her fiancé, then the tears came. Great big splashing tears.

The tears drowned the words she wanted to say and she choked on the mixture of sadness and sentiments. Eduardo could just make out a pitiful, "Sorry. I'm sorry." He wanted to be angry but she was obviously on the verge of a serious panic attack.

Enfolding her in his arms and stroking her hair, he

soothed her as she sobbed like a child in the safety of his embrace.

When he judged she had composed herself enough, he joked, "Okay, race you down the hundred flights of stairs. One diamond engagement ring is the glittering prize."

CHAPTER THIRTY-SIX

Battle of Wills

Serena refused to back down. She argued her case.

Waking in the luxurious setting of Eduardo's waterfront mansion, her first sight was of the rose pink Miami sunrise that formed beguiling patterns in the sky and heralded the promise of another pink-cloud day.

Serena worked her charms provocatively and endeavored to match the enticement of the sunrise.

Her soon to be husband was a man who religiously exercised at dawn in his home gym with a personal trainer whose overseeing of Eduardo's fitness regime ensured that the fifty-year-old looked ten years younger.

Stretched out on top of the covers, showing off naked, tanned limbs, Serena was propped up on the pillows of Eduardo's custom-made supersize bed.

She raised her hands above her head, yawned, and stretched out in a seductive pose, ensuing that her beautiful body was shown off to best advantage.

Eduardo stepped into his shorts, pulled a T-shirt over his head, and perched on the end of the bed to do up his running shoes. Not impervious to the female charms on display he was nonetheless determined not to be distracted. He was conscious that the trainer had raised the bar and a grueling workout was scheduled. All before he had even started a day's work at the surgery.

"I said, I invited my birth mother," Serena repeated.

"I heard. What do you want me to say? You know my opinion."

Eduardo was not about to call off the wedding, but he was distinctly unhappy about the situation. Following the massive row and subsequent dramatic events at the Empire State, the engagement ring had still not been found.

Eduardo had filed a police report and was still awaiting the insurance payout. The diamond-studded wedding band he had designed was still at the jeweler's, and a replacement engagement ring was being crafted. An exact replica of the lost one.

He would love to know who had picked up the dazzling diamond ring as it flew off the rooftop of New York's most famous landmark.

Likely the finder had assumed a jewel that size was probably a fake.

"So against all my advice, you've invited your birth mother. On your head be it," he told Serena.

"I've taken contingency measures," she assured him, attempting to wheedle her way into his good books. "Kathleen's best friend Concepta is her plus one and will keep her in check."

"Now you really are playing me for a fool," said Eduardo.

"No one, no one in the world can guarantee the behavior of an alcoholic. I'm frankly amazed that this friend would even agree to take on such a responsibility. She knows your mother a lot better than you."

Serena had to admit, "I think the excitement of attending such a high-profile celebrity wedding is the attraction."

"God, preserve me," Eduardo had reached the end of his patience. He raised his voice in frustration. "I don't want to hear ANYMORE about it."

In a last ditch attempt to win his approval, Serena played what she saw as a trump card. "Even Maria has agreed that it is a very kind gesture and she thinks it will be a once-in-a-lifetime experience for Kathleen," said Serena.

Serena was not about to reveal the full extent of her conversation with Maria about her decision to invite Kathleen to the wedding.

"You're still the official Mother of the Bride," she said, as if it could possibly have been any other way. "No one will even know who Kathleen is, but it will be such a thrill for her. At least allow her to be there for one important event in my life. Not just the birth."

The last comment stung Maria, as Serena knew it would, and she looked away rather than acknowledge the tears in her mother's eyes.

"It's only one day—well, a weekend," Serena tried to justify herself. "You've had me all my life."

Maria showed an uncharacteristic flash of anger. "Yes, and I'd like to know how your life would have turned out if it had been the other way around."

Serena knew she had gone too far. "You've been the best mother in the world to me," Serena admitted, as she choked back her own tears. "Please don't break my heart now. I won't invite her without your blessing. Please, mama. Please."

Serena knew she had used emotional blackmail on Maria and she was not proud of the fact, but she really did feel it was a matter of honor that Kathleen be allowed to attend the wedding.

Eduardo gave her a withering look. "Maria won't try to deny that Kathleen is your biological mother, she has shown a very compassionate attitude, which is no less than I would expect of her. However, she doesn't know that we have invited a raging alcoholic likely to run amok and spoil the whole wedding."

Serena refused to be silenced. She desperately wanted Eduardo to agree with her decision and at least share the burden with her.

"Concepta is in charge of all arrangements, I talked to her on the phone," she explained. "She will shop for a dress with Kathleen and travel with her from New York for the weekend. I've advanced her—not Kathleen—money to cover all their expenses."

Serena swung her legs off the bed onto the light wooden flooring and walked toward the bathroom. As a parting shot she informed Eduardo, "For our peace of mind, I think you'll agree it's the best solution: the two of them will share the pool guesthouse. We can keep an eye on Kathleen and she won't be in an impersonal hotel somewhere. Concepta says...."

Eduardo had heard more than enough and allowed his temper to get the better of him. He shouted as she closed the bathroom door, "Spare me the details. Subject closed. I just pray you know what you are doing."

CHAPTER THIRTY-SEVEN

Wedding Party

"The wedding is off," Serena told her mother.

It was the first Maria had heard of it and she needed to make a very subtle judgment between normal prewedding nerves and a genuine crisis.

"Keep calm and trust Mom. I'm sure we can work it out," Maria said soothingly. "Do you want to come to me or shall I come to you?"

"I'm coming home—when I've packed my suitcase." Serena milked the drama for all it was worth.

"Don't do anything hasty," Maria cautioned.

Less than an hour later, Serena flounced into the apartment and threw a copy of one of the celebrity gossip magazines onto the coffee table in front of where Maria was settled down with one dog on either side of her.

There on the front page, an extremely fuzzy photo that the magazine claimed to be Dr. Eduardo Vasquez enjoying a lap dance on his stag night in Las Vegas.

"Dr. Betrayal," the headline screamed.

Maria gently pushed the dogs to opposite ends of the padded lounger and patted the vacant place for her daughter to sit down. Serena put her feet up and her head on her mother's lap.

"I'll never live it down," sobbed Serena. "How could he do this to me? I could kill him with my own bare hands. I can't go through with the wedding."

Maria wished she could take the hurt her daughter felt and make it her own. She felt that familiar feeling of a dark hole opening up in her soul. The first thing was to figure out a strategy. No way would she approve of Eduardo's actions, if the story was true, but there had to be better evidence than one murky photo in a questionable gossip sheet.

"Have you spoken to Eddie," Maria asked.

"No, I will never speak to him again," Serena claimed.

Maria looked puzzled. "Then how will you know if it's true? Surely he deserves the benefit of the doubt."

"He's left several messages," Serena was forced to admit. "I haven't returned his calls."

"Then do so now," said Maria sternly. "We can't begin to make sense of this until we have both sides of the story."

"Go on," she ordered, "go into the bedroom and make the call."

For an hour, Maria sat and anxiously waited for Serena to reappear.

When she did make an appearance, Maria was relieved to note that she was all smiles.

"Eddie's lawyer has sorted it," she said happily. "It's a case of mistaken identity. It wasn't him at all but someone else in his party. The magazine is going to print a retraction, the photographer cannot prove it was Eduardo, and now the lawyer is asking for damages."

Maria listened and hoped what she was hearing was true. By the time the lawyers had finished arguing about retractions, damages, and denials, the wedding would be over. She was glad to let the lawyer deal with the whole messy situation. Her only concern was to keep Serena on course and believe Eduardo's explanation and the lawyers' assurances.

"Crisis averted," she told Serena, "now put it all behind you. It isn't, it never was, and you and that handsome hunk Eduardo are to be married in a matter of days."

Maria put on a mock serious face. "I was really worried I was never going to get you off my hands. I've got used to having this apartment to myself."

Together they laughed.

Please God, let it be alright, prayed Maria.

Please God, let my birth mother behave, prayed Serena.

*   *   *

Serena's wedding gown from one of the most exclusive bridal boutiques in the Beautiful City, Coral Gables, was a fashion sensation.

The backless creation held together with a single jewel-encrusted button and a halter neck drew gasps of admiration as she made her way down the long aisle of the Gesu Catholic Church.

Draped from her tiny fitted waist, it cascaded down to a flowing fishtail skirt below the knee, the skirt, layered over half a dozen tulle ballerina petticoats, was covered with tiny seed pearls that danced in the shimmering light of the chandeliers and altar candles. Serena's trademark long flowing ringlets were arranged on the crown of her head. She looked like an angel.

The congregation would have to wait until after the conclusion of the marriage ceremony when she was already Mrs. Eduardo Vasquez to be treated to the full splendor of the front of the gown. A sweetheart sculpted top was encrusted with shimmering white jewels and a stiff collar framed her flawless features and revealed a huge pair of drop diamond and pearl earrings. A wedding gift from her new husband.

Photographs of the dress, flashed around the world, would appear in newspapers, magazines, and on television shows nationally and internationally. Copies of the dress would be styled for retail sale.

Serena was a red-carpet celebrity princess and her husband Eduardo attracted almost as much attention for his dashing good looks and Miami's take on a traditional tuxedo. His outfit was an azure blue tuxedo with blue leather loafers—worn without socks. Styled after the eighties television star Don Johnson in *Miami Vice*, only a man as handsome and self-assured as Dr. Vasquez could carry off the look.

From the day of their wedding, Serena and Eduardo were destined to join the A list of celebrity power couples.

* * *

Concepta tried her best to ensure that Kathleen stayed on the straight and narrow. Fortunately, she showed little interest in drinking and instead spent most of the time crying at her good fortune and the blessing to have in her life the lovely girl she had given birth to thirty years before.

The two stayed quietly for two days before the wedding in the guest cottage enjoying the luxurious amenities and had come out only when invited.

Serena winked at Kathleen on her way out of the church. It had been decided that her other mother should be allowed in the wedding photographs but not in a prominent position, a compromise to which Serena had reluctantly agreed.

However, she reached out to Kathleen and squeezed her hand. "Thank you for being here today. It is very special to me," she assured her. "See you at the reception, Concepta has the address. It's just a couple of blocks away and most of the guests are walking."

Congratulating herself on how well everything had gone, Serena watched from the top of the stairs as Kathleen and Concepta entered the marbled reception room, took the gold-embossed escalator to the banqueting floor, and emerged to be greeted by Serena and Eduardo in the receiving line.

Eduardo stiffened and imperceptibly turned away as Kathleen reached out to shake his hand. Kathleen shot a worried glance at Serena and then looked to Concepta for assurance. Her fragile ego began to crumple. She had felt so happy. Now she felt like the wicked fairy at the feast. She was not welcome. Only pretending to be an honored guest, she realized she was the girl who had given her baby away. She had no right to be there. Oh God, if only the floor would open up and swallow her.

Walking quickly away frantic to hide her shame, she knew where she was headed. At the entrance to the reception room was a twenty-glasses-high champagne fountain. The gold liquid flowed and guests were being handed the sparkling crystal glasses for a toast.

Amidst the laughter, the merriment, and the elegant sound of a classical string quartet that welcomed the guests, there came an almighty crash.

The tower collapsed, more than fifty champagne flutes broke ranks and rushed crazily toward the pink marble-tiled floor. Shattered glass splintered everywhere and an ocean of champagne bubbles danced impudently over the well-heeled feet of wedding guests.

Eduardo reacted at the sound of the first smashing glass and rushed toward the cries of confusion and panic. Catering staff were already diplomatically guiding guests into the next room far away from the chaos as they cleaned up the mess. Serena waited anxiously to hear what disaster had befallen the highly efficient and oh-so-organized caterers. Reporting back, Eduardo's face was contorted in anger.

"Take one guess. Your birth mother helped herself to a glass of champagne from the bottom row of the fountain and brought the whole glass structure crashing down. She certainly is a real alcoholic; one glass is too many, and a thousand is not enough."

Kathleen was mortified, Concepta distraught, and Maria the problem-solver stepped in to salvage the situation. She whisked Kathleen and Concepta off to the ladies' restroom.

"I'm so sorry, I'm so sorry. I didn't mean to do it," Kathleen tried to explain and apologize at the same time. "Please forgive me. What must you think of me? I was only going to have the one glass. Just to steady my nerves."

"Don't upset yourself," said Maria. "It's all under control. It could have happened to anyone."

Concepta gave her a quizzical look and even Kathleen knew that wasn't true. Kathleen decided to push her luck. She didn't hear the door of the restroom open.

"I'm pretty shaken up," she said. "Could I maybe have a small brandy?"

Serena stormed up to Kathleen and without a trace of pity told her, "It's time you left. I came to tell you that I never want to see you again. You betrayed my trust and let yourself down. I have nothing more to say to you. Get out of my life, Kathleen."

Kathleen knew when she was defeated. Concepta convinced her that no good could come of them refusing to leave. Before she could do any further damage, Kathleen was sent home in disgrace from the reception, accompanied by her faithful and embarrassed friend Concepta.

The pair were discreetly escorted off the premises by Eddie's driver, taken to the house to collect their belongings, and driven to the airport.

Kathleen, already emboldened by the small amount of champagne she had managed to drink while the tower crashed all around her, was hopeful there would be supplies in the car.

She was outmaneuvered. Eduardo had warned the driver to remove the alcohol. Kathleen sat in the back of the car, arms folded, lips pursed, "I'll get a drink at the airport," she said defiantly.

Concepta, sad and disappointed at the outcome of one of the best days of her life, packed and left Serena a letter of apology. She hurriedly scribbled a message on the back of the printed Order of Service, of which between them the women had stuffed at least a dozen in their handbags.

"We are both very sorry for what happened. Kathleen is too upset to write this letter. I know you said you never wanted to see her again but your mother is not a bad person who needs to learn to be good. She is a sick person and I for one still believe she can get well. Maybe one day that will happen. Thank you and have a happy life. You deserve it. Love Kathleen and Concepta."

CHAPTER THIRTY-EIGHT

The Heat Is On

"Whose name is on the list this week?" asked Dr. Eduardo Vasquez, as he poured rich ruby wine into gold-rimmed Moreno glasses for his prominent and influential guests.

Only one conversation existed at the dinner parties of his well-heeled friends and medical colleagues. No one even discussed real estate any more or the huge killings they had made on the stock exchange. They had more pressing concerns on their minds.

The Drug Enforcement Agency was targeting "pill mill doctors" and several had already gone to jail. Many more feared imminent arrest.

He was not about to admit it, but Eduardo knew that his name was moving ever higher up the list. The doctor whose name was currently in the frame was one they all knew.

Eduardo proposed a toast "Let's drink to him—and his criminal defense lawyer."

The laughter had a hollow ring to it.

Investigations had been ongoing for several years, but

they had previously been secondary to the government's determination to disassemble the South American cartels. Every time a major player like Pablo Escobar or drug kingpin Joaquin Gusman "El Chapo" ("shorty"), the leader of the Colombian criminal organization, was killed or jailed, the public were reassured that the war on drugs was being won and the bad guys were being brought to justice.

The heat died down and other drug-dealing activities slid back under the radar. Prescription drug dealing on home territory did not engender the public outrage reserved for gangs operating an illegal trade in cocaine and marijuana. There seemed little urgency to move against the perceived reputable medical profession until the scale of the problem was revealed and facts that could not be ignored began to come to light.

Major pharmacies like Walgreens and CVS Caremark paid fines of millions of dollars for failing to maintain controls over the distribution of massive amounts of drugs such as Oxycodone and other powerful painkillers. These drugs were diverted to drug addicts and dealers operating in the black market.

Thousands of pain clinics had spread across the nation, and South Florida, which already had a reputation as the medical fraud center of the States, operated as a tourist destination for patients hooked on pain medication.

The Department of Drug Enforcement had started to aggressively pursue crooked physicians they claimed peddled prescription drugs and made their fortunes.

Serena had long since given up making moral judgments.

"I always put the interest of my patients first," Eduardo

never tired of telling her. More and more she saw through his mask of self-righteousness.

Her husband claimed, as he had done way back at the beginning of their relationship, that he was a caring professional doing the best for his patients. She chose not to hear the argument that claimed the "pill mill" clinics were responsible for a trail of death from painkiller overdoses. Criminal defense lawyers made as much money as the doctors, finding new and imaginative ways to protect their clients, and prove their innocence. No one doubted that some of the methods might be considered "unorthodox."

Popular wisdom claimed that many cases of potential medical malpractice suits were settled out of court, with the families of dead addicts accepting payments to assist with "expenses."

Serena cringed; she knew what was coming next and she dreaded it. The spare room joke.

"Did you hear about the lawyer whose wife threw him out because she was so angry at him cluttering up her spare room? The room was stacked wall to wall and floor to ceiling with dollar bills."

Eduardo never lost control or got drunk enough in public to admit that he too stored his spare cash in a locked room upstairs in the six-bedroom mansion. Serena had suspected so for the three years of their marriage.

After the dinner party guests left, Serena confronted him. Eduardo denied again and again that he was hiding anything from his wife. "Trust me," he shouted. "Don't I deserve at least that from you. You know I am under immense pressure, I need your support not your accusations."

Fearful of yet another row—there were far too many of them in their house these days—Serena let the subject drop and went to bed.

Eduardo as usual stayed up drinking. With the lame excuse that he had an early start in the morning, her once passionate, loving husband now often slept separately from her. Their lovemaking was almost nonexistent and his moods and anxiety were more and more unpredictable.

Her love for Eduardo was slowly being killed. The major changes in his behavior and his attitude toward her meant that she no longer believed or trusted him.

* * *

The very next afternoon the story began to unravel.

Serena came home unexpectedly from the television studio and found Eduardo stuffing paper money into an already-filled room. The supposed joke about the lawyer and his spare room full of money was alive and well in her home. Except in this scenario it was a doctor not a lawyer who was the hoarder. Or should that be money launderer?

Spotting an unknown car in the circular driveway at the mansion initially aroused her interest. A burly African American, with exotically tattooed arms and an unnaturally muscled body, had stood guard.

As she drove past the car heading for her usual parking spot, Serena squinted into the open trunk. It was filled to the brim with dollar bills.

Another man she had never seen before appeared from the house. He carried a square wooden wastepaper basket.

Serena stepped from her car and he walked toward her and blocked her view, as the guard closed the trunk.

Senses all on alert, Serena sidestepped the stranger who did not move to try and stop her but did pull out his phone and dial. Breaking into a run, Serena had increased her speed; she had completed enough half marathons for charity to know how to pace herself.

Taking the stairs two at a time, she had surprised Eduardo who turned to look out of the upstairs room expecting to see his helper.

Serena almost skidded to a halt on the polished wooden floor in a side corridor of the house she had never had occasion to visit previously.

What she saw shocked her and it did not take more than a few seconds to calculate there was no good or legal explanation for the contents of the room.

Money. Wall to wall, floor to ceiling—money.

Eduardo had busily and meticulously moved a large pile to make way for the new supplies on their way from the trunk of the car in the driveway.

Serena looked at him contemptuously.

She spat out the incriminating words, "Drug dealers in white coats" and walked away before he could answer.

* * *

Serena was not the only one to have discovered her husband's secret activities. His name had gravitated to the top of the list. DEA agents operating with warrants had already tapped his work and home telephone and his movements were constantly under surveillance.

The high-profile life that he enjoyed through his wife's celebrity status meant that the couple were always on show in public.

Rivaling J Lo, Beyoncé, and Madonna as the city's most famous residents, Serena and Eduardo, the glamorous pair, posed in the hottest fashions, direct from the world's runways. They graced red-carpet events, top ticket shows, and dinners, fundraisers, clubs, restaurants, and charity occasions, all perfect photo opportunities to promote their image as media stars and attract ever more sponsorship and product endorsements.

Serena and Eduardo Vazquez were big-time movers and shakers.

They enjoyed an enviable lifestyle and owned multimillion dollar homes on Flame Island, Miami Beach, and in New York. They traveled internationally to join the other beautiful, feted people on their yachts and in vacation homes; Serena and Eduardo had arrived.

But having it all was not enough. For some individuals, as Eduardo was fond of explaining when talking about alcoholism and addiction, all the money in the world, the homes, the cars, the boat, the clothes, the jewelry, the fame and fortune was never enough.

"I believe," he would expound, "that some individuals are born with a dark hole in their soul."

Serena suffered the agonies of betrayal and being let down by her husband, but she knew there was a part of her that still loved him. Where could she turn? She hated to admit to her mother how much of her dream had been shattered. Her life was falling apart.

"Please, don't give up on me. Tell me what I can do to make it up to you?" pleaded Eduardo in desperation as he ran after her and fought to come up with an explanation for the money cache. Serena sat on the top step of the curved staircase. Eduardo slumped beside her, legs straight ahead, his back to the gallery banister.

For the first time, Serena admitted to herself that she saw not the handsome features of the man she loved, but the face of a tortured soul who tried too hard to achieve and compete and survive. In his efforts to have it all, he was destined to lose it all.

Serena listened in shock as he explained what he proposed. "Some of my colleagues have left the country and set up practices in other countries," he said, "ones like Cuba that don't have extradition treaties with the United States.

"It might not be forever, but the authorities are closing in on people like me. A Plan B is essential."

Serena, who had so hoped for a happily ever after, was skeptical. "What happens to me?" she asked.

Eduardo had obviously given it some thought. "Everything needs to look as normal as possible," he informed her. "You stay here and carry on with your life, your career, your charities, and your friends. Maria might even agree to move in to keep you company. To all intent and purposes I am on an extended trip. That's true," he said using his best "please believe me" smile.

"I won't deny that I have not always behaved honorably. But situations develop over time and I was put in a position where I had to offer my patents the same services as they got from other practices. I'm not a bad person."

Serena gave him a sidelong long as he used the same excuse Concepta had given for Kathleen's unacceptable behavior at the wedding reception.

"Please stand by me, Serena," her husband pleaded. "The lawyer will sort it out. No charges have been brought. For the time being, he suggests I remove myself from the situation and the country."

"When will you go?" asked Serena doubtfully.

"Now, today," Eduardo admitted. "Plans are in place."

"You were going to go without telling me?" she said, realization slowly dawning.

"Only to protect you. The less you know the better. I promise I thought only of you."

Serena stood up, brushed the seat of her pants where she had been sitting on the step, readjusted her clothes, and looked at her husband with contempt.

"Do what you have to do," she said, "and spare me the details."

"Serena," he said as he jumped to his feet, grabbed her shoulders, and stared deep into her eyes. "I have a confession to make. You need to know. I'm sorry."

Serena waited; she guessed what was coming next.

"I'm not a drug dealer in a white coat."

He had always recoiled from the dreaded accusation.

"I am a drug addict. I know how my patients feel because I am one of them. I too suffer from the disease of addiction. When I go abroad I intend to check myself into a rehabilitation program."

Saddened but not altogether surprised to hear about her husband's drug abuse, Serena decided one last time to give him the benefit of the doubt. She walked away from Eduardo.

"Good luck with that," she said. "Goodbye, Dr. Vasquez."

CHAPTER THIRTY-NINE

Letting Go

"Hello, Dr. Traynor. I am Serena Perez. Very pleased to meet you. I came as quickly as my schedule allowed."

Serena had collected an impressive entourage since arriving at the hospice direct from the airport where she had flown in from her Florida home on a private jet and been transported to the New York hospital that was home to the Catholic Cancer Center.

She was not inclined to elaborate and show off her importance by boasting that she had been delayed hosting an "at home" fund-raiser for the female Presidential candidate who was on a whistle-stop tour of South Florida.

Nor was she about to admit that it was only after her VIP guest had departed, full of thanks on the wave of a hugely satisfying fund-raising opportunity, that Serena had decided to fly to see the patient in the hospice bed who she had been informed would not make it through the night.

"I know who you are, Miss Perez," Dr. Traynor assured her. "Even overworked hospital interns watch television.

And I could not fail to be impressed that you chose to marry not a member of the entertainment industry, but a medical doctor."

Serena smiled and nodded her head in acknowledgment of what was obviously intended as a compliment. She had no intention of admitting to him, or anyone else outside her closest circle, that the marriage was over in all but name.

Even the celebrity gossip machine had not caught up with that information. It always amazed Serena how much a high-profile person like herself could actually keep quiet if they did not have friends or relatives selling stories to the media.

She was blessed with a loyal and tight-knit group who had her best interests at heart and who saw it as their role to protect, not exploit her. Although she was well aware the press were not above making up stories, the less details they were spoon-fed by insiders, the less they were able to prove and expand on their suspicions. Confidentiality agreements signed by staff members at the TV station and at her home were strictly enforced.

Serena enjoyed a secluded existence, cherry picking her interests outside of the nightly television appearances on her network show. She and her mother Maria, along with her personal assistant, lived in the marital home and she traveled with trusted aides and confidants.

Serena and Eduardo had not publicly admitted that they were separated and had not lived together for many months.

Contact with her soon-to-be ex-husband was conducted through his lawyer's office. Serena had distanced herself physically and emotionally. As far as she was concerned, her husband's betrayal of her and everything she and her family stood for had been compromised from day one of their meeting.

Serena knew she had been used; she was adamant that it would not continue.

"It's true," she had told Maria, "what doesn't kill you makes you stronger. Finally I feel like I have grown up and accepted responsibility for my own life.

"I am certainly not a victim and like the one time First Lady Hillary Clinton was famously quoted as saying, 'I am not some little woman 'standin' by my man' like Tammy Wynette.'

"Hillary certainly showed millions of women how to maintain their dignity and prove how powerful they could be out of the husband's shadow."

Serena had chosen to walk away from her flawed husband and not be tainted by his confessed addiction or ongoing criminal mentality.

She had also thought she could walk away from her real mother, but that had proven more difficult.

Dr. Traynor steered her down the interminable hospital corridors, behind them a sedate procession of nuns, nurses, and administrators.

Serena was more than a match for Dr. Traynor's fast-paced walk and reasoned talk. She was well used to striding out through the long corridors of a television station on her way to deliver breaking news and interpret complicated national and local scenarios in an intelligent and concise manner.

"There are many similarities between our jobs," he said, as if reading her thoughts.

"On a daily basis we deal with matters of life and death and try to make sense of them to the people whose lives have been personally impacted and who won't have the luxury of moving on to the next big story tomorrow."

"Well put, doctor," said Serena. "It can be hard to strike a balance between becoming too emotionally involved yet also knowing that without compassion we can't be uniquely useful to our fellow human beings."

The two shared a moment of understanding and were thankful for the unique insight that illuminated their deeper motivations.

"Kathleen was asleep the last time I looked in on her," he said in a tone that did not deny the affection he felt for a sick and dying patient who at best was cranky and at worst downright impossible.

A wave of cold fear washed over Serena. Behind the closed door of the private room, she knew her biological mother lay dying.

The woman who had given birth to her had now completed her life circle and was close to the end. She had pleaded for Serena to come, Serena had resisted. Her birth mother had won the battle if not the war. Her daughter was at her bedside.

Quietly closing the door behind them, Dr. Traynor approached the bed and gestured for Serena to take up a position on the other side.

Bundled up in the bedclothes with just hands and face visible, Serena hardly recognized the features of her mother.

ELLEN FRAZER-JAMESON

Kathleen lay perfectly still and Serena experienced an agonizing sense of loss when she thought the lady in the bed had already departed this world.

Dr. Traynor bent his tall body down to within a few inches of Kathleen's right ear and said, "You have a visitor."

There was no response.

"Kathleen, can you hear me? It's Dr. Traynor. I have someone with me. Do you want to see her?"

Still no response.

Serena looked at the doctor who had cared for her mother and assisted her in the last stages of the terrible disease.

"Is she still alive?" she asked, stepping further away rather than closer to the bed.

"She's been in and out of coma for several days now," the doctor admitted. "Our policy is to allow her own body to regulate her waking and sleeping, but we also monitor her constantly and administer medication to keep her pain manageable."

At the words pain medication, Serena recoiled. The doctor continued.

"We don't believe in decisions that will prolong the patient's suffering especially at this late stage, but patients have different pain thresholds.

"Some patients constantly ask for more medication and others want to see how far they can push their own endurance. Medication is administered at set intervals but if the patient doesn't request the relief, then we will let them wait until they do feel the need. Other patients forcefully demand ever greater and more frequent doses of the chemical respite."

Serena urged him to go on. "And what kind of patient is Kathleen?" she asked, although she felt she could guess the answer.

"As they advance and more medication is prescribed, most patients become dependent, or addicted if you like. As they are so close to the end of life, it is not the most major of their problems. However, a patient like Kathleen who has previously displayed tendencies toward addiction, is a prime candidate for becoming severely dependent while under the end-stage medical care, and their discomfort when denied the drug can be extremely distressing to them and the medical staff."

Dr. Traynor finished his explanation and told Serena point blank, "As a doctor it raises moral questions when we're anxious to regulate medication but the patient demands more than we think necessary.

"Patients can be very persuasive not to say manipulative," he admitted.

"I really appreciate you taking time to explain it to me," said Serena gratefully. She was beginning to get an insight into some of the issues and dilemmas she had previously questioned.

Even as Dr. Traynor talked he kept his eyes fixed on the patient. He stood by the bedside and squeezed Kathleen's hand. At the first sight of her awakening, he leaned down again to speak directly into her ears and look directly into her eyes.

"Kathleen, look who has come to see you," he said.

Kathleen's eyes flickered open briefly and closed. It was

a moment or two before she opened them again and a tiny spark ignited as she gave an indication that she could see and hear.

In a small voice she asked, "Did she come? Did my daughter come?"

Serena felt herself choked up with tears as she reached for her mother's hand.

"I'm here," she said. "It's me, Serena. You asked for me and I came."

Kathleen clutched at her daughter's hand and held on tight though she had little strength left in the rest of her body.

"You came. Thank you. Thank you."

Kathleen began to cry, deep wracking sobs. Tears spilled from Serena's eyes and splashed silently on to the front of her mother's hospital gown. Mother and daughter mirrored each other, struggling to gain clear sight so they could gaze at each other. Never before had the two had such a clear vision of the person who shared their lifeblood.

Dr. Traynor had moved to a discreet distance across the room. Now he stepped forward as he observed Kathleen endeavor to push herself up on her pillows.

Kathleen shot him a ferocious glance. "She's my daughter, I have to talk to her," she said. "It feels like I've waited forever."

Serena could hardly bear to see Kathleen in such distress and discomfort and her tears gushed forth.

"There's no hurry," she said. "I'm not going anywhere. What did you want to tell me?"

"Sit down," said Kathleen.

Serena did as she was told. She knew a mother's orders when she heard them.

Kathleen's voice could not sustain the volume or authority but she was determined to have her say. It was as if she had practiced it over again and again in her head.

"They tricked me," were her first words. "Mother Michael tricked me into giving you away. I never forgave her. She ruined my life and I'm not the only girl she treated that way. I wanted to keep you. I loved you from the moment I saw you. I loved you even as I carried you inside me. No one could have persuaded me to give you away but they stole you from me."

Serena worried that Kathleen would overstretch herself. Her mother was able to deliver just a few words at a time and then she would lapse into long silences. Serena was prepared to wait. She reflected on the revelations as they spilled from the lips of the dying woman. Surely she deserved the chance to tell the truth of her story now? Before she finally reached the end?

"Don't rush," said Dr. Traynor, "I'll ask a nurse to come with water for Kathleen. Would you like a coffee?"

"Tea, please," said Serena. "I'm Irish, like you."

As she turned her attention back to Kathleen, Serena was worried that she had gone back to sleep or slipped into a drug-induced coma.

No, Kathleen looked alert and anxious to continue her story and explain exactly what had happened as she gave birth at the convent.

"While I was in labor, Mother Michael withheld pain medication from me until I agreed to sign the adoption form. Of course I didn't know what I was signing but I did know that I needed that pain-relieving injection."

Kathleen now relived the scene in her head as clearly as if it were happening all over again.

"For the want of that painkiller, I bought myself a whole lifetime of pain."

Serena felt perspiration break out on her forehead and she thought she would faint. In a cruel twist of fate, the substance that was supposed to have relieved the pain had robbed her mother of her beloved child.

Kathleen was well aware of the irony of the situation, though whether she had identified the direct link previously, Serena did not know.

"God punished me for what I had done," Kathleen said over and over again.

"You were the one who suffered," said Serena, trying to placate the ever-more agitated patient. "I had a wonderful life. You have nothing to feel guilty about."

Kathleen nodded and then in a torrent of words, as if she was now frightened she would not have time to finish what she needed to say, she revealed the punishment she believed God had visited upon her.

She clawed at the top of the bedclothes with her thin, weak hands and her voice barely audible as she confided in her firstborn.

"You had a good life and I'm sorry for the times I hurt you when I turned up and behaved badly. Please believe me,

I never meant to make you unhappy. I was always so scared when I was around you; I needed a drink, Dutch courage, to take away the fear. The feeling that I wasn't good enough and you would know that I wasn't worthy of you.

"However, you should know that you were luckier than my second baby. I refused all medication when she was born. Even though I really wanted it, I was too scared of what might happen if I didn't have all my senses about me. I refused to take the relief but I paid anyway.

"God took away my wonderful husband, Kieran, and our baby girl.

"She lived just one day. Like a beautiful butterfly she lived less than twenty-four hours. God took my second baby away from me because I had been wicked and given you away. He never forgave me and I never forgave myself."

With a huge sob expelling from that dark hole in the soul, Kathleen grabbed Serena's arm, dug in her ragged nails, and begged, "Forgive me? Please forgive me. Then I can die in peace."

Serena cradled her frail mother in her arms and they cried together.

"I forgive you," said her daughter over and over again. "I forgive you. God forgives you."

The night sky was pitch black outside the hospital room window.

From time to time a doctor or a nurse, or a nun or a member of the catering staff or an administrator would tentatively open the closed door, look in, and retreat. None chose to interrupt the intimate scene.

Mother and daughter reconciled.

Serena had one question that she longed to ask her mother. It was now or never. She took a deep breath and in a quiet voice asked, "Who was my father?"

Kathleen looked lovingly at her daughter and gave the slightest nod. "You have the right to know. His name was Marco Sanchez and his family was Hispanic—like yours. From him you got your dark Spanish good looks. He was a charmer and," she paused as Serena held her breath and prayed she would hear every last detail, "a star performer. We went to school together in New York. He was not the love of my life—but he gave me the love of my life. You."

Serena grasped her mother's hand. The end was very near. "Thank you and bless you," she said.

Serena's heart was wide open. "I love you, mother," she said even though she did not know whether her words could be heard as Kathleen slipped in and out of a coma. "You are not a bad person who needs to be made good. You were sick, now you are restored. God forgives you."

Kathleen exhaled one more soul-shaking breath as the life left her earthly body. Serena clasped both hands over hers in prayer and told her, "Your soul is restored. You are free."

Epilogue

On a bitterly cold winter's day, accompanied by her mother, Maria, and trusted family friend, Concepta, the television star Serena Perez was one of just half a dozen mourners at her birth mother Kathleen's funeral in the Catholic Church of the Sacred Heart in New York City.

Although she had not been close to her mother, the deathbed confession and the pair's reconciliation had opened up a deep well of grief in Serena. Fearful that she was in danger of feeding that dark hole in her own soul that had so cruelly driven her mother and her addicted husband, Eduardo, Serena had tried to find solace in her charity work in the community.

She had always enjoyed helping out at the soup kitchen in NYC and now she regularly joined the Matthew 25 Mission to feed the homeless at a Community Church on Miami Beach.

Here she observed the multilayered levels of assistance where the homeless were fed and offered medical attention as well as access to services to ease their transition off the streets into housing and rehabilitation programs.

"It's amazing how a haircut can add to a homeless person's self-esteem," Serena told her mother. "Nearly all the people who come for the free meals have a drink or drug problem. Addiction is so common and these people are at the raw end. I want to help."

Maria heard her daughter's concerns and rejoiced that she had been blessed with such a loving, caring daughter. Kathleen had much to be proud of and thank God, Serena did not appear to have inherited the gene or inclination toward the alcohol dependency.

Still, though, she sensed a deep well of sadness in her beloved daughter and was desperate to help.

On the private Gulfstream jet back to Miami after their New York trip, mother and daughter sat close together and held hands. "Poor Kathleen," said Serena. "Her life was so sad and filled with loss. I feel like I have survivor's remorse, as if she sacrificed her life so that I could have all the best things. My life was perfect and I had the love of two wonderful parents. Did I steal Kathleen's chance of a good life? Maybe if she had been able to keep me, she could have built a life for us and having me would have made a difference to her.

"Now I feel bereft, as if I keep losing the people I love; my father, Humberto, my fiancé Karl, my husband Eduardo, and now my birth mother, Kathleen. The grief gets deeper all the time.

"Please don't think this is any reflection on you, Mama, but sometimes I struggle to find a meaning in life and a reason to keep on living."

Marie had suspected that Serena was going through a

deep emotional crisis but this was the first time she had admitted as much. It was as if the intimate confines of the plane high up in the clouds had made her examine her very existence.

"I've been giving our situation some thought. I believe it's time to move out of Eduardo's house and restart our life afresh," Maria told her with as much enthusiasm as she could muster.

"Let's travel," she encouraged Serena. "Take a special vacation. I've never been back to Cuba but I'd love to go. Now that the restrictions on traveling there have been eased, it would be my dream to take you to the places where I grew up and show you my roots, my upbringing. Reconnect with the places and people who made me who I am. Your father and I always said we would go one day. You and I can do it in his memory. We could go as ambassadors of the Copper Bridge Foundation to promote joint art, literature, and culture alliances between Cuba and the United States."

Serena nodded thoughtfully. "Yes, I'd love that," she said, and added, "I'm willing to move out of the mansion, but my life is still in limbo as long as I don't know where Eduardo is or whether he is ever likely to come back. A part of me is really reluctant to take those final steps and divorce him. He's my husband and somewhere deep inside I still feel a deep connection to him. If I could separate the addict from the person, I know I could learn to love him again."

Maria knew this was not the time for her to offer an opinion; her daughter had the right to make the major decisions without her influence.

"But you are right," Serena continued her chain of thought, "it is time to move on—at least from the house."

The pain of separation and loss that Serena had experienced when she had previously moved out of her family residence was not in evidence and she thankfully relied on her mother to arrange the next planned relocation.

"It hardly felt like I made any impact on the house at all," said Serena. "I was playing a part, one that did not suit or satisfy me."

The lawyer refused to admit whether or not he knew the current whereabouts of Dr. Eduardo, but he did agree to arrange a call to a safe phone number.

"I have only the information Eduardo chooses to reveal," he said. "He contacts me, I do not contact him."

Serena was strangely excited to hear Eduardo's voice; he sounded good but then he always could get the show on the road and talk the talk.

He had news for her. The treatment program he had undergone had worked.

"I am clean and sober," he told her. "Despite the fact that I still have problems, my life is better than it has been for years, my whole way of looking at the world has changed. Before I was in despair with my existence in black and white; now I have the wonder of a new world in color.

"It's an amazing feeling. And, guess what, this is the best part: I am allowed to help the other patients. I am in an inspirational program where they understand the disease of alcoholism and addiction—and have very successful recovery rates with patients.

"I still can't give you too much information but here,

though I am not licensed to practice as a doctor, as a recovering drug addict, I can be uniquely useful to other sufferers."

Worried that there had been no response from his wife, Eduardo asked, "Are you there, did you hear what I said?"

Serena was crying too hard to respond; from a place deep in her heart she felt a wellspring of gratitude and a sense of hope. "It feels like my heart is unfreezing again," she said, "like the first time I saw you. Did I ever tell you my first thought was that I wanted to kiss you? I wish I could reach out now and hold you close."

Scenes from the movie of their marriage played out in her head. With a rush of joy and spontaneous emotion, Serena remembered wonderful times they had shared, the intimacies, the promises, and the certainty that this was the man with whom she wanted to spend the rest of her life. She truly believed that he had loved her. She knew she loved him. Her heart rebelled. "I will not give up on us," she said. "The flame still burns in my heart. I refuse to walk away. Maybe there is a future for us."

On the other end of the line, Eduardo could hardly comprehend what he was hearing. He had never meant to hurt his wife; he deeply regretted the anguish and pain he had inflicted on her. His spirits rose as he dared to consider that maybe he could reignite a tiny spark of the love they had experienced before his sickness overtook him.

"Are you ever coming back?" Serena asked.

Eduardo was silent for a moment. "I can't make promises, Serena," he said. "There is much to take care of legally, financially, and medically. I need to deal with it—one day at a time."

"That works for me," she told him, feeling a genuine acceptance for whatever course her life was now destined to follow.

Choosing her words carefully, she told him, "A trip to Cuba is in the cards, for me, very soon. Havana sounds like a wonderful place. I hear they have very progressive treatment centers there."

Eduardo laughed; his beautiful wife never failed to take his breath away. Without being told, she knew. He had not needed to tell her. The love link had led her to him.

Before she hung up the phone, Serena made the sound of a kiss being blown. "I love you," she said, in a small, whispered voice, just loud enough for her husband to hear.

"Love you too," he replied, "and don't ever forget it."

AA Pledge Adapted to Cuba

Just for Today . . .

I swear by the lives of those I love most dearly, that during the next 24 hours, I will abstain from the toxic substances that enslave me, and I will avoid situations and conversations that I might be tempted to use. I will hold in my mind the thought that the artificial pleasure they give me creates great suffering for those who love me and keeps me from reaching my life goals. My parents' suffering is enormous and when they brought me into the world they had other aspirations for me than drug addiction. I too have other dreams, and suffer from my addiction. For the sake of my loved ones as well as for my own, I must recover from my addiction.

About the Author

Ellen Frazer-Jameson is a professional communicator working in media, print, and theater. A former BBC broadcaster and Fleet Street journalist, Ellen is a published author, producer, theater director, and performer. She co-presented the largest late-night audience show in Europe on BBC Radio 2. Ellen lives in London and Miami Beach and to relax dances Argentine tango.

Ellen's other books include *Seven Steps to Fabulous* and *Love Mother Love Daughter* (Red Door Publishing). Ellen is currently working on a follow-up to *Love Mother Love Daughter.*

You can contact her through her website at www.ellen frazerjameson.com.

Author photo courtesy of international photographer Dora Franco
www.dorafrancophoto.com

www.ingramcontent.com/pod-product-compliance
Lightning Source LLC
Chambersburg PA
CBHW061315170626
46817CB00001B/193